THE VIPER OF KERMAN

To N and P

I.

IT WAS UNTHINKABLE that anyone from Anareh could have ditched this bludgeoned, broken corpse into the qanat. No villagers would have polluted the deep subterranean artery that irrigates their pomegranate orchards, date palms and pistachio trees. The crime seemed most repellent to the muqannis, the men who spend their lives hunched in the waterway, tending every sinew of the tunnel as it runs limpid mountain water for thirty miles beneath the deserts of Kerman. Shreds of this man's skin and fragments of his shattered skull now defiled the water with which they brewed their tea and washed before prayers.

The deep shaft was accessed through a narrow opening a little over sixty yards above the watercourse. Flip a stone down there and you won't hear a thing. It was hard enough for the team's rickety windlass to hoist up sodden bags of mud and gravel in the clearance work but now the muqannis had to strain every fibre to heave out the murdered man. When the distended cadaver was craned into the evening sunlight, Abbas the blind, by far the strongest of the digging team, linked his hands under the corpse's arms and wrestled him out into the dirt.

As Abbas had told them a couple of hours before: this was no accident. Lowering himself into the conduit to daub up cracks after September's earthquake, he had immediately sensed a disturbance in the flow of water, spilling round a large obstacle, as if part of the qanat's roof had caved in. He reached into the water, expecting to press his hand into a pile of sediment but recoiled as he planted his palm squarely and unmistakably on to the cold contours of a corpse's face. To a blind man there was no question of what he had just touched.

'God have mercy,' he gasped and slumped on to his haunches. For a couple of minutes Abbas collected his thoughts and waited for the drumming of his heart to recede. Tentatively, he returned his hands to the body and carefully appraised what he had found. He had never conceived this level of violence against a man. His knowing fingers found the wrists tightly bound with electric flex and cuts sliced across the man's back, deliberately done, as if with a scalpel.

At the surface, all four muqannis and Jahangiri their broad-shouldered foreman, gathered round the dead man, voicelessly mouthing prayers. His legs were contorted at improbable angles, his chest and back a livid hulk of smashed ribs, blade wounds and purple weals. But it was the face that would haunt them: the eyes imperceptible behind swollen, black nests of contusions and the cranium folded around itself where a withering blow had staved in the forehead. The youngest of the muqannis, Hosseini, swung round and retched.

'Motherfucker Arabs. Only motherfucker Arabs would do this shit. No Iranian could do a thing like this,' he sobbed, veiling his embarrassment with rage and flailing his hand in disgust at the body. 'We never had this shit before he came, before he came back with his army of motherfucker lizard-eater Arabs. It used to be just real Iranians round here. It should just be real Iranians round here.'

The other muqannis shared Hosseini's fears about the viper's return to his home village, the shady security apparatchiks and the comings and goings of blacked-out cortèges purring through the streets at all hours. But they knew enough of Tehran's intrusive Byzantine politics not to make trouble.

'He could be a Baluchi. Ask me, this looks like a drug killing,' said Rezaie, one of the older labourers, deftly extinguishing Hosseini's unwise foray into politics.

'Something like this was always going to happen with the latest wave of cartels pushing up from Zahedan. It's screwed up everything. Let's say our friend here tries to cut the other traffickers out of a deal; this is what they do to you. It's a lesson to the others. Cruel bastards, the Baluchis. Very cruel, even to their own.'

No one believed the man before them had been a Baluchi drug runner but they all murmured in convenient agreement and cursed the changing of the times. Truth be told, there were few in Anareh who did not surrender their cramped limbs to the opium brazier each night, and even fewer who were not nodding acquaintances of the Baluchi peddlers, privy to their intrigues and gossip. If there was a rotten apple in the cartels, they would have heard about it by now.

Jahangiri knew his boys needed his wise counsel more than ever but taciturn as he was he needed to play for time and quoted from one of the few surahs of the Koran that was still fresh in his mind: the table.

'Whoever slays a man, if not as punishment for murder or for corruption upon the earth, it is as if he has slain all humanity.'

Despite the sage nods of the old guard, Hosseini, to whom the rhyming Arabic prose had just been an impenetrable jumble, was impatient.

'Shouldn't we just bury him, boss?'

Jahangiri ran his hand through his beard and told the boys to wait. He retreated to his beloved 1977 Land-Rover and gently tapped an unfiltered Homa on the bonnet before lighting it, his invariable ritual since his days back on the front where the chain-smoking began.

'The boss will know what to do,' Rezaie assured the lads.

It was the most beautiful part of the evening. Under the midday sun, the mountains of Kerman will disappoint any traveller seeking the snow-flanked magnificence of the Alps. They are almost amorphous, a bulbous excrescence heaped up on the edge of the desert. But as the shadows lengthen and the heat ebbs away, the rugged outlines of the Jebal Barez become more clearly defined, as if etched out with charcoal. It was the time of day when Jahangiri felt closest to his God, al Hadi, the eternal Guide.

To the men who work them, the qanats are a sublime testament to the ingenuity and tenacity of their forefathers. Tourists may fill their photo albums with the turquoise tilework of the Safavid mosques or the bas-reliefs of tribute-bearers at Persepolis, but only if they stare out of the window on their flights across the desert will they appreciate the apogee of Iranian engineering. You might be forgiven for thinking the air force had been out for a practice, laying a bombing-run of craters down from the mountains to each town and village. Those craters contain the access shafts, many easily over a hundred yards deep, puncture-holes leading down into the qanats, lifelines hewn more than two millennia ago. To break the Persians, you break their qanats. The thirteenth-century Mongol invaders, those devils loosed from Tartarus, quickly saw that bringing Persian towns to their knees was child's play, pouring bucketload after bucketload of sand into the underground watercourses.

Keeping the water flowing is hazardous work and Jahangiri had hauled out many bodies over the years. He had lost many friends down in the underworld: bitten by snakes, poisoned by build-ups of gas or crushed by cave-ins when fitting the nars, the ribcage of an ageing qanat. Worst of all, there were those, like his own father, who drowned when they triggered turbid dambursts in the clearance work. Yet he could accept all those deaths – the whims of the capricious waterway itself – more easily than this aberration, a man disposed of as if he would be unnoticed or forgotten in the current. This was the work of callous, spoiled, city boys, the new order that thinks water just flows out of a tap and that thirsting date palms can survive on a few inches of autumn rainfall. These people, he thought, these people. Corrupt upon the face of the earth. They understand nothing of the sanctity of it all, the way the whole fabric fits together. They have no inkling that Jahangiri and the old masters still exist, lovingly memorising every twist and turn of the qanat, measuring out gradients with candles in the pitch black, not too steep or the rush of the current will eat out the supporting walls. Is there no respect for our kind any more, for the old ways?

Still, he also knew there was no question of retribution; you cannot fight such shallow-hearted men. This could only be the viper's latest vendetta, albeit bungled. That being so, should they just do what Hosseini said and bury the body under a pile of stones, somewhere off towards the mountains? He inhaled a dense lungful of perfumed tobacco. Impossible. We are not those kind of men. He ground the Homa butt into the dust and dragged a tarpaulin out of the back of the old British workhorse.

'Here, let's load him up.'

Two of the muqannis rolled the mangled body on to the tarpaulin and threaded a rope through the eyeholes, trussing him up like one of the pahlavans, the peripatetic, chain-sundering escapologists who pass through the village twice a year.

'Are you really sure about this, boss?' Hosseini asked. 'I mean, nothing but trouble is bound to come of this. If they wanted him out of the way and we just put him out of the way, then everyone's happy.'

Jahangiri turned up his nose in distaste.

'We'll take him to Hajj Mahmoud for the proper rites. That is the way we do things. That's the way we have always done things.'

'He hardly needs the rites. How many times did you keep telling us that the water of the qanat is holy water? Isn't this corpse already cleansed?'

At Jahangiri's stony indifference, Hosseini tried a different tack.

'Hajj Mahmoud is hardly his father's son: he's a simple akhond, a sermoner who'll expect a fistful of greens for reciting prayers he doesn't understand.'

The foreman had heard enough.

'We'll get him down to the mosque then make a police report. End of story. Finished. If you've got any sense, you'll play dumb from now on.'

Brushing off a scorpion that had crawled on to the tarpaulin, the muqannis heaved their sorry burden into the back of the Land-Rover and piled in beside it. Jahangiri noticed that Rezaie eased the door closed with a respectful click rather than his customary slam, as if somehow trying not to rouse the deceased. The foreman churned up a great cloud of dust as he followed the easy gradient of the qanat back into Anareh.

Shortly before turning in that night, Jahangiri's wife, Sousan, poured him a glass of arak. She knew he was still digesting what it could all mean for him and his dear, dear boys. He downed the caustic firewater and fixed the central floral medallion of the carpet with a tired stare. Although the police had made no mention of it, it occurred to him for the first time that he had moved evidence.

Shortly after dawn prayers, he heard the splutter of an unfamiliar jeep directly outside his house. The driver killed the engine and cranked up the handbrake. Visitors. Jahangiri chased his chickens into their coop and invited his guest inside the caramel mud-brick walls of his courtyard.

Colonel Nouriani appeared rather too stately for a Revolutionary Guardsman, with a dapper, well-trimmed beard. He did not sport the stubble and paunch that had become the hallmark of his unit's corpulent top brass. Under his arm, he cradled an ornate silver samovar, an exquisite piece of Russian handiwork, a bauble fit for the villas of the Caspian littoral rather than the dusty villages of Kerman. Their hands pressed across their hearts, the foreman and the officer launched into the ceremonial gauntlet of courtesies that must be exchanged between host and guest. Jahangiri invited Colonel Nouriani to sit on a wooden bed-frame decked out with kilims. Sousan, clad in a white floral chador, dutifully brought out piping glasses of tea, accompanied by bowls of coarse sugar cubes, diced apple and walnuts. The soldier poured out effusive thanks and, once again, pressed his palm across his heart with a bow. Sousan smiled with appreciation and beat a hasty retreat, kicking off her sandals as she slipped through a bead curtain back into the kitchen, her inner sanctum.

Nouriani had immediately noted the thin white scar down the foreman's cheek and the pink blotches that distinguish the survivors of chemical attacks.

'You did your time on the front, I see.'

'Majnoun,' Jahangiri replied, with sadness rather than pride.

It was a name to conjure with, the supreme pyrrhic victory of the war. A quarter of a million men dragging their way through the marshes, against maybe only ten thousand Iraqis. But the Iraqis had the tanks, artillery, gunboats and poison gas.

Majnoun. What a name. Majnoun the delirious lover of classical Persian verse. Majnoun, the crazed Romeo.

'Then we served together,' said Nouriani respectfully, but he could sense Jahangiri was in no mood to swap stories from the battles of the Kheibar offensive.

'Mr Jahangiri, I bring you this samovar as a token of appreciation from Ayatollah Baharvand.'

The foreman protested and insisted that, while he was obviously always at the service of the Ayatollah, he could see no reason why he should merit such a fabulous ornament.

'The Ayatollah read last night's police report on the recovery of the body of our martyred comrade, Sergeant Ahmadian, and was fulsome in his praise for the courage and dedication of the muqannis. He was most insistent on the point.'

Jahangiri protested twice more before summoning Sousan from her domain. The samovar, she assured the colonel, would take pride of place in the reception room, where he, and even the Ayatollah himself, would always be welcome. After she had scurried back into the kitchen, Jahangiri expressed surprise that the dead man had been a Revolutionary Guardsman.

'He was attached to Baharvand's security unit. Directly under my command, in fact. But the Ayatollah always insists that his boys do some of the regular security patrols, being part of the community and all that. He was murdered by some drug-runners out on the road to Deh-e Tofangchi. I'm sure you know the roadblock, just where there are outcrops coming right down to the road on both sides.'

Of course he knew the spot. Everyone does.

'Four days ago, he pulled over a SAIPA pick-up with a couple of hobbled camels in the back. He had been told to keep a special eye out for camels. There have been a couple of big hauls cut out

8

of the animals' bellies in the last few months. And the drivers were Baluchis, so he had justifiable suspicions.'

Jahangiri shook his head wearily and picked out the most brain-like of the walnuts.

'He called over the other guardsman on the roadblock and the two of them told the Baluchis to get out and open the back of the vehicle. That is when they set on him. You saw for yourself what they did to the poor devil. Savages. Baharvand got really worked up that no one gives a damn about all our lads dying like flies down here on the borders; he called it the forgotten war. We are drafting a statement for all the state networks. People have got to know about the sacrifices being made.'

'What happened to the other soldier?'

'The traffickers shot him in the chest and left him for dead. But he survived, el Hamdulillah. He told us the whole story.'

Jahangiri grimaced and concurred that it was all a very ugly business. Nouriani smiled, complimented the foreman on the excellence of his courtyard and lifted himself from the wooden bed-frame, puffing out his chest and ironing out a couple of wrinkles in his khaki uniform.

'The Ayatollah sends his best regards to your muqannis, the whole team. He always reminds us he is at heart a farmer and that little matters more to him than the Anareh estates where he was born, kept alive by the ancient qanat, he always adds.'

Jahangiri laughed politely and shook the guardsman firmly by the hand.

'God protect you my friend,' he said, repeating his thanks to the Ayatollah for his generosity and his concern for the dying art of the muqannis.

He waved the jeep off and closed the lime-green metal gate that separated his courtyard from the road. He was amused by the notion of the viper as a keen agriculturalist rediscovering his roots in Anareh. He pictured the former secretary of the Supreme National Security Council checking the ripeness of his pomegranates and fretting about the aflatoxin count in his pistachios. But Nouriani had struck him as a decent sort, even though his story had been an assortment of clumsy lies.

Six hundred and fifty miles northwest of Anareh, Seb Maynard, third secretary at the British embassy, was working late on a memo, trying to muster an interest in the parliamentarians' latest attacks on British companies. London's inability to grasp the irrelevance of the Iranian parliament – an unruly kindergarten – became doubly infuriating when Leila, prima donna of the uptown social scene, was throwing a party he really needed to get to by half nine. Alas, there was also a maverick president to keep an eye on. Ahmadinejad was due to give a speech, a fixture that did not seem to be airing on state TV. Seb thought it best to keep refreshing the website of the official news agency, just in case old Mahmoud lobbed another political grenade, vaunting another unlikely atomic breakthrough or baring his teeth at the Israelis. But nothing yet. Almost absent-mindedly, he double clicked on the bulletin about the soldier killed in the glory-bringing jihad against drug smugglers in Kerman and printed it off for the drug liaison officer. The story was ordinary enough but the camels had some novelty value and because two Baluchis had been arrested the mousy pair who cover human rights could squeeze it into their bulging dossier of impending executions.

Ultimately, Ahmadinejad was a no-show and Seb finished his memo by ten to nine. Even supposing some parliamentarians were mouthpieces for bona fide powerbrokers, only the big names such as BP, Shell and British Gas were politically toxic enough to find themselves in the cross-hairs. And they were up shit creek anyway. The majority of British companies, supplying valves and tubing to natural gas projects which the lawmakers had never heard of, could keep flying in under the radar and clocking up tidy profits. The problem was not so much politics as projects drying up. Even though it was the fourth time he had to spell this out for Whitehall, so his despatch flowed pretty easily, there was little sign the penny would drop. He guessed his polished opus would land on Friday lunchtime and the long weekend would already be getting under way. The Mandarins would be slipping out to catch the 16.05 from Paddington for a couple of days gouging divots out of moorland golf courses or gibing round the tranquil reaches of the Helford. The memo on British interests in Iran would be forgotten.

But that was hardly the point for Maynard the rookie. He still savoured the prestige and exoticism of his first posting even though no Iranian officials would talk to the Brits any more. He had that thrill that comes with night shifts, loyally flying the flag while the rest of the world tucks into dinner and watches telly. He still enjoyed a secret frisson when he glimpsed his own ghostly reflection in the office window after dark, the left side of his face picked out by the lamplight. All night essay crunches in his lodgings on Walton Street had the same magic, just the two of them, him and his reflection, grappling with the battle of Hattin while the rest of Oxford slept. He had outshone the rest of the Keble contingent who had ended up counting beans at Goldman Sachs and Deloitte. They had the cash, but not the cachet. If he ever needed evidence to prove his geopolitical significance to the city Apaches, he could tell them about the hammer wrapped in a tartan handkerchief in his drawer. He had orders to smash the innards of his computer if the boys in black were to storm the embassy. And most importantly, the square-mile brigade didn't have invitations to Leila's extravaganza, a mini-skirted debauch where debonair young diplomats were

11

bound to strike it lucky. Tragically and unjustly, Leila herself was looking to land a po-faced German first secretary but her entourage always seemed to include an army of beguiling lovelies who were unfailingly keen to sink their claws into naive western boys. He was up for a bit of clawing. He whipped his tie off the hook on the back of the door and used his reflection in the window to knot an immaculate half Windsor.

Stepping back to his desk, he scribbled a note to Rice-Jenkyns across the top of the agency bulletin and slipped it into the out-tray. And that was the last time he gave any thought to the murdered sergeant. Within a fortnight he would be working eighteen-hour days as the tinder-dry nation around him crackled into flame. Every newspaper in the world would splash across its front page that picture of the tankers burning off Bandar Abbas, columns of black smoke billowing into the crisp blue sky of the Persian Gulf. Maynard would deftly splice together his telegrams to London: the litter of bombings, burned-out tanks and high-level hits woven together in consummately wrought prose, laced with official utterances and off-record gen. But the Iran Mandarins in London knew none of the pieces were fitting together. A resurgence of the People's Mujahidin, the old enemy from the early revolutionary days, or a concerted al Qaeda campaign could never explain anything on this scale. They just did not have that kind of strike-power or organisational ability, no matter what the ghouls in the Tehran ministries wanted you to believe. Seb Maynard's paymasters kept asking for more, although no one at the embassy could even pick out the corners of the jigsaw. However, that murdered soldier in the qanat could have explained it all. After all, he had never manned a road-block in his short, devoted life.

On the Thursday night in October that Ahmadinejad failed to deliver a speech, Maynard had no greater concern than the tides of Tehran traffic which were still in spate at nine fifteen. It was past ten by the time he pulled off the Sadr highway and squeezed the Range Rover into a spot outside Leila's tower block. Two weeks later, she would be one of the first to bail out, flashing her French passport at the grudging customs officers at Mehrabad airport.

When the lift doors crunched open on the seventeenth floor, the muffled throb of Persian pop beckoned. He rang the buzzer of 17-3 and a grinning, portly waiter in a waistcoat quickly ushered him inside. A huge flat-screen plasma television was pumping out the latest hits from the California, Tehrangeles. On the screen, three scantily-clad women on a flying carpet were wailing about their broken hearts while twenty or so bright young things jived away to the beat. Around the dance floor, Seb could make out the regular rogues' gallery, many of them nodding to him as he headed to the drinks table. There were the film-makers, sculptors, entrepreneurs and management consultants who always used these occasions to give the diplomats and journalists their low-down on what was really going on in the Islamic Republic. Seb resisted the amber come-hither of the bootleg Bells and mixed himself a Smirnoff and pomegranate juice. At least the Armenian booze-dealers weren't still pushing that Skyy vodka the US troops in Iraq had been selling off at bargain basement rates. It was good to be back on the Smirnoff. Seeing one end of the table barred by a crisps magnate haranguing *The Times* correspondent about the myth of Kurdish discontent, he headed out on to the balcony where Leila was holding court, leaning languidly against the balustrade, surrounded by half a dozen impossibly glamorous twenty-somethings.

'Sebastiaaan joon,' she cried, kissing him three times. 'I was worried you weren't going to make it.'

'Sorry, yes, imprisoned in the office. But I could never miss this view,' he replied, throwing his hands up at the snow-capped Alborz as if he were a ringmaster introducing the next act. The mountains had a leering, imminent menace, racing towards the apartment like a breaking wave. 'Look at that. Fantastic place you've got here.'

'Aw, chérie. You have a drink, wonderful. Now, do you know everyone here?'

Only a few of the faces on the balcony were familiar but he greeted them all as warmly as if they were old friends.

'How are things with Britain, the Old Fox?' asked Reza, a rock guitarist with slicked-back hair, whom he remembered to be a bit of a wiseacre.

'Pretty good, pretty good,' he said, taking a measured first sip of his vodka and pomegranate. 'I have just this minute sent off our latest instructions to the Supreme Leader, mapping out how Iran is to be run. What I like to call the gameplan.'

They laughed heartily, enjoying the running Iranian joke that the British still run the country. Well, it's a joke at parties in Kamranieh. To many Iranians, it is a sincerely held belief that Britain is still as mighty as when wily classical scholar Monty Woodhouse helped the CIA oust Mossadegh in 1953. Seb had unwisely once suggested to a sweet-seller that perhaps, just perhaps, the Americans ran the world these days. The shopkeeper scoffed at the idea and pointed out that this is where the British had been at their most devilishly cunning. The Old Fox had made it look as if the Americans ran the world so mad Arabs would attack New York instead of London. Presented with the logical conundrum of bombs in London, the sweet-seller neatly explained that the British occasionally had to attack their own people to justify their imperialism, a view regularly aired by the Iranian government. Seb would face regular grillings in the bazaar on why his government had ordered the murders of Dr David Kelly and Robin Cook out in remote countryside. Seb always insisted he was not at liberty to speak for the assassination team at MI5 but he added, with a note of confidentiality, that it was assumed that men with beards were seen as being natural allies of Iran. The bazaaris always seemed to enjoy the joke but never agreed to lower their prices.

'So what are you planning to do with our country this month, you evil imperialist?' joked an achingly beautiful girl in a silver sequined cocktail dress. She gave Seb a wide-eyed, expectant look that he found irresistible.

'Oh, you know, the usual. A continued ruthless exploitation of minerals while launching a renewed crackdown on parties. We British can't stomach parties, all the alcohol and mini-jupes. We see very much eye-to-eye with the leadership on the whole mini-skirt issue.'

Again the party-goers got into the spirit of the running gag but talk of a crackdown touched a nerve. The woman next to Miss Sequins, her nose sculpted into a little ski-jump by the cosmetic surgeons, said many of her friends weren't venturing out into the party scene any more because of all the raids. It was like going back to the pre-Khatami era. Some friends of friends had gone shoe shopping up at the Tajrish bazaar in north Tehran, supposedly safe territory, when a troupe of gorillas pulled them into an alley and accused them of 'bad hejab', flouting the country's dress codes by showing a provocative four inches of naked shin and letting too much hair spill out from their Armani headscarves. Tempers frayed after one of the beardy-boys called the girls whores. They were bundled into the back of a van. Passers-by pretended that they couldn't see what was going on.

'Were these intelligence guys?' Seb asked.

The girl shook her head.

'No, but that's the problem. They had no idea who the hell they were. Morals police? Basijis? Judiciary? Some religious brigade run by God knows who? That's the point, you can't do anything because you don't know who you are up against. So these guys take the girls miles out of town to some empty warehouse. Really scary. You know the sort of place: broken windows and wiring hanging out of the wall. Then they take the girls' mobiles, jot down all the numbers and sift through the text messages. After that they make them sit on benches and grill them about personal stuff. Do you drink vodka? Do you have boyfriends? How do they fuck you? Everything. Then, finally, they made them take off their shoes and shoved their feet in buckets of cockroaches.'

Reza slammed down his glass on the parapet. 'Man, that's some fucked-up shit. I bet they get off on that. There are some serious crazies walking around out there, man. That Dr Freud knew a thing or two. Boy, those guys sure aren't getting enough.'

Everybody there heard stories like this but that was no reason for them to bottle their rage. They could never accustom themselves to this world. A spectacled documentary-maker in a beret, who had been shaking his head in dismay throughout the story, mentioned, almost in passing, that the police had confiscated his archives on Tuesday, which accounted for the last ten years of his work.

Seb asked what he was doing to get them back.

'They gave me a chit,' he explained. 'But when I took it down to the station they said it wasn't valid. I'll try to get some back-up from the ministry of culture people but I really don't hold out much hope of them managing to do anything.'

'Jesus. Sorry, that's awful.'

As the rest of the group commiserated with him, the radiant hostess took Seb by the arm and pointed to the luxury penthouse of a block of flats across the road.

'They raided that place a couple of weeks back. It wasn't even a party, just a soirée with a few fifty-year-olds having a bottle of wine or two. They tried to talk or pay their way out of it. But that just pissed the gorillas off even more and they pulled guns. One woman freaked and chucked herself out of the window, that's twenty floors down.'

Seb stared wide-eyed at the pavement beneath the building. The apartment was one of the most exclusive in the city, built before the revolution by French engineers who insisted it was earthquake-proof.

'Some people said she had been shot in the back but her husband told me she just jumped.'

'Fucking hell. I'm impressed that all the raids aren't scaring you off.'

Leila lolled her head to one side and smiled flirtatiously.

'You gotta keep partying, I guess. It's the only way I can show how much I hate them.'

Once these stories start, there's no stopping them, Seb knew. All Iranians have a horror story to tell and ninety percent of them are true. The rest of the party melted into a fug. He lost count of the vodka and pomegranates and disgraced himself on the dance-floor. The nympho from the Austrian embassy got it together in the kitchen with a twice-divorced factory-owner and, at some stage, the pugilist from *The Times* had performed his usual party trick and lost his rag with the crisps magnate, poking him in the chest and shouting across the room that the man was a dangerous nationalist and probably a fascist. Somebody was going to snap his neck one of these days. Like a loyal lapdog, Seb kept bounding over to Miss Sequins, who finally rewarded him with a fifteen-minute tête-à-tête on a gaudy Louis XV chaise longue beside the dance-floor. It transpired not only that she had a name, Negar, but also a job, working as an accountant for one

17

of the biggest car makers, Iran Khodro. She left it agonisingly late in proceedings to tell him about her boyfriend, at which point Seb's diplomatic side kicked in and he made uninspiring small talk about automakers and declining foreign investment. Sensing that she had made a tactical error with this naive Englishman, Negar steered the conversation back to her boyfriend who was firstly a good-for-nothing and secondly always in Sweden, where she was convinced that he had a string of other beautiful Persian girlfriends. Seb decided not to snap up the bait. It sounded all too complex for his liking. He looked at his watch. Two fifteen. The tiredness hit him suddenly, his head was throbbing and he made his farewells. Negar was one to keep on file for future reference.

He reached the high-walled sanctuary of Gholhak, the leafy British embassy residential compound, by half two. It was little wonder that the Iranians wanted this 'occupied territory' returned to them, citing reams of spurious ancient parchments, but Seb always shuddered to think what would happen to the Qajar residence, immaculate flower beds and bottle-green parrots if oil ministry philistines got hold of the place.

Jasper, Gholhak's ginger moggie, had curled up on the end of his bed. There was profound suspicion around the compound that Jasper was in the direct pay of Iranian Intelligence. No-one quite knew where he appeared from and a Filipina maid intermittently took him off for operations which no one had ever thought he needed. But despite the fears that his scarred belly was riddled with transmitters, Jasper still had a free run of diplomatic dinners and soirées, tuning in to top-level chit-chat. Rather than wake the slumbering secret agent, Seb threw open the French windows at the end of his bedroom, startling a fox that scampered off across the croquet lawn. He pulled on a sweater, poured himself a carafe of water and settled in one of the rattan chairs on the veranda, wondering where the nightingales had got to. It was three weeks until his twenty-sixth birthday and life was treating him well.

Seb was still sleeping off the excesses of the previous night, when a family sedan, a silver Peugeot Pars, pulled into the viper's estates and was promptly surrounded by a swarm of black-suited security guards. The man in the back seat was irritable and had done little but complain to the driver about pot-holed provincial roads all the way from Kerman airport. Where was Anareh anyway? From what he could make out through the tinted windows, it hardly even felt like a real village, more an accretion of vassal homesteads parasitically feeding off the sprawling Baharvand farms. He had put aside this Friday to celebrate his daughter's birthday and had planned a picnic out towards Damavand. He had protested briefly about the summons but the viper's emissary in Tehran had spelled out that non-attendance was impossible. The burliest of the thugs escorted Jafari to the steps of the main villa without even granting him the common courtesy of a greeting. It was only ten yards to the entrance but the visitor, shuffling along in an ill-fitting grey polyester suit broke into an instant sweat. The way the meat-head continually fiddled with his ear-piece played upon his nerves. If he were picking up some instructions through that thing, his sunken, dead eyes showed no flicker of comprehension.

Jafari was impressed by the elegant simplicity of the villa. The crimson Heriz carpets in the main salon must each have been worth thousands of dollars, tens of thousands perhaps, but the vulgar trinkets of the Tehran nouveaux riches were nowhere to be seen. It was a family pile worthy of the great houses of Kashan, with a lofty wind-tower planted squarely in the middle of the roof. The security honcho pointed to the corner of the room, again without uttering a word. Wondering whether the brute was in fact dumb, a great asset in Ayatollah Baharvand's world, Jafari nestled himself against the hard cushions ranged up against the wall and admired the lattice-work of the alabaster ceiling.

The viper thought it important to make them wait, sweat them a bit and establish the proper pecking order from the outset. Apart from a servant who brought in some tea and a bowl of cucumbers, Jafari was left alone for half an hour, an eel wriggling through his guts as he tortured himself over why he should have been summoned.

At quarter to eleven, the pencil-thin cleric entered the room, threw back his mantle and stretched out a hand. He had mastered the quick approach that left seated guests stumbling. Jafari only just made it to his feet in time and was immediately enveloped in the embrace of the Viper who expressed surprise that the director of programming at state television had never made it down to the Anareh estates before.

Jafari explained how delighted and honoured he was to be invited and enquired whether the wind-tower really managed to keep such a spacious villa cool through July and August.

'Oh indeed, indeed,' the Viper said, waving his hand airily and placing himself against the wall opposite Jafari. 'I really cannot abide air-conditioning. I feel it eats up the lungs. There's something so healthy about the wind-tower.'

The kow-towing civil servant remarked that some of his staff at state broadcasting had passed him the cleric's profile in the previous week's *Time* magazine. It was a well played card. Kristina Kowalski had shared Jafari's interest in the wind-tower on her trip to Anareh and been won over by the old man's undoubted charms. He was particularly pleased by the description of himself as 'an architect of the 1979 revolution' and she had found one of the European ambassadors, French he seemed to recall, who hailed him as the 'most cerebral and charming of Iran's nuclear negotiators'. He even thought that he had coped rather well with the question on how he won the sobriquet viper. In his eccentric but fluent English, he joked that if everyone was calling the hardliner Mesbah-Yazdi 'the crocodile' and the hard-nosed pragmatist Rafsanjani 'the shark' then he probably had the least painful bite of the turbaned class. He realised the western press was likely to fete any bigwig who was critical of the president but that was no reason not to bask. He made all the right noises about personal freedoms and Kowalski remarked that she detected a tear welling in his eye when he described Iranian youngsters turning to drugs and emigration as the only ways of escaping social restrictions. She had little idea that the more cynical, careerist Shi'ite clerics master the art of crocodile tears shortly before puberty.

'Yes, but you can never trust the western media. All this nonsense about my business interests. I have my little farm here and that's quite enough for a man of my years. They must think I am "the shark". I wrote a letter to the editor, but nothing yet.'

More tea arrived and Ayatollah Baharvand asked whether all was well at state television. Jafari proudly explained that the network was producing a new series of feature programmes on Iran's mosques, to be shown for an hour each evening, profiling various jewels in the country's architectural crown.

God, that sounded dire, Baharvand thought. As if Iranians weren't all scrambling for satellite anyway. What was it with these little men in suits like Jafari? Why were they always trying to impress the clerics with their holier than thou credentials.

'Excellent, excellent. It sounds a fascinating series.'

He sipped a little tea through the sugar cube pinched between his teeth and decided enough time had been wasted.

'Now, what news from your brother, my friend?'

Jafari felt the electricity shoot down his spine. If Baharvand had any leverage over him it was through his brother. The old man was calling in his debt.

'He is doing very well, hajji. He and his family send you their fondest regards.'

Bullshit. The Commie bastard probably still hates my guts.

'And do pass my best wishes on to them. They are still in ... where was it? Hamburg? Hanover?'

'Hamburg. Yes. His wife is German: Annika.'

'Aha.' Baharvand fixed Jafari in an icy gaze and chomped the end off a cucumber. 'And remind me, how many children do they have?'

'Just the two, Dariush and Maryam.'

'Ah, good Persian names at least.'

'Oh, of course, and they both speak the two languages, Persian and German.'

'And they write Persian?'

'Yes, yes, Alireza taught them the script.'

'That is a relief. I do hate all these Californians who pretend to be Iranian but can't even write their own names any more. Idiots.'

Jafari laughed politely but feared that any discussion of his brother was steering the conversation into turbulent waters. He would never forget that icy November day in 1981 when he embraced Baharvand in a courtyard outside Evin prison, impervious to the driving rain. Baharvand, probably the most powerful judge in the country, had happily torn up the death warrant of Alireza Jafari, a harmless communist firebrand from the Tudeh party. In the loyalty of his brother, he saw a more useful investment. The grateful brother had exactly what was needed to be a great player in the fledgling Islamic Republic. Not talent, but the total lack of it. Hossein Jafari paraded a dazzling mediocrity. One type of leader in the wings was the commander who had led an insane, suicidal charge across the Iraqi minefields. The other was a Jafari, the dogged time-server, who would do well. Those men would be destined to run the country. Jafari had that profound lack of imagination required to go far. Baharvand and his ilk would be kept at arm's length.

And Jafari did worm his way up. He now ensured Iran's terrestrial viewers didn't get an unseemly flash of unveiled female flesh at football internationals and had their purgative spoonful of mosque architecture before bedtime. Baharvand saw the US embassy siege as one of the most preposterous and self-defeating farces of the early revolution but realised the fiasco would produce a handful of men who would go on to greater things. A couple of times, Jafari appeared on evening television corralling a handful of blindfolded American diplomats. Unlike several of his fellow hostage-takers, Jafari had even lacked the self-awareness to rebrand himself as a reformist under Khatami. He was exactly the sort of man you could trust to safeguard the morals of a nation on the brink. Despite an unfortunate oversight when he had allowed some traditional Qashqai musicians to sing live on air at the Persian new year, he had reduced official programming to a turgid lifelessness that teetered on brilliance.

'I am going to need some help from you in the next few days, my friend,' Baharvand continued, dusting another decapitated cucumber in salt. 'I fear we are once again heading into a period of national turmoil and that you and I will both be needed to steady the ship, perhaps state television far more than my own humble efforts.'

Jafari thought it best to say nothing.

'In the next ten to fourteen days, you will be joined in Tehran by groups of Revolutionary Guards and technicians answerable to me. You will work with them and put your resources directly under their control.'

Jafari could not disguise his alarm.

'What should I do if I receive contradictory instructions through the normal channels?'

'You ignore them. You are answerable to me and my commanders. I have agents deeply rooted in certain opposition elements lobbying for greater democracy: students and others. I have it on good authority they are planning protests very much on the scale of 2003. This time I will ensure that these demonstrations receive a full and unedited airing on state networks.'

Jafari shook his head. Baharvand had clearly gone insane and could easily be reeled back to earth.

'We will be taken off the air. They'll know this could spark nationwide unrest. Even big celebrations after football wins are off bounds. You know all this. Troops will be sent round and that will be an end of it. With the greatest respect, what you say is impossible, Ayatollah. I'll land up in jail, or worse.'

At the far end of the salon, there entered a short figure enveloped in a black chador. The old woman padded barefoot across the carpets and settled next to the Ayatollah. It was well-known, almost as a point of political folklore, that the Ayatollah's wife, Massoumeh, had always been a vital policy maker back in Anareh. Baharvand continued to advance his plans, as if oblivious to his wife's entrance.

'The military elements are of no consequence to you now. These are being handled separately. You will learn what is happening more or less by the same channels as everyone else. I, along with commanders such as Colonel Nouriani, will be delivering pre-recorded messages throughout the day. Naturally, these will pass through you. There will be separate messages

24

regarding, for example, the closure of borders and airports for which I will also rely on your services.'

'This is madness, Ayatollah.'

Massoumeh had no time for such insubordination.

'You are not privy to the full plan and you will not be. You have only to do your part. You have only to assure your staff that you are working legitimately in tandem with our people. Play your part and all will be well. You will be well rewarded.'

But Jafari was now panicking.

'Ayatollah, I really don't have the faintest idea what you are planning but you really cannot pull this sort of thing off any more. There really aren't the old loopholes in the system, they have sewn everything up. It will never work. Whatever it is.'

Baharvand smiled considerately.

'When I started my work at the Supreme National Security Council during the war, they put me in charge of weapons procurement. People remember all the secret meetings to buy arms from the Americans but the bread and butter deals were with Romania and Bulgaria. There were several strands to relations with Eastern Europe: learning heavy-water technology, training asymmetrical forces and a whole host of such enterprises. I got to know the countries and their leaders well, along with our opposite numbers in the security set-up. I do not pretend to know what happened in Romania in 1989 when Ceausescu was shot but it taught me the importance of television and how valuable you could be to me, my friend. Some of the Securitate people who used to oversee our weapons' shipments simply kiss off the revolution as a coup from inside the regime, with the Soviets and Americans pulling the strings of course. They realised they were going to lose their own hides so toppled Ceausescu as soon as the crowds got rowdy. Curiously enough, that nasty little dwarf-man was meeting me here in Tehran when the whole thing blew up back in Romania. The brilliance of the matter is that the world still believes there was a home-grown, popular uprising that cast off the shackles of Communism. Television gave the world the good news. People can be too petrified to be spontaneous, they needed a little help along the road.'

Jafari had understood only snatches of what the cleric was saying but fathomed the enormity of what was being placed before him.

'OK, maybe you can do that stuff in a little country, in a Romania or a Bulgaria. But by God, pull the wool over their eyes, here? No, no, no.'

Massoumeh's patience ran out with the ungrateful little pen pusher. She had shown her loyalty to Baharvand, the visionary, back in 1982 when she flung herself between him and a mujahidin assassin. She even had one of the bullets still lodged in her. How dare this pimple of a man not fall into line?

'Listen, our friend. It is only natural that you have little sense of the scale of the resources backing us but you can be rightfully confident of success.'

She paused and examined the sweaty official.

'When you return to Tehran you will find that your wife and children are already in our care. You will explain to any inquisitive friends that they are taking a holiday.'

Jafari stared in disbelief at the gaunt cleric but elicited no reaction. Massoumeh continued: 'We hear and see everything. Our people are already deeply imbedded in state broadcasting. If there is even the slightest suspicion on our part that you are about betray us, then your family will die. They will return to you, safe and sound, as soon as we have concluded our business.'

Jafari had suspected from the outset that he would have little choice in agreeing to whatever plan the viper had in mind.

'Your brother in Germany will also die,' Massoumeh added with a relish that Baharvand himself found a touch distasteful. He decided to try and reassure the terrified civil servant by mapping out more of the practicalities.

'The day itself should not take you by surprise. I will arrange several meetings with my technicians before then. You will know exactly what I will want transmitted and when. Much of the material is already pre-recorded. My film teams will know where and when to film major public and student protests. Your men will co-ordinate with them and do exactly as they say. Do as you are told, exactly as you are told, and you will have nothing to fear.'

'That will be all,' Massoumeh added. 'From here on in, we are watching every step you take.'

As the silver sedan ferried the unwilling but loyal conspirator back to Kerman airport, Nouriani joined the viper on the steps of his villa. The chirp of cicadas had imperceptibly swollen into a roar.

'There's good news from our people in intelligence: apparently, our watchers are chasing their arses over the mole. They got nothing from him before we took him out, nothing. It sounds like we managed to squeeze far more out of the bastard on this side.'

Baharvand nodded but remained impassive.

'I take it that you have disciplined the men who threw the mole into the qanat. It caused a lot of upset in the village.'

Nouriani insisted that the men had been punished and apologised for their stupidity.

'Very good, colonel, very good. Now, tell me, back in the early days, do you remember any mention of a Danish shipping office down in Abadan, Janssen's?'

'No, Ayatollah, I'm afraid that doesn't sound familiar.'

'Really? A pity that. It's a fascinating story. And I think it is time that we put them back in business.'

2.

ANDY TREVARTHEN EMERGED from Barons Court tube at dusk and headed off towards Fulham Palace Road, past the contented regiments of terraced houses and their convivial front rooms where families were settling down for supper. One father was laying out an electric train-set and a group of boisterous young professionals were watching the Arsenal match, empty lager cans strewn across the parquet. Andy had always been fascinated by that time of day, lighting-up hour, when the English, a supposedly reclusive people, could be most easily spied upon. For at least forty five minutes, their homes were no longer their castles. Walk through any city at twilight and you get a series of stolen glimpses through the glass wall down the centre of the ant colony: the children's tantrums, the violin lessons and the marriages on the rocks. He never quite decided whether it was latent exhibitionism or whether he had simply been born into the secret world and was somehow just fated to observe. Always from the outside.

On the other side of Charing Cross Hospital, he was relieved to find the florist was still there. As ever, his strategy was to abrogate all responsibility and let the sales assistant call the shots.

'Hi there, I'm after something for a girl's eighteenth. I am afraid I'm not very good at this sort of thing. What should I be looking at?'

The woman's name tag said Dot but she looked at least twenty years too young to be a Dot. Maybe there had been a revival, an Indian summer for Dots.

'OK, well, we can do any of these,' she said, pulling out a photocard of different bouquet combinations.

'And all of these are OK for birthdays? Well, I rather like this one, with the pink roses and the freesias.'

'Oh yeah, that's a popular one. Do you want me to do that up for you now?'

'That would be great, thanks.'

The middle-aged spy had never understood flowers and he was never convinced that Juliette had either, which presumably lay at the heart of the problem. She had always seemed delighted to get them but they were quickly tossed to one side.

The price took him by surprise but he thought it better not to protest now Dot had tied everything up. He extracted three ten pound notes from his wallet and set off towards Beryl Road. The amethyst sky had turned to granite. It was drizzling.

The burly sea-dog himself opened the door to number 76, wearing an incongruously feminine apron.

'Chained to the kitchen sink again Anoush?'

'Hey Andy, come in out of the rain. How's life?'

'Not so bad.'

Andy brushed his feet on the doormat and gave the beaming Commander Bozorgmehr a great bear hug.

Najmeh appeared at the top of the stairs and melted at the sight of the bouquet.

'Oh Andy, no, you shouldn't have.'

She hurtled down the stairs and threw herself into his arms.

'They're sooo beautiful. Thank you so much.'

'Not at all. Happy birthday. What are you up to?'

'Well, it's with the girls tonight. Then Mum and Dad are taking me out tomorrow.'

'Very nice too.'

Andy was the only one of Dad's crowd that Najmeh would never introduce to her own friends. She got highly protective about him. And she knew Mum had the hots for him. She sort of did herself. A bit. But with plausible deniability. Dad's regulars were a disaster. It was a bit better now but when she was thirteen bringing her girlfriends round to Beryl Road meant running a deadly gauntlet. Who would we have tonight? The monarchists in silk ties and gold necklaces were probably the worst, lecturing teenage girls from Hammersmith on Iran not really being Muslim, the mullahs being Palestinians and the Shah being a born statesman who understood what was good for the Pear-shans. And their English was so crap. And, oh, you just wished they'd stop scrounging Burgundy off Dad and do something vulgar like get a job.

Najmeh's friends had initially been intimidated by Dad's poker crowd. They were, admittedly, a bit lecherous. But the girls had warmed to them in the end. One in particular, Ali Mostofi, a mustachioed property shark who had been in the navy with Dad, gained such a notoriety for witty repartee and unseemly comments to under-age girls that, for a while, Najmeh's classmates jostled to get invites on poker night. In a way she felt Ali was a remedial linchpin of Anglo-Iranian relations. While the girls at school got the stage-managed flag-burnings and 'Death to America' chants on the evening news, they could always get an antidote from Ali and the poker-night lads polishing off the Johnnie Walker. Mum had put an end to poker night last year, snuffing out years of glorious tradition.

But Andy didn't fit the mould of Dad's friends. It was curious that such an unassuming man should prove quite so compelling.

31

He was a bit stockier than on his last visit and was greying round the temples. He must be getting on for his mid-fifties now, she guessed. He wasn't tall and always seemed shabby round the edges, wearing scuffed shoes and a tweed jacket that should probably go the journey. Not even all those years in Paris had managed to spruce him up. He was unlooked after, in need of work. Why Juliette disappeared like that she could never work out. Andy had something very special. Maybe it was the mellow voice and the composure. Always charming, funny and shrewd but equally closed and unfathomable. Those family holidays on Juliette's farm outside Roscoff had been highlights of her childhood, with Andy and her dad teaching her how to sail while Juliette taught her the sort of French she would really need to know.

Andy enquired after Mum who was down in Richmond, catching up with tittle-tattle south of the river. Najmeh filled him in with the latest: the dreary French A-level texts and her work at a café; before springing back upstairs to put on her glad rags.

Andy followed Anoush into the kitchen where a couple of raw mincemeat kebabs had been skewered.

'Hopefully this drizzle'll stop in a minute and we can barbecue these beauties outside,' Anoush said, pouring out a couple of glasses of Chilean Merlot. '*Be salamati.* How's things in Paris?'

'Oh, dull. Mainly Maghreb stuff though we have a few Iranians blowing around. There's a glut of émigré types – and not just mujahidin – who seem to think that they can give us the crown jewels on undisclosed enrichment facilities, for a price. But none of it matches up with the Israeli intel.'

'And the real world? See anything of Juliette?'

'On and off. She is still with that computer programmer, Marko with a k. I've got to that age when I can admit that he seems lovely, actually. Very settled. What she needs these days.'

'Fuck that. I hate this guy.'

Loyalty was one of Anoush's finest qualities.

'Aaaaanyway,' said Andy, trying to divert conversation from his estranged wife. 'It seems somebody has sent up a flare.'

'A huge one, through Mohsen Karimi.'

'Well, well. Mohsen Karimi, eh? He doesn't say much, but when he does, you gotta listen.'

Mohsen was one of Iran's finest exports, now chief economics correspondent on *The Times*, and the sort of journalist who made Andy wonder whether straight-down-the-middle SIS men had any function. For years you would forget that he was a born-and-bred Tehrani as he put Mervyn King through his paces on how to run the Bank of England. But two years ago, he had penned one of the most brilliant pieces on the Islamic Republic that Andy had ever seen in print. It was so brilliant, in fact, that he worried Mohsen would be pushed under a tube. He had laid bare the sprawling financial interests of leading clerics who had always insisted they could barely afford their mantle and turban. Baharvand had been particularly well researched, he seemed to recall: Kermani copper mines, hefty percentages from Revolutionary Guard rackets and money laundering operations all around the Danube, using his old arms' dealer friends in the Securitate to set up phantom steel-makers. And then there were all the semi-legitimate enterprises: the consultancy fees paid by western oil firms looking to get a slice of the action in the South Pars gas fields. Wisely, Mohsen made no mention of the narco-trade but he clearly had sources that Andy would kill for.

'Yeah, Mohsen. He sends you his regards. He invited me out for lunch yesterday. Said it was urgent. We went to that Hungarian place off Soho Square that the hacks always go to. He said that Mehran Baharvand, the Ayatollah's nephew at HSBC, had got in touch. They are old friends those two. Then he just came out with it: Mehran Baharvand needed a coffee morning with us.'

Coffee morning. Rendezvous two. Fascinating. Mohsen was hardly panicky and was worth every penny of his retainer.

'That's a big call for Mohsen. How much does he seem to know?'

'It's hard to say, but he let on that baby Baharvand thinks he's under very heavy surveillance at the moment. Apparently he said Janssen's would have to be re-opened.'

'Ha! Did Mohsen know what that meant?'

'He said Baharvand wouldn't tell him what it meant but it would show us that he was serious. I said I didn't get it either and that the message would have to be passed further up the food-chain.'

'Probably for the best,' Andy said, holding his glass at the base and swilling the wine distractedly. The second rendezvous intrigued him. Things hadn't been this exciting for years. The second rendezvous meant all the trimmings: the safehouse in Wilton Square on Monday, along with the Yanks and the Israelis. He was already mulling over how many teams of watchers he'd need to walk through in relays, from Essex Road to Old Street. It sounded like Baharvand might have a tail, one of those leaden-footed clowns run by the Iranian embassy. It should be pretty easy to remove one of them from the picture.

'OK, tell Mohsen tomorrow that the coffee morning is on. Monday. 7 a.m.'

There was a gentle drumming as Najmeh skipped down the stairs and tugged on her high heels at the bottom. The two greying men in the kitchen assured her she looked divine and was bound to knock them dead.

She swung open the kitchen door and peered up pessimistically into the heavens.

34

'Mmm, it's stopped for now but I'd still better take a brolly.'

After her dad had satisfied himself that he knew where she was going and that she had her mobile, she disappeared into the night with a cheery wave.

Anoush swept up the *Daily Telegraph*, a bag of charcoals and a box of firelighters. Andy followed him out into the little concreted garden at the back.

'Do you hear from Mohsen yourself?'

'Rarely. The last time he came to find me he was after a story: the cover-up on the al-Yamamah arms sale to the Saudis. You remember, the arms deals between Britain and the Saudis which rasied billions of dollars, the kinky-sex slush fund that the Serious Fraud Office could not investigate because of the public interest.'

Anoush poked some screws of newspaper under the piles of charcoal.

'I didn't know too much about it,' Andy continued. 'I hadn't heard the banter from back at base camp. Maybe I should start leaking more now I am in my dotage. Mohsen put together a tart polemic arguing that British foreign policy was morally bankrupt. It helped that he hates the Saudis so much. He mentioned that a senior diplomatic source had resignedly told him that the national interest "now meant little more than the triumph of profit over principle".'

'And that was you?'

'I fear it may have been,' Andy replied, lighting a Gauloise in the nascent flames of the barbecue. 'I am turning into a trendy lefty at last. Almost a hippy. Only a few more years until I turn into a full-blown whistle-blower.'

'You can't fool me. I seem to remember you rather enjoyed your time pretending to be a journalist.'

Andy laughed and conceded a palpable hit.

'That was more about gorgeous Czech girls than the freedom of the press but yes, it had something to it. I missed it when they finally said I was leaving the field and being put under diplomatic cover for the rest of my years.'

Anoush poured out another couple of glasses of wine while they waited for the haze of blue smoke to subside and the charcoals to build up to a flaky white heat.

'So old-man Baharvand would have told Mehran about Janssen's, you reckon?'

'He must have done. I suppose it's ancient history now but I do feel that family is still taunting us.'

It was infuriating that the viper's clan should slither back into their lives after it had taken Andy almost twenty years to work the poison out of his system. For years he had hoped that the mujahidin would exorcise his demons for him and blow up the cleric's car. God knows, the bastard had it coming.

Baharvand's kangaroo court in Abadan had found it impossible to work out which of the suspects actually had been the agents that Andy was running out of the shipping office. When in a generous frame of mind, Andy sometimes reckoned that Baharvand, then just a humble judge, might have been about to show clemency. But April 1980 was the worst possible time to be on trial. The judiciary in Tehran was baying for blood when separatist Khuzestani Arabs seized the Iranian embassy in London. They needed a ruthless show of intent in the oil heartlands that would let Saddam know he had no hope of fomenting dissent among his Arab brothers on the eastern side of the border. On the same day that the SAS stormed the embassy, Baharvand hanged everyone: five British agents and eleven Khuzestanis Andy had never heard of. The women were raped before they died.

Andy had made it out just before the arrests and had been

shuttled through the mountains by Kurdish networks that could bundle him across the Turkish border. The escape routes had been built in the mid-70s by a brilliant agent-cum-carpet trader in Sanandaj. Generous retainers had been paid to Kurdish rebels ever since. Base camp seethed that half the money probably ended up with Marxists – the Komaleh – but could hardly begrudge their men an escape route. One evening, gathered round a campfire in the Zagros mountains, a peshmerga leader had told him that a British spy, although shot twice through the arm, had caught the Iranians with their trousers down and had made it to Kuwait in a stolen yacht. The peshmerga bellowed with laughter and joked that the Revolutionary Guard were a troupe of schoolgirls who stopped work at three o'clock to go and buy pastries. Andy couldn't help but join in. It was the first time he had laughed in a fortnight. Commander Anoushiravan Bozorgmehr's overworked guardian angel had been conjuring miracles again.

If anything, the bullet wounds in Anoush's forearm, seemed more pronounced than ever, like a python's bite. Najmeh still believed he'd picked them up in a disastrous training exercise that became more explosive on each retelling. After she heard that the Shah's illustrious imperial navy organised swimming lessons in the Persian Gulf with snipers posted on the foredeck to keep the sharks at bay, she believed any form of stupid accident was possible.

Anoush wielded the two spitted kebabs like swords before laying them across the coals. He laid a few tomatoes on the grill to blacken as the fat bubbled out of the mince and hissed on to the charcoal.

'Where you staying tonight by the way? With Cyrus?'

'Yeah. He sends you his regards. When did you last see him?'

'Not for a few months. I popped into the bistro this summer

and he seemed even more chilled than ever. If that's possible. He's taking the Buddhism thing very seriously these days.'

'Sure. Old Dalai Cyrus. I realised I would need to pop in here for my fix of something that died in pain before going back to his place. He always has a little saucepan of some vegetable curry on the boil. I can have that for pudding.'

'Is there any hope that we might see you next weekend?' Anoush asked, testing one of the kebabs with a fork. 'Nazila has been spreading rumours that one of her banquets could be imminent.'

'Oh definitely. I am trying to delay my return to Paris so I can go and spend a few days down in Cornwall with my mum. I will make sure I am around for Nazila's feast.'

'Let's just hope Baharvand doesn't screw up your plans.'

'Again.'

Gloucester Road was only a couple of stops east on the Piccadilly Line and Andy cut a drab figure amid the party-goers debouching into the rain. He dug his hands into his pockets and headed for the warm glow of Bistro Eveline. Rain was tipping in cupfuls off the baldachin and Andy couldn't work out whether it was a brisk night's trade or not. As promised, the light was on in the garret directly above and he tried the bell.

'Hey Andy, come on up.' The door buzzed for a couple of seconds then sprang open. Four storeys above, Cyrus was waiting for him. Miles Davis and the smell of curry wafted from within.

'Great timing. How was Anoush?'

'En forme. He wishes you well. How's business downstairs?'

'Oh, so-so,' said Cyrus, pulling his most inscrutably toad-like face. 'So-so' to Cyrus probably meant a full house and a stream of compliments to the chef. 'Benny's safely at the helm down there. You should try this. It's a little concoction I have been playing with. It's like a basic dhal but with a coconut and lime twist.'

'Aha, have you been delving into al-Baghdadi again for the next big sensation? Secrets from the thirteenth?'

'Not quite Andy. This one's from Delia actually.'

Over the last twenty years, the Gloucester Road garret had been one of Andy's main refuges. Every time it seemed inevitable that he would be sacked or Juliette had stormed out again in a whirl of Gallic exasperation, there was always a safe-haven up above Bistro Eveline. It seemed to sag under the weight of all the books, many of them in Hebrew, French, Arabic and Spanish. Andy would never take a book when he stayed but would stretch out from the divan where he slept and pluck out a tome on a subject about which he knew nothing. It was in this room that he had first encountered Marquez and Hesse. He was always particularly intrigued by the Central America section, the reading matter from a fiery interlude when Cyrus decided that he was a red-bandana revolutionary and disappeared to a coffee plantation in Guatemala. He returned three months later as peaceable as he had been when he first burrowed out of Iran.

Most mutual friends who joined them over tea or Courvoisier up in the garret always felt Andy and Cyrus belonged to a better, more gentlemanly age: the diplomat and the restaurateur. There were few men who seemed to have built up such a profound reservoir of arcane knowledge, their conversations meandering through Liverpool strikers, Syrian politics and scenes from 1950s' films that no one had heard of. Only a handful of people knew that Andy first approached Cyrus with a view to blowing his head off with a Browning 9mm.

Pushing through the mountains of Kurdistan back in 1980, Andy had been acutely conscious of a supreme irony: this was the Great Game, the alluring chimera that had tricked him into joining the service in the first place. An impressionable romantic destined for a sporting second in Persian and Turkish, he saw himself in the mould of a Sykes or a Griboyedov, defending his nation's interests in the passes of the Zagros and giving black-shirted assassins the slip in the back alleys of Diyarbakir. While Middle England fretted about the dangers of punk and quaffed Mateus Rosé, he would be out there, compass in hand, stretching out maps on the bonnet of his Land-Rover and building contacts among the Baluchis.

As an undergraduate, Andy had affected a scorn for the city, boasting that he was only at ease on storm-buffeted Cornish cliffs or traipsing round the barrows and stone circles of Bodmin Moor. So what could have given him more exhilaration, more of a sense of actually existing, than those night marches across the mountains with the peshmerga, the point-man singing of yearning and lost-love under a silver crescent moon? Everything he had ever sought had been before him. At dawn, the guerrilla column would weave through the oak forests of the high ground, gazing down on the rolling green fields below, a transplanted Dorset dotted with almond and pear trees. They waded through the coruscating streams of ice-melt that tumbled into the valleys and watched the hypnotic wheeling of the eagles catching the thermals over the dolomite ridges. The pastel blue skies were scarred only by puffs of cirrus.

He had been so wrong. The tingle of adventure had evaporated in a moment and he didn't give a fuck about the beauties of the Zagros in early summer. His whole life had been numbed by a black tide of failure, inadequacy and guilt that would envelop him and grind him down to nothing. Even when the peshmerga excitedly pointed to a brown bear scuttling back into his cave, Andy could only see his agents, his friends, choking and jerking in their death throes, strung up on pick-up truck cranes. He had been trusted with too much too young and men who trusted him completely had died because of his ineptitude. They were twice his age but had insisted that he was the boss. They brought him jerry-cans of wine, the fruit of clandestine foulage in the bathtub. He was just a schoolboy floundering out of his depth. In the cliffside camps, he would rarely sleep, reliving his basic trade-craft mistakes again and again as the jackals scrambled around the rocks. He felt embarrassed and worthless in the presence of the Kurds risking their lives for his. Taking him back to what? No career in the service, that was for sure. How could they have misjudged him so badly? And how could he have allowed them to coax him into believing that he could have been a real spy?

He couldn't bear the thought of returning to his parents' house; his shame in the presence of his father would be unbearable. Only his admiration for his Kurdish guides stopped him pitching himself off a cliff or putting a bullet through his temple. He could hardly let their efforts go to waste. Passing through a forest one morning, he told Ardalan, the paterfamilias, that he should go on alone. They should not risk their lives for a simple pawn. He told him he was finished as an agent and that his war against the mullahs was over.

The craggy-faced peshmerga, the man who looks death in the face, just shook his head and told Andy not to worry. But the young spy delved deeper into the self-loathing welling up within him. He told Ardalan that the Brits were never going to do anything to help the Kurdish struggle. The RAF had bombed and gassed the Kurds in the 1920s and they were still two-faced snakes today. Albion would always be perfidious.

Ardalan nodded sympathetically. He understood.

'That's not the point, my friend. We do not really care who you are. But when we have got you across the border into Turkey, then we can tell our families that we spat in the faces of the Iranians.'

Andy had never felt so insignificant.

A week later, when his sanity had almost entirely unravelled, one of the younger peshmergas decided the forlorn Englishman needed cheering up.

'You are wrong to hate yourself because the Iranians killed your men. The Iranians will always kill our men. The only repose of the heart is to kill them. They send a column of Revolutionary Guards into our hills. We kill them. Then we put their heads in boxes and leave them on the road for their comrades to find, so their women can cry, as our women cry.'

The teenage fighter gave him a wide grin and passed him a Turkish cigarette. His words had hardly been a balm and Andy instinctively felt revolted by them, but their echoing rage would be ringing in his ears when he decided to kill Cyrus.

On 11 June, Andy got his wish. The peshmergas gave him his final instructions on how to slip across the Turkish border but agreed it was best if he did the final leg alone. It was so easy to cross that many people joked they did it by accident. His guides had sketched out a map in thick pencil so he could negotiate the Zangmar river and avoid the sentry posts around Maku. With his matted beard, muddy shalvar and sun-hardened features, he should arouse little suspicion. After a cursory round of handshakes and 'good lucks', they disappeared down a defile. That year's Pulitzer would go to Jahangir Razmi's photograph of a group of Kurds before an Iranian firing squad, some crumpling while others still stood tall, a split second before their executioners fired. Andy never found out what happened to his peshmergas.

Just before nightfall, he crossed a dirt track where two valleys opened up before him. The Kurds had said he should take the northernmost one, hunker down for the night there and then make his rendezvous in Turkey just before dawn on 12 June. His guides had not mentioned the concrete hut-cum-pillbox, twenty yards up the mountainside at the opening of the valley but it was perfectly possible that it had been built in the last few weeks. His first guess was that the paraffin light inside belonged to a shepherd but he felt a strange delight when a lone sentry in khaki stepped out and waved. The first ten days in the mountains had burned the knees and lungs but, quite suddenly, one morning, he realised he'd become a lot fitter. He once again felt that dangerous, unbridled immortality that comes with the tough-guy courses with the service. The incitement of the young peshmerga had hit home. He wasn't going to cross into Turkey without finishing one of the bastards himself.

'Salaam, brother,' shouted the figure in khaki, waving vigorously. 'You can't go down there.'

Andy gave a gesture of surprise and walked steadily towards the guardpost, fingering the Browning in his pocket. He weighed up the man. A gendarme with an affable, amphibian smile. In the wrong place at the wrong time.

'Don't call me brother,' he barked as he slammed the man hard in the face and split his lip. 'Just because the Iranians fucked all our mothers doesn't make us brothers.'

Andy let his bloodlust run free and kicked the gendarme hard in the spine as he reeled round. He pulled the terrified man up by the scruff of his uniform and flung him hard against the metal door of the sentry hut which burst open, sending the dazed gendarme sprawling across the floor. Andy drew his pistol and stepped inside with the measured froideur of the professional assassin.

At first it was the cosiness of the place that stopped his hand: the little carpet, the tea on the camping-gas cylinder and the piles of books. The gold lettering of a blue hardback volume was picked out by the paraffin light. *Les Chouans – Balzac*. Andy lowered his gun. Who the fuck is this guy? What the fuck am I doing?

'Vous lisez Balzac en français?'

Cyrus craned round, blood dripping from his lower lip, equally bemused by the farce unfolding. The Kurdish psychopath now wanted to talk about Balzac.

'Ah, oui monsieur, d'habitude c'est très ennuyeux de garder la frontière. De temps en temps il y a un Kurde obsédé par Balzac qui essaye de vous tuer mais, généralement, c'est un bon endroit pour lire les classiques.'

Andy laughed almost hysterically at this dry description of himself as a murderous Kurdish Balzac groupie, and slumped to the ground beside the gendarme. It was dark outside.

'You on duty here all night?' he asked, reverting to Persian. He read the name tag on the breast of frog-face's uniform. Danielpour. Jewish.

'Yes.'

'No relief? Checks?'

'No. We're miles from anything.'

He didn't seem like he was bullshitting.

'Good. Right, you should probably get some tea going.' Andy gestured to the pot with his pistol. Andy's father often insisted that the ritual of getting the kettle on was vital in a crisis, particularly when you felt control seeping away. He would recount how, during some God-awful bombardment at Monte Cassino, he just told the boys to get a good brew going. Their faces, which had been riven with terror, were promptly oblivious to the shellfire bursting around them.

'I just saved your life,' Cyrus said in English. 'As payback, I think it's only fair that you not kill me.'

'That does sound fair. Where did you learn English?'

'Beirut. The American University. The valley you were about to go down was mined four days ago. If you take the ridge to the left, you'll be fine. We're twenty minutes walk from Turkish territory.'

'So you've all been warned about the Zionist imperialist spy, eh? You should keep an eye out for him. He sounds a mean son of a bitch.'

'I doubt he'll come this way. I'll file another quiet night report.'

Cyrus lit the camping gas and blew out the match, sending a wisp of smoke through the hut.

'Good move. What about your lip?'

'They know I'm pretty clumsy. I'll say I fell over going for a piss.'

'How on earth did you end up here?'

'I got drafted six months ago. Until tonight, it's been great. I get long, boring sentry duties and catch up with all the greats. The only downside is I have to do some patrols on a horse; I hate horses! Hate them.'

Andy and Cyrus that night found they shared a hatred of horses and a love of football. Cyrus was a pacifist who dreamed of going to London to continue his studies and open 'a little place'. He reckoned he would be able to get out of Iran in the next couple of years, which was not before time. He had no idea how bad things were about to get but added, with a wry smile, that a Jew should always have his boots on and be ready to leave. One of his socialist friends in Tehran had, one month before, been subjected to a mock execution. Five times he had heard the pistol click behind his head. It was definitely time to wipe the patina of dust off his suitcases.

Like a stranger on a train, Andy felt few inhibitions with

45

Cyrus. He told him that he would definitely give him a hand with the 'little place' once he arrived in England and that he would have put all this spying nonsense behind him by then. He would have gone back to Cornwall and bought a little farm.

'How do I find you?'

Andy thought that he would trust Cyrus after three years of trusting no one. He had half resigned himself to death anyway. Still, he wasn't sure that he wanted to hand out his family address to a man who may later be tortured.

Andy picked up *Les Chouans* and wrote a name and address on the frontispiece: Arnold Douglas. Lancing College. W. Sussex.

'He was my old French teacher. A colossus of a man who has been teaching French for thirty years. In his whole life, he has been to France once and didn't care for it much. When you come to Britain, send him a postcard with your address. Sign it Danielpour. I'll make sure it gets to me.'

It seemed academic. Danielpour would probably never get out.

Cyrus was astonished at how childish the instincts of a spy become. It all felt like a playground game.

'Are you not going to tell me your name?'

'Andy. For now, just Andy. So how did you end up as a gendarme?'

'I got lucky. There were nine of us in the recruiting office and we pulled straws. The others are in the army.'

'Not reading Balzac,' Andy mused.

'Certainly not reading Balzac. And I landed on my feet up here in Maku as well. It's the best job you can get. We are under a great little sergeant, Mohammadi. He runs his own mini-empire and pushes the officers around, we get provisions weeks ahead of everyone else and all the soft duties.'

'Fantastic. What's his secret?'

'This is the really nice bit. You'll love this,' said Cyrus, pouring out a glass of tea for Andy.

'When we arrived we were shit scared of the officer, he was even called Islami. He had a thick black beard and walked around with his copy of the Koran. But he was like butter in Sergeant Mohammadi's hands. 'Yes, Sergeant Mohammadi', 'Of course, Sergeant Mohammadi'.

'At first we thought the trick just lay in the chaos of his filing system. Mohammadi's office is a bunker full of thousands and thousands of chits and documents. Only he knows how the whole operation works so he has made himself indispensable. But we pressed him a bit over the arak a few weeks ago and it all came out. He's really got Islami by the balls. Mohammadi delved into his files and pulled out a photograph of a parade in 1976. And there he was: our commander, immaculate and clean shaven, being given a gong by the Shah himself.'

'Ha ha, typical.'

'And Mohammadi had more. He asked whether we'd ever noticed Islami with his sleeves rolled up, his hands wet after preparing to wash for prayers. Yes, of course, we always saw that. Well, you always see him making a big show of going to prayers because he never actually goes. For a simple reason: he doesn't know how.'

'He must do.'

'Nah, Mohammadi has known his commanding officer for ten years. He lived for fast cars and fast women. He never set foot inside a mosque.'

'Ah, the joys of a revolution. I'm surprised you ever want to leave Maku.'

'Brother, this revolution is totally screwed in the head. My sister lives up in the Caspian. Lovely place. Lovely flat. All lovely. Then two months ago all the sewage engineers were sacked and replaced by bearded Islamists who could run the water treatment operation in a more revolutionary way. So the whole town stinks of shit.'

Andy sipped his tea and got Cyrus to tell him about *La Comédie Humaine*. With about a hundred novels, the gist wasn't really an option. So he settled for highlights.

Cyrus didn't remember dozing off but, by the time he woke at half four, Andy had already crossed the border and rendezvoused with Mac from Ankara station, who promised him a slap-up breakfast in Dogubayazit. A chisel-jawed Turkish officer congratulated Andy on an excellent escape and drove them to an army base, where menacing battle-lines of tanks were ranged behind the barbed wire. The Turk didn't hang around long. His own country had enough to keep him busy, simmering with tension since the killings at Kahramanmaras. If that weren't enough, the Kurdish east would always keep military intelligence on its toes. Mac filled Andy in on the things he might have missed: Tito was dead, Mount St Helens had blown up rather spectacularly and Euro 80 was under way.

There was only time for a shower, some western clothes and a plate of scrambled eggs. The area was swarming with Iranians and it wasn't a good idea to hang around too long. A few senior officers came into the canteen to shake Andy's hand, but he didn't have the energy to relive his escape and suspected they just wanted to worm out some information on his peshmerga guides. He pretended not to speak Turkish. Mac was furious that so many of the top brass had got to know the story and became increasingly impatient about the helicopter the army had promised.

The canteen was decked out with black and white photographs of Ataturk and the Ishakpasa Sarayi, the rococo pleasure palace that attracted adventurous tourists to the wilds of eastern Turkey. Through the window, Andy could see bare-chested commandos doing chin-ups and wrestling each other into the gravel with knives. This place must be hell in winter.

Andy asked the Scot from Ankara station whether he was for the high-jump.

'You'll be debriefed at the embassy but that's not the impression I get. Off record, I think everyone is rather impressed, actually.'

Impressed? Maybe the service was like they always joked. The darkies swing but the plucky schoolboy makes it out through the mountains in a *Boy's Own* adventure and gets a medal. He imagined the pick-ups in Abadan again and felt sick, pushing away the plate of eggs half-eaten.

'Thought you'd be ravenous.'

'No, sorry Mac, I'm not feeling so good.'

Mac was right: Andy was still in a job. Our man in Abadan had reconciled himself to seeing out his days on his Cornish farm and opened his debriefing with contrition. To his surprise, his interrogators didn't seemed too worried about the end of the network and spent at least half the session grilling him for any gossip about Kurdish mobilisations that he may have heard of on the trek through the Zagros. Sure, they understood young Trevarthen would take the hangings hard but he had been safely insulated from more important networks in Khuzestan. Janssen's had provided a steady flow of workmanlike intelligence from the docks. But there was better stuff out there. He hadn't really landed everyone in the soup. Old loyalists from the Anglo-Iranian era, BP men, were shipping up an excellent picture on the fundamental question: oil security. Almost too much data to process, in fact. The prickly issue of Arab discontent was well covered through some inspired joint operations with Baghdad.

49

All in all, the men round the table seemed rather amused that Andy had thought he was so important.

It was generally accepted at base camp that he had failed simply because he was outgunned. It could have happened to anyone. On a bright note, his escape was brilliantly executed and he would be pleased to know that Commander Anoush Bozorgmehr had been granted asylum in the United Kingdom.

Andy got a valedictory pep talk from a fusty colonel, now long-dead, who had fought the Soviets by Queensbury rules, while they irradiated bourgeois intellectuals and snapped thermometers up their penises.

'The most important thing is that you get straight back at 'em. The way you freeze up is to spend months or years licking your wounds. That kills a man's confidence. We're going to be sending you behind the Iron Curtain as a courier, newspaperman, get you listed as a foreign correspondent somewhere.'

Suddenly exhausted and finding it difficult to maintain a purchase on reality, Andy accepted a month's leave and promised to learn how to type.

Leave could not have been a worse idea. He continually recalled that bit of Seneca – that bit all schoolboys had to read – where it said you could watch the countries and cities recede over the stern of your ship, but your own failings would always hound you down.

And they did hound him down, into a tiny rented room in Hania, in a back street running down to the quayside opposite the mosque of the janissaries. He'd arrived thinking he could put it all behind him by picking up Scandinavian girls over ouzo and tavli at beachside tavernas. Instead, he didn't rise from the sagging mattress on the wrought-iron bed – not even to eat. He just smoked cigarette after cigarette and stared up at the peeling plasterwork of the ceiling, following the spidery, jaundiced lines of damp where the copper pipes had leaked in the room above. Every train of thought led back to the same place: the cockroach-infested cells of Abadan prison. The wilder flights of fancy led to that little village in Kerman where Baharvand came from, whatever that place was called: something to do with pomegranates. *Anar*. Anarak. Anaran. Anareh. He'd get across the Pak border somehow and slit the Ayatollah's throat.

He realised that he had not feared the sack but had craved it. But they just gave him a manful pat on the back and said 'better luck next time.' What the fuck did they know? Like Dostoyevsky's Raskolnikov, he had murdered the pawnbroker woman and her sister with an axe and needed to confess. He wanted Siberia and they just gave him another job.

Mrs Dhaskolayannis was worried about the new lodger. Such a nice, polite boy but he didn't seem to be going out at all. He left open the windows to the crumbling little balcony and she could hear that he shouted and sobbed continually in his sleep. Unlucky in love, she thought. And such a pity. But he wasn't going to sort things out in there. She would take him some baklava in the morning.

But he wasn't there the next day. He just left a wad of drachmas, far more than needed to cover the rent and the damage. You can never read these quiet ones. He had awoken just after four. The little city was perfectly quiet apart from the dull chug of a lone fishing boat setting out from the harbour. The screaming was in his head. There was an untouched pitcher of lemonade on the table. He downed a couple of glasses but the screaming just got louder and an anvil was pressing down on his shoulders. Water. He went into the little bathroom and flicked the switch, wincing in the cold glare of the bare light-bulb. He turned the taps on full and stared into the lifeless, hazel eyes of the trained killer before him, distorted by a tarnished mirror that had already cracked down the middle. He yelled until his lungs were empty, pressed his left palm hard against the wall and whacked the mirror again and again with his right fist, oblivious to the glass ripping his knuckles. His head was reeling, he couldn't breathe and that screaming just wouldn't stop.

He came round feeling icily clear-headed but his hand stung like hell. He could hear a polite knocking on the door and a man saying something, rather timidly, in Greek. Was there a fire? He realised he was lying on cold, blood-smeared tiles.

'Are you all right in there?' The same voice. Thickly accented but speaking English.

'Fine. Yes, sorry, I'm fine.'

Twenty-seven years and two nervous breakdowns later, Andy still dwelled in the shadows. On Saturday nights like this, he could come up for air and watch *Match of the Day* with his old friend but he would never really dispatch the ghosts. Beside the television set, there hung a miniature of a nineteenth-century Polish aristocrat: Ewelina Hanska, she of Bistro Eveline. Cyrus insisted she was the only person who loved Balzac more than he did. To the diners downstairs, he explained this sentiment with the detachment of a literary aficionado. In his heart, he knew that a copy of *Les Chouans* – not even one of his favourites – had once saved his life. A few months after he arrived in London, one of the first questions he asked Andy was whether he would be dead if had left his copy of Balzac in the gendarmerie in Maku that night. The spy admitted, in all honesty, that he had no idea.

3.

ANDY HAD KNOWN the Spartan safe house on Wilton Square, a strangely verdant corner of Hackney, for the last twenty-five years. He had often worked there until dawn, sharing gherkins and plum brandy with Black Sea skippers and Hungarian army officers. Too often their treasured little secrets, on movements of Typhoon-class submarines and the bed-swapping antics of Soviet generals, were far less interesting than the peripheral morsels they would accidentally let slip. The rooms where Andy grilled that motley band of cold warriors now had the cosy familiarity of a grandparent's house; you felt instantly at ease there but always looked around with interest for any alterations: new kettles and electric-heaters generously provided by the UK tax-payer. Somehow that lurid Charles and Diana cheese dish always managed to survive. Couldn't somebody just drop the bloody thing?

He had arrived at six. A cold, hostile Monday morning. Spitting rain. Arriving for the morning slots in the old days, he would test his skills by observing the milkman. He knew which households around the square took one pint, which took two. It was his morning ritual, aligning his thoughts for the interrogations ahead to the chink of the milk bottles and the electric whirr of the milk float. Andy had formed a one-sided comradeship with that milkman. But Britain was now a country that bought its milk in plastic containers from the supermarket. Britain was not a country that Andy Trevarthen, an increasingly morose defender of the realm, particularly liked any more.

By six thirty, a couple of his lads dressed as Thames Water lackeys had erected a little tent across the square. They were both armed. Moments later Andy got a coded text assuring him that Mehran Baharvand was safely en route. He had been followed from his Chelsea villa by Amiri, one of the Iranian Embassy's least talented footpads and perhaps the easiest to remove from the picture.

Baharvand's cab had come to a red light at six twenty-two and Amiri's Vauxhall Corsa purred to a standstill three yards behind. The security man was tired after yet another dull, pointless night watching Baharvand's house and he stared into the refracted blur of the traffic light, not bothering to flick the wipers and brush off the specks of rain. The Baharvand scion was a banker and there was nothing unusual about his early start. Amiri hadn't even noted the cab's registration, the official grounds on which Alef Baa would later sack him. He yawned.

From nowhere, two police motorbikes blocked him. The light went green and Baharvand's cab sped away with a splutter, like a smoker clearing his chest. Amiri revved his engine, blasted his horn and swore in Persian at the riders but the tall Met officers were unmoved. One of them continued to block his path and casually tapped the bonnet to encourage the irritable foreign gentleman to stop churning the motor. The other slowly dismounted, slid up his visor and gestured that the Iranian should roll down the window.

'You no have right. I am diplomat.'

'We know exactly who you are Mr Amiri. You, sir, are a panty-sniffer. We would very much like you to accompany us to the nearest station and help us with an investigation into the theft of lingerie from department stores across London over the last four months.'

Amiri's English was not good enough to understand and he blasted his horn again.

'I am diplomat. Islamic Republic Iran. Please I go.'

A police car had pulled up behind the Corsa, its blue lights pulsing through the rear window. The dismounted cop grinned and pulled out a CCTV still of Amiri making one of his regular truffle-hunting expeditions to the lingerie department at Selfridges. The Iranian intelligence man blanched at the image.

'Ambassador Movahedian very angry, no?' said the policeman. 'You come now, then all over. No ambassador. We no tell ambassador. You come now.'

At the ambassador's name, Amiri just slumped over the steering wheel.

Andy got a second text saying that Baharvand's tail was helping the police with their enquiries and smiled only at the efficacy of the detention; he had long ceased to be surprised by the sexual vulnerability of diplomats. There had been many instances when he had to help pick up the pieces after vulnerable English public schoolboys thrust their faces into the ample bosoms of a Polish or Czech honey-trap. As for the Middle Eastern embassy staff, the service filing cabinets sagged with transcripts of calls to saucy chat-lines and snaps supplied by obliging cherubs. Amiri's penchant for frilly knickers would promptly end his undistinguished career with the Iranian intelligence service.

Avi and Max arrived together at ten to seven. They'd both had daughters late and the girls attended the same Jewish primary school in Cricklewood. They saw each other a lot socially, at school events mainly. The only thing they seemed to disagree about was Iran. Baharvand was in for an interesting ride. In his previous incarnation, Avi was one of the Israeli F-16 pilots who had taken out the Iraqi nuclear plant at Osirak in 1981. He had few doubts that the Iranians were cruising for the same treatment. Max, his softly-spoken, stocky cousin at the CIA, was looking for any other way out of the Persian labyrinth.

Avi slapped Andy on the back and Max shook his hand with a puckish smile. Andy asked about the swastikas that had been sprayed over the wall of the school by a group of Asian youngsters. Max grimaced.

'Yeah, Rachel is still a bit shaken up but I think we all reckon it's a one off. And we've got one of your plucky British bobbies there for the next three weeks.'

'Sure, sure. No worries there now,' said Avi in his booming, unruffled Israeli drawl. 'But let's hear it, Andy. What's baby Baharvand got for us? You've excited a lot of people back home, and in Langley too it seems.'

Max nodded in polite agreement.

'No idea. I am just a bit worried that safe-house coffee won't meet the exacting standards of a City banker.'

'Oh yeah, he'll clam up if you give him that instant decaf shite over there,' joked Max, surveying the safe-house's utilitarian kitchenette.

Despite the bonhomie, Andy was a Cold War man and he didn't much care for the cousins and the Israelis having a stake in this. He had grown up in an age when you kept your secrets more closely guarded from the Americans than from the Russians. Your hard-won product used to be a valuable, tradable commodity. Over Iran, Britain was now boxed in. A joint US–Israeli sting in Oran had unearthed a British-Pakistani liaising with Algerian al Qaeda. They hauled the kid into some warehouse on the dockside, beat the living crap out of him and shot one of his knee-caps off. He talked. Everybody does. So the Yanks cut a deal. After a well-stocked bomb-making lab had been dismantled in Bethnal Green, the cousins and the Israelis could share anything the Brits got on Iran for two years. Andy didn't like it, but he'd have to lump it.

There was no unpleasantness over the quality of the safe-house coffee. Baby Baharvand opted for PG Tips, served in a souvenir mug from Hampton Court. Andy was taken aback by how similar the nephew was to the kingpin back in Anareh. The figure across the great mahogany table might have been clean shaven and dressed in a crisp Savile Row suit but there was no mistaking the same piercing eyes and the same bullish strength of his physiognomy. He was thirty-three years younger than his uncle and looked like the hanging judge Andy had known back in the revolutionary days.

'Now you, I know very well, are Mr Trevarthen,' he said once the round of handshakes and good mornings had been dispensed with. 'But am I to have the pleasure of knowing the names of these two gentlemen?'

Baharvand's English was impeccable with a mid-Atlantic accent that flitted between New York and London as he spoke. Andy noted his oily sales' patter had picked up idioms on both sides of the pond.

'They are just Mr Trevarthen's friends,' said Andy curtly.

'I understand,' the banker replied and laid his mug on the table. 'I realise that you must all be very busy men and I cannot use up too much of your valuable time. As you have probably surmised, I am acting as a messenger on behalf of my uncle, Ayatollah Ali Baharvand. He has a deep respect for the talents of Mr Trevarthen and could think of no better point of first contact for his proposal.'

Baharvand had taken a short breath before the word 'proposal' and now examined the faces of the three secret agents to see if the carefully rehearsed opening gambit had impressed his audience. The men were open and sympathetic, fixed on him, not taking notes. The whole thing must be recorded anyway, Baharvand correctly assumed.

'My uncle's frustrations as a nuclear negotiator have been well documented and his feelings on this matter will lie at the core of what I have to say. What is less well known, but vital as background to the proposal, is his attitude towards policy within our region. My uncle still loathes the Shah and what he represented: I cannot pretend otherwise. SAVAK imprisoned and tortured him. This is not something he will ever forgive. But he always thought the Shah's regional policy was, let's say, coherent. He saw Israel and Turkey as the logical strategic allies of Iran. Sunni Arabs can never be trusted as partners for Shi'ite Tehran. Never.

'So my uncle now finds himself in a position where he believes his own sentiments could chime with those of western governments. He believes that Iran's national interests would best be served by putting declared enrichment work at Natanz on ice for ten years. Iran should also mothball the other enrichment facilities, the ones the International Atomic Energy Agency in Vienna knows nothing about. Furthermore, the Ayatollah has arrived at the conclusion that few policies are as destructive as our pig-headed intransigence towards Israel, a nation with which we must strike a peace deal to deliver on our true potential in the market-place. Although we are already OPEC's second biggest producer, we are being held back as an energy supplier because of our foolish stance towards our natural ally, Israel.

'Up until now, it may have proved academic that an influential cleric had a political vision that shared much common ground with what the West wants. Now the picture is different. In two weeks, Ayatollah Ali Baharvand, on behalf of Tehran, will offer this ten-year atomic freeze and a deal to recognise Israel. In return, the United States should re-open its embassy on Taleghani Street and end its trade embargo against our country.'

The western agents remained impassive. He was their Joe. They should work him over, not go fawning to him. Andy decided to be systematic.

'You said Tehran was operating uranium enrichment facilities other than Natanz, unknown to the IAEA. Which sites would you be referring to?'

Baharvand shrugged and spread out his palms in a profession of innocence.

'I am not myself an expert in these matters, I fear, Mr Trevarthen. My uncle has permitted me to tell you only that such sites exist. As to their whereabouts, such details will naturally be made available to you once you strike an accord with the Islamic Republic.'

Andy smiled drily.

'Which is the truly fascinating question, Mr Baharvand. How does a geriatric cleric who has retired to grow pomegranates down in Kerman persuade Ahmadinejad and the Supreme Leader to offer a humiliating deal to the West?'

'Are you aware how much the ruling caste is hated in Iran, Mr Trevarthen? Not just by my long-suffering people but by all kinds of elites across the nation. My uncle has decided to lead the backlash. And we don't just mean the students and the poor forgotten people of Iran, though they, naturally, constitute part of the equation. What we are talking about here are the business leaders, the bazaar, the army, the oil-men, the technocrats sick of mumbo-jumbo in the ministries. My uncle does not represent the unreal opposition peddled in Washington, detached mujahidin émigrés and fantastical pie-in-the-sky monarchists. This opposition is the real backbone of Iran, nationalists who did not care for the Shah but feel the nation is now going the wrong way. For years my uncle has been rearing these men. Now he is ready to institute the new order.'

A heavy, treacly rain was oozing down the window panes.

'So, supported by such men, Ali Baharvand is planning a coup d'état in two weeks?' Avi asked.

'Coup is a strong word. Small aspects of the operation will resemble a coup. But if you could see the way the alliances and family-trees of real power-brokers in Iran have been forming in the last few years, you would realise that the ruling class is there and ready, a ruling class that would embrace my uncle's vision. The top layer needs to be skimmed off but in a few bold strikes the state will be presented with a fait accompli. These men are sick of being the international bogeymen. They are willing to make a deal on Israel and the nuclear facilities for the good of the nation and, most importantly, because it makes sound commercial sense.'

Avi leaned forward.

'Bold strikes? Do I smell more traditional Iranian bloodletting?'

'Bloodshed of some degree is, tragically, always inevitable in Iran. I am sorry, but that is how our nation is, gentlemen. Mr Trevarthen has seen this. He will attest to this. But if you ask whether we are planning executions, whether we are planning a purge, then the answer is no. People just tend to fight to the end in my country.'

'Hoveida didn't fight to the end. He was just shot through the neck,' Andy interjected.

Easy Andy, Max thought. Play it cool, this man could be a god-send.

'It won't be like Hoveida. My uncle never wanted the prime minister to die. That was Khalkhali's doing.'

'So you don't have a wish-list of leading politicians to be executed?'

'Of course not.'

'So, why do we trust your uncle?'

'My uncle knows, Mr Trevarthen, that you of all people have the least reason to trust him. That is exactly why he has chosen you. But what you ask is legitimate. What you are asking is: why my uncle is angry? Why is Iran angry? Let me explain it to you. You can tell your public that this transfer of power is all about civil liberties, that it is about freedoms. That makes good stories in the papers. Your politicians can make pretty speeches. But if you want to understand where the pressure for change really comes from in Iran you have got to look at the money-chain. The money-chain and our wounded national pride.

'My uncle helped lead a revolution because he wanted Iran to become stronger. And what has he seen happen? He has seen Turkey and these upstart Arab despots across the Gulf overtake us economically. The current government of Iran is wrecking our economy and turning us into the brain-drain capital of the world. The West has always looked to battered students and women's rights activists for hopes of change in my country. They are a side-show. Cut through the mystique, gentlemen. Just see that Iran is like any other country. Political earthquakes do not come from airy dreams of liberty, they come from price-hikes and the frustration that you cannot make a profit.

'Mr Trevarthen has followed my country for years but perhaps you gentlemen do not quite have a full picture of its economic frustrations. God has given us the second biggest oil reserves in the world and we have squandered them, clumsily damaging fields that will now never give of their best. We

61

inherited an oil industry that could, with a following wind, pump six million barrels per day. Now we struggle to pump three point something or other. And output is dropping all the time. Because of our international histrionics and greedy Ali Babas in our political system we cannot get investors. My uncle wants the big contracts to go to BP and Conoco. Does that surprise you? Your oil men have a lot to gain from my uncle.

'Under these apes we have now, any investor who comes to Iran will be insulted and fleeced. People are too scared to do any business with foreigners. We used to be a land of traders, on the Silk Road. Now we will be accused of treason and arrested if we sign contracts with outsiders. The oil companies have tried but we offered them lousy commercial terms under the buy-back schemes. The Turks tried to set up a mobile phone network and run an airport. Renault are trying to build their Logans. So what do we do? We insult them in parliament and accuse them of cultural imperialism. We renege on deals we have signed. We change the terms again and again. We simply steal money. We chuck our own officials in jail for signing deals with major foreigner investors. You remember the deputy-minister who signed the contract with Turkcell? He's now in jail as a supposed Israeli spy. Really! Companies that seem to be a success in every other country in the world slope off to their stock markets and tell their shareholders that their projects have hit the rocks in Iran. It happened to Shell. It happened to Statoil. They lost in Iran. They could not beat the system. Iran, holder of the world's second biggest natural gas reserves, cannot even produce liquefied natural gas because we cannot get the investment. A few flakes of snow and we have to cut our exports. Our nation is a laughing stock. What I am describing is a catastrophe, gentlemen. We are our own worst enemy with this nuclear tough talk and decades-old anti-Israel cant. All our best people are in

London, Paris, Hamburg and California. We just need the signal to go home and get the economy working again.'

Andy had heard this sort of plaintive cry from the business class a hundred times before.

'Ali Baharvand cannot shake a wand at Iran's piece-of-crap economy,' he said. 'It doesn't need a few tweaks here and there. It's a state dinosaur staffed by people who do three-hour days and drink a fuck of a lot of tea. Even under a more benign political system, many investors will take one look at the way Iran is held together and walk away.'

Baharvand knew Andy was playing devil's advocate. Iran was too rich to be sniffed at. He liked him.

'Let me put it like this. People make one hell of a difference. Only three years ago, it still felt like a different world. There was some hope that Iran could find a way through. Down in Kerman, as I am sure you know, my father and my uncle have considerable interests in the copper industry. Some of the mines were on family land. Drumming up project finance in the Middle East with HSBC in Dubai, I used to deal regularly with the head honchos in the copper business. They were smart men, former mining engineers who loved the industry, international men who had worked in the States and in Chile. On my last visit to the state copper company, I found they have all been replaced by former Revolutionary Guards, pasdaran in polyester suits. The corridors and offices were stuffed with Ahmadinejad's henchmen and they didn't give a damn about copper. In the old days, the managers used to reel off their production data without notes. They lived the data. Ahmadinejad's men do not know which column to read the figures from. But they pray round the clock and go home early. It's the same in every industry. Shipping. Aluminium. Wheat. You hold an oil industry tender: you know it's going to be won by Revolutionary Guard engineering subsidiaries like Khatam ol-Anbia who won't be able to do the job. Look at the new ambassadors. Peasants. Only three years ago, within this lumbering state sector, there were men with plans that international lenders could deal with. We could make money in the Islamic Republic. Now that is a thing of the past. There's an internal coup going on in the country. Men loyal to certain blocks in the Guards are taking over the asylum. Everyone else can go screw themselves. But the rest of society is furious gentlemen. The rest of powerful society.

'Most importantly, the bazaar is with us. Never fall into the trap of seeing the bazaar as a spent force. Those little carpet stalls are still just the public faces of million-dollar trading enterprises. OK, they have branched off into real estate these days but they are still a force to be reckoned with. If you gentlemen do not share Mr Trevarthen's familiarity with the revolutionary era, you may not recall that it was the bazaar that toppled the Shah in 1979. He so despised them as a bastion of conservative power that he even planned to drive a road right through the middle of the great covered bazaar in Tehran. Now everything the bazaaris try to do, they find some Revolutionary Guard friend of the president in their way. They are furious.'

Max lifted a podgy finger to break the flow and pose his first question.

'When you say that various business classes who have been knocked off their pedestals are "with you", what does that mean? Is this just a natural support base that knows nothing of your uncle's putsch? Just how many people do know about the Ayatollah's plans?'

'Look, this again is really territory where only my uncle himself would be properly qualified to speak. But the sense I have is that the number who know that a transfer of power is in the offing is very, very small. Only the essential protagonists of the operation need to know. The rest are a group that my uncle knows he can rely upon as soon as the transfer of power is complete. Please don't use the word "putsch". Implementing revolutionary change is all about gauging the mood and this is what he can do better than anyone else in the country. It used to be the case that the money-makers, the men who pulled the strings, were more or less content with the status quo. They could live their private lives in their palatial apartments and no one worried. Now they find themselves feeling as hostile towards their rulers as the human rights activists, students and labour unions. We have come to a head here.'

Max did not look impressed.

'Really, Mr Baharvand? You see, my big problem with what you are saying is that I think Mr Ahmadinejad is still actually very popular in Iran. Even if block voting from basijis and their kind, the paramilitary Islamist volunteers, helped get him through the first round, the guy still got seventeen million votes in the second round of the election back in 2005. You can't rig that. Sure, some studenty types might not like him on one side and the moneyed class might not on the other. But the vast majority of Iranians like it when he tells the Americans to get stuffed and reassures them they are on track to become a serious nuclear power. The boy from Aradan is like them and he's done good.'

This was fascinating but frustrating. Max enjoyed unstitching stories but that normally meant picking holes in little pieces of careless trade-craft that failed to gel. Who gave you the camera? Who do you report to? Who does he report to? What did you do with that train ticket? Max could not remember the last time he had had to grill someone on his appraisal of the state of a nation. Half an hour ago he had seen Iran as essentially stable. Now a smooth-talking financier was telling him that it was on the brink of meltdown.

'There are two ways of looking at that,' Baharvand replied, unhurried. 'In the 2005 election, Ahmadinejad, perhaps ironically, was viewed as the candidate from outside the system. People voted on economic grounds. Ahmadinejad was the folksy redistributor of oil wealth. He was their Robin Hood. The majority of the people are not judging the president on how well he is bloodying Bush's nose or how many trips he makes to see comrade Chavez. They are judging him on his economic performance and he is, quite frankly, not doing well. We have seen petrol stations torched in this absurd crisis over gasoline. How an oil state can get to the point where it has to import and subsidise on this scale just defies human reason. If that weren't enough, you should have seen the last Labour Day demonstrations: tens of thousands chanting "Forget Israel, remember Iran". I saw intelligence agents rounding up the press and ordering them not to report what was going on. So, on the one hand, the voters who held out such hopes for basic economic improvements simply have not got them. The oil windfall goes into shady religious organisations and is never seen again, well, until it stokes up inflation.

'On a second and more important level, the current Iranian regime is causing you more trouble than you can manage. Tehran is going hell-for-leather for an atom bomb and should be there in a couple of years. And what is your answer? You do not have one. Sanctions cannot deter these men. Air-strikes would open Pandora's box. Iran would mobilise its asymmetrical forces round the world, fomenting violence in Iraq and launching terrorist attacks in cities across the globe. God knows what would happen to world oil prices when Iranian fighter-jets start taking pot shots at tanker traffic in the Strait of Hormuz. No, you are totally snookered over Iran. You need a far better deal and my uncle is going to give you that.'

66

The glib and impassioned boardroom pitch may well have won Baharvand friends in the City but the men round the table were getting increasingly irritated by the vagaries and patronising didacticism of the financier. Tell us something we don't know.

'Everyone round this table,' Andy said, 'spends rather a lot of their time building up pictures of Iran, talking to people across the spectrum. We all have our own images of the Islamic Republic and what you have said is naturally of value to us. But we are, first and foremost, practical men Mr Baharvand. We want to know dates, facts, figures, military loyalties, the names of the leading conspirators, everything. And most of all, we want to know why you are being so good as to tell us all this? If you say the Ayatollah is just going to seize power, fait accompli, what do you need from us?'

Baharvand nodded without any sense of chastisement, simply acknowledging the logic of the request.

'In a sense, I can probably answer those two questions together. My uncle has been fascinated by uprisings across the world over the last decades: Romania, Pakistan, Venezuela, Thailand, Fiji ... You name it, he has trawled through the reports, even met the protagonists. The psychology of seizing power has become something of an obsession to him. He calls his plan "the Romania model" as this was perhaps the country he got to know best from his days buying armaments during the war. According to him, the end of Ceausescu all started with some genuine popular discontent, even though this could have been stirred up by outsiders like the Soviets. Then people around the president, Moscow's Communists, saw the time was right, quickly toppled him and made their overtures to the West with promises of democracy.'

This was all familiar territory to Andy. Ceausescu's sullen secret police had twice bundled him into a car and, to his great relief, deported him. At least it always made exciting copy for the comic.

'And how does this Romanian model transplant to Iran?'

'From Wednesday, the student movement is going to resume demonstrations. Big demonstrations. Like 2003. Some of the labour groups will come out in support. Down in Ahwaz, the Arabs will join the struggle for greater freedoms. The Kurds too. The Ayatollah has friends in all of these groups. It is just a matter of lighting a few small fires and by Sunday we should have a blaze.'

Andy checked the flow.

'What student groups are these? Which cities? Which unions? Which Arab parties? Which Kurdish parties? Who are the leading figures in these groups? Do they know Baharvand is going to support them? Do they know he is going to seize power? Please try to be as detailed as possible in what you tell us Mr Baharvand.'

'I am sorry, I can understand your frustrations, gentlemen but I really am just the messenger. The humble errand boy. Part of the strength of this operation is how little each of the various groups knows. What I do know is that no one being exhorted to join in the popular protests knows the full extent of my uncle's plans.

'And this is the point where you come in. From Thursday morning to Sunday, I think we can safely assume that Iran will boil up into one of the biggest stories in the world media. One of my uncle's principal allies I can name: Hossein Jafari, director of programming at state television. The public will have images of popular discontent that they never dreamt could ever be beamed into their homes.'

Avi raised his eyebrows.

'How on earth is Jafari loyal to the Ayatollah, and not the leadership? The Supreme Leader appoints him, doesn't he?'

'It's personal,' Baharvand said. 'He helped him out once.'

'How?'

Baharvand shook his head. 'Sorry.'

'OK, Mr Baharvand, so where do we come into this?'

'Well, crucially, we need the world to rally behind this popular rising in Iran. Bush, Brown, Merkel and Sarkozy must stand up and back the protesters early. Just on the necessity for democratic reform. They should know in advance what's going on. My uncle will then make sympathetic noises in the Iranian media.'

'You hardly need us for that. These things tend to have a life of their own. With the bad blood over the nuclear programme being what it is, all of the US and EU leaders will be champing at the bit to have a dig at the Iranian leadership,' Andy said.

'When my uncle speaks out in favour of the protesters, he should be supported. And western leaders should have an understanding of which way this is going, so they can help him consolidate power in those first, fragile weeks.'

Poker faces. Andy prodded him again.

'So, all you want is for us to lay the ground for a coup? Convincing democratic leaders that this is a democratic thing? That Baharvand is going to turn Iran into Switzerland?'

The banker delved into his pocket, pulled out a disc and slid it across the table.

'It is heavily encrypted. The first code is Shiraz, the cross code is Janssen's. With the apostrophe. Your tech people should be able to unravel the rest. The final data is a set of co-ordinates. Those co-ordinates could prove to be a thorn in our flank: an impediment to everything moving off as smoothly as it could. This is no cause for alarm. As things stand, I would say that my uncle has an eighty per cent chance of pulling this thing off. The twenty per cent danger-area that could unseat him lies in those co-ordinates. I think the sites will already be known to you. Guard bases with commanders who are unpredictable or whom we will never make see sense. Nests of basijis, Islamic paramilitaries. With judicious co-operation in removing these co-ordinates, I think my uncle would be guaranteed one hundred per cent success.'

Jesus Christ. So that's why he's here. Now we cut to the chase.

'We will, of course, study these co-ordinates carefully,' Andy said. 'But are you really telling me a few air-strikes will neutralise your opponents to an extent that makes your uncle's plan water-tight? You may be right. Maybe most Iranians are pretty hacked off with this current state of affairs and powerful groups are genuinely angry. Maybe you are even right that an influential heavyweight such as your uncle could engineer those forces to the extent that he could overthrow the system. But a huge and well-structured part of the present system will want him dead and will do everything to thwart him. Obviously, the regressive nuts who enjoy a good stoning and want Israel nuked are a minority. But they are a minority with huge financial resources and a spider's web of brilliant networking. You cannot liquidate them from the air. They'll hate you and stand in your way for decades. They are determined to pull Iran back to the Middle Ages and a little internal coup is not going to stop them.'

'Mr Trevarthen, you really must not see these people as such a nebulous and elusive force. They have their leaders like everyone else. Even a couple of their most senior ayatollahs, men they will follow, are close to Ayatollah Baharvand. The ruling caste are veering towards messianic cultism. The Ayatollah and his allies represent a real return to the old ways, the true faith. Other figureheads can be removed from the picture. But the herd at large is not something that will vex us for long, Mr Trevarthen.

These are people who will come over to us when they see on which course history is taking them.'

History? Who does this guy think he is? The banker sensed the growing air of scepticism from across the table. Avi had the strongest experience of fighting this larger enemy: the brooding, conservative children of a revolution that was still only in its infancy. He had fought them in Lebanon.

'What of Hezbollah?' he asked. 'Is Iran just going to cut off one of its own limbs? Weapons, money, a national mission? All over? Just like that?'

'I think my uncle believes that the children of the revolution are now old enough to stand on their own two feet. Of course, the Shi'ite world is of importance to us but Iran itself must become the focus now. Pan-Islamic interests are treading us into the dust. Will Iran help the transformation of Hezbollah? Yes. They are our children. Will we continue to arm them in the same way? Of course, not. Those days, the days of Dr Chamran should already be long behind us.'

'But they are not,' Avi said, as a resigned afterthought. He could never imagine Iran saying farewell to Hezbollah.

Baharvand was silent for a few moments. 'I think, we have it then, gentlemen. Are there any other questions?'

Andy laughed.

'We have only just begun, I am afraid. You'll be calling in sick for at least the next three days.'

Max took the initiative while Baharvand was on the back-foot.

'Let me put something to you, Mr Baharvand. A tale I heard from an Iranian-American businessman last month. Let's say he makes car windshields. Or sorry, windscreens. He doesn't make car windscreens, but I don't want him roughed up. He's a friend of mine. He came across a good business proposal. In Germany,

71

he found a stash of cheap but good glass with kite-mark security. So, he thinks, excellent, I'll import this into Iran, sell it for European car models there and increase my profit. He researches the law and notes down the import tariff that he'll be paying down the docks at Bandar Abbas. Let's say it is twelve per cent. The numbers all add up. Things are looking good.

'A month later his glass arrives in Iran and he goes down with a haulier to pick it up. Some Revolutionary Guard commanders present him with a bill. A huge bill. But the tax is only twelve per cent, he says. Well, no, they say. We are changing the rules. We see that this German glass is very cheap. We know what you can sell this for as windscreens in Iran. You are making too much profit.

'So what does my friend think? He thinks "fuck off". You cannot stand in the way of business. What I am doing is just good, old-fashioned trade. Any judge will see the matter the same way. So he takes it to the courts. And, guess what? He doesn't seem to find anyone there who seems to be able to just read the import tariff sheets with a clear mind. It just says "windscreen glass - twelve per cent" but, oh no, everyone wants some more.

'Now as you say, the Revolutionary Guard and their friends might be doing more and more of this. It is impossible to do business with Iran without somehow doing business with the Revolutionary Guard. But you know who my friend was up against? He was up against Ayatollah Ali Baharvand's men. That your uncle has plenty of friends and illicit income from parts of the Revolutionary Guard and the courts, I do not doubt. I dunno, maybe these men can help him pull off a coup from the inside. But what I do know about Ayatollah Ali Baharvand, is that he is a racketeer like everyone else. The reason he needs our help now is that other parts of the Guards and other crooked members of the establishment are making more money than he is. He wants our help taking over the show so that he can make as much loot as he used to.'

The Ayatollah's nephew was impressed by the CIA man. Here were people who knew how to drive a bargain.

'Look, Ayatollah Baharvand knows how the real Iran game is played. He is not one of these powerless, stupid reformists like Khatami that the West idolised for years. My uncle is a real operator. And he could be the West's man. You have everything to gain from him.'

'But do we? The fact that you are coming to us now suggests he is already losing his edge. His friends in the Revolutionary Guard are the ones who are outnumbered. Your uncle's men aren't just striking deals with the big fish any more. He isn't just charging some enormous "consultancy" deal for brokering an oil contract. He is left picking on small businessmen, squeezing out the last rial from car windshield importers at the docks.'

'I do not think that this is a constructive way of looking at the problem. There are other perspectives. So much of this transfer of power is based on the personalities: the commanders, the war heroes we do have on board. And in coups, the military never just splits down the middle and flocks to their respective flags. This is the point: most commanders just wait patiently in their barracks until it is clear who is going to win.'

'Some just roll out the tanks and shoot into crowds,' Avi said.

'Hence the co-ordinates. We know those men.'

'Hence the co-ordinates,' Andy echoed, pocketing the disc. 'Ok, let's start this at the beginning. There are things we need to know, either now or very, very soon. Try to memorise them. Make a list of every nuclear facility from uranium mines through to the yellowcake production at Ardakan and the uranium hexafluoride output at Isfahan. The heavy water at Arak. The military installations at Parchin. Kalaye Electric. List everything.

73

Set up the jungle telephone with your uncle. We're going to keep you as our point-man. Come back to us with how much activity will be going on at these nuclear sites over the next ten years.'

Max chimed in.

'We'll need the Ayatollah's exact wording on all of this. And particularly we'll need exact wording on Israel. We'll need to know how much the Iranian public will be told and how much will be just between us.'

Andy looked up at the clock. It was going to be a long haul. Baharvand had the same feeling. Does tonsillitis get you three days off at HSBC, he wondered? Maybe tonsillitis and a fever would do the trick.

Andy arrived slightly late at the ziggurat down on Vauxhall Bridge. Legoland. Base camp. It was half six and he was famished, but if Emperor Lomax summons you to his marbled chambers, then the legions march through the night on an empty stomach. He was puffing away on his pipe, filling his glass-walled office with a heady Latakia blend that reminded Andy of his own father, exiled to the summer house. Regulations on smoking in public places certainly did not apply to the Emperor.

Lomax looked up from the piles of Hackney transcripts and snorted out an 'Aaa-HAA', still biting the pipe-stem between his teeth.

'Good to have you back with the family, Andy.'

'How you doing, Callum?'

'Very well. Take a pew, old man.'

Lomax was wearing his Balliol tie. They'd known each other at college but it would never have occurred to Andy to buy the tie. But there again, it would never have occurred to Andy to learn how to play golf or join a London club. And probably partly because of that, it would never have occurred to those who decide such things to give Andy a knighthood. For Callum Lomax that was only a question of time. In deportment he was already Sir Callum. Not that Lomax or anyone else in the service looked down on Trevarthen. Perhaps only Callum knew Andy as a damn-fine first-change in the college XI, but everyone knew the other stories. Not just the escape with the Kurds, but that remarkable weekend in Budapest which became more intriguing every time Andy declined to discuss it. Men like Lomax spent their whole lives running networks out of embassies, and doing so very shrewdly. But they still reserved a jealous affection for those like Andy who led careers that should really have disappeared sometime in the 1930s.

'Well, this is one hell of a thing,' Lomax said, taking his pipe by the bowl and stabbing the stem into the piles of transcript. 'I am briefing the PM at nine tonight. Condy has already read the thing. Guess Bush'll have a look soon. Mossad are all over it. We are telling the French and the Germans a little something to keep them sweet.'

'How much?'

'Not a lot. Don't worry. Still like 'em as little as you do. Haven't gone funny. We have said something along the lines of: we expect some kind of pro-democracy street trouble in Iran. Baharvand might speak out in favour. We should probably put together a joint statement, encouraging democratic reform in Iran.'

'That's probably about as much as the embassies need to know too. The ambassador is too much of a liability. Not really the sharpest crayon in the tin either, so best to keep them guessing while this bubbles on, even if it gets nasty.'

'Absolutely agreed. On the money again, Andy. PM doesn't like the ambo much either. Married to the daughter of some massive Tory donor.'

75

'Aha. Right. That I did not know.'

'Now, look. You are aware I could just go in and give the stock security appraisal of this guy Baharvand to the PM. But what do we really think? Even if it's just a hunch. Few people know that bloody country and that bloody man as well as you do, Andy. Want my opinion? He'll be dead by Christmas. But he looks like he's just going to plough on and cause one hell of a stink, whether we help him or not. And he'll probably cause a fucking global oil crisis, whatever happens.'

'As you say, it's always hard to trust him but I cannot work out what his game is yet. It doesn't add up. Baby Baharvand dropped some hints that he'd like to open some lines with Israeli agents in Iran. Alarm bells, of course. Essentially, Avi wonders whether the whole thing isn't an elaborate ruse to flush out the few surviving field-men the Israelis have got inside the Islamic Republic.'

'Likely?'

'There would be far simpler ways of doing that. It's not inconceivable but it would be a sledgehammer approach.'

'But you don't really believe what we see is what we get, do you?'

'No, I don't. Baharvand is an impossible man to understand. The viper. Max is right that he's a crook who feels power seeping away from him but, again, something on this scale would be wholly unwarranted. Baharvand might well be about to make a power grab but I'd be pretty surprised if he then went through with this nuclear and Israel proposal. It sounds like a suicidal package to go into office with. But you'll never find me underestimating the bastard. He is still a brilliant tactician and one of the few men who has always been able to judge the primal moods of Iran. The big throws of the dice, he always seems to win.'

Lomax nodded.

'Thanks. That's what I needed to hear. Of course, you'll head up our team on this with Catherine. She says she'll talk to you again.'

Andy's tension dissolved into a short laugh.

'Sure, of course. It'll be good to work with her again.'

Responsibility and promotion meant nothing to Andy. For many within the secret world, unable to share successes, even with close friends and family, the verdict of one's peers means everything. Andy had ceased to judge his life by those standards. Possibly even as early as the disaster at Janssen's, that side of him was dead. If a job came up, particularly an interesting one, he'd be keen to do it, but seniority gave him no spring in his step. The Lomaxes thrived on the jostling and backstabbing, weaving their way between contending ambitions. Andy judiciously avoided base camp.

'They just want me to get a reassurance from you.'

'That I am not still on a one man hate-mission to get Baharvand killed?'

'Something to that effect.'

'He seems to think I am an old friend now. My main feeling towards the man is more one of fascination, I guess. Janssen's was a very long time ago. I can play each ball on its merits, I can assure you of that.'

A cricket metaphor would always lead Lomax to concur with the validity of your argument.

'Naturally. Personally, I never had any doubts.'

'I take it the military bods are going to be there tonight? Have you had the co-ordinates processed?'

'Of course. Yes, one or two places we had no idea existed actually. We haven't the foggiest whether he wants us to drop bombs on munitions or people.'

'I hope we can get an instant knock-down from the top. I already told Baharvand there was no chance we would put any British weaponry or special forces at his disposal.'

'Wise. But Christ alone knows what the Israelis and the Yanks will make of all this. They might already be briefing the pilots and fuelling up. It's a real embuggerance this sharing malarkey.'

'In the politicos we trust then.'

'Mmm... The Israelis won't really buy into any of this appeasement baloney will they?'

'Well, they know Iran better than any of us on the ground and they have a real sense of what a schizophrenic quagmire the place is. It's really hard to know how it would go down. Well nigh impossible. If you were to suggest to me that Iran can sometimes veer towards casual anti-Semitism and that the Iranians rallied round to donate money and jewellery when Israel attacked Lebanon, then I'd say you were correct. If you were to say Iranians often claim to hate the Palestinians far more than the Jews and resent their Arab solidarity with Saddam during the war, I'd say you had something there too. Iranians will often hark back to Cyrus liberating Jerusalem and talk about themselves and the Jews as the two great peoples of the Middle East, the peoples who should carve it up between themselves.

'If you told me an Israeli had turned up in the streets of Tehran and everybody had come up and shaken him by the hand I would believe you. If you said they had pelted him with stones, I'd say that could happen too. Israel is an impossible question to weigh up in a country as screwed in the head as Iran. We cannot read how Iran would react if it heard there were to be a deal with Israel. Schizophrenically probably. Like on everything else. Just on that little part of Baharvand's thinking, we cannot read the nation. As to every other tortured layer of his proposal ...'

Andy threw his hands up in feigned despair.

'What a bloody country,' Lomax sighed. 'I had better not tell the PM that no one has the faintest idea how this will play out.'

'No, probably not an ideal way to preserve our budget.'

'Right.' Lomax banged all his papers into neat, heavy rectangles. 'You go down the corridor and be nice to Cath. She still loves you.'

'Everybody loves me, Callum. Good luck with the prime minister. Not that you'll need it. Caledonian mafia.'

'Ay, Tartan triads.'

Cath Spedding had cleared her desk and was heading out, clutching a file. Andy caught her by the filing cabinets. She still had that remarkably martial way of dressing that played up her femininity. She was wearing the sort of broad-lapelled greatcoat that would have suited a defeated infantryman in Napoleon's Grande Armée as he retreated across Russia's frozen wastes.

She sprang towards him and kissed him. Then recoiled and punched him in the chest.

'No, you are a total bastard. I must remember that.'

'Indeed. Pub?'

'Why not? Just the one. I've just got to run this file down to the crime people. Parsian. You know him?'

'Mo Parsian? Of course, old friends.'

'Well, he's back in the UK, making a nuisance of himself. He's a specialist in making sure that our *Guide Michelin* restaurants don't run out of caviar during the ban.'

'Oh, that sounds his style. Not from the Iranians though?'

'No, he's using Azeri poachers.'

'Ah, friends from his meat pie days?'

'You've lost me.'

'You haven't heard that one? Parsian a most extraordinary operator. He ran meat pies and chips to the

Norwegian and British oil workers in the early days of the Azeri oil boom. Made millions. Please don't let them lock him up. He could be very useful to us one day.'

'You are not serious.'

'He's sharper than ninety per cent of people in the service. Perhaps more honest.'

'Andy, stop it. He's a crook.'

'The man is a genius, I am proud to call him my friend. Never liked sturgeon anyway. Very ugly fish. Big snouts, like the French.'

Cath peered over the top of her spectacles.

'You bastard. After all this time, you bastard. Just give me two minutes to make sure Parsian gets deported, then you can buy me a brandy.'

'Done.'

He noted she had her first white hairs. Was that premature?

The pub was yet another sign, as far as Andy was concerned, that London was going to the dogs. The furnishings looked like an IKEA catalogue and most of the pumps were given over to fizzy, lifeless lagers. Andy only ever praised a pub if there were gnarled rafters, sawdust on the floor and a demijohn of pickled eggs. His era had long passed. The music in London was too loud. And there was never a tune. This place was a bag of shite and the barmaid looked surly.

He seated Cath at a small table and went to the bar, taking a place beside a burly bar-fly in a Barbour jacket. His hair was matted and his red forehead was flecked with dots of waxy sweat.

'She'll leave you, you know.'

Andy thought for a moment that the comment could not possibly have been directed towards him. People just don't say that sort of thing.

'Her? Never. Honest as the day is long.'

'Yeah, exactly, twenty-four hours mate.' He laughed at his own joke. 'That's what women do to you. That's what women do.'

He can't be saying this. The pub's not full but he's quite loud. Cath can hear. She thinks it's all quite funny.

'We probably deserve it.'

'No, we bloody don't. Well, maybe you do. I didn't.'

Until that moment Andy hadn't realised quite how drunk the man was.

'Seventeen depots I had. Cars from everywhere. And all for my bloody family. Then divorce. Out of a clear blue sky, mate. Never heard from them again. Just hear from the fucking Child Support Agency.'

Thankfully, the barmaid came to take his order.

'Same again, Dave?'

'Of course, darling. Now, if I didn't know you were already spoken for, I'd ask you for a kiss.'

The barmaid made a face as if she had bitten deep into a lemon. Andy began to feel genuinely sorry for the old soak who plodded off to a small table at the other end of the bar and raised his pint in a mock salute. Andy nodded back.

'Sorry 'bout him. He's such an arse.'

'Sounds like he's had a rough ride.'

'We all have a rough ride. He's just a twat. What'll it be?'

Andy carefully settled the pale ale and the cognac on to the table and folded his overcoat into a bundle.

'Cheers,' Cath said cheerily. 'I think I will leave you. You are a wastrel.'

'Fair enough. How's Otto?'

'Otto is Otto. Boring and reliable. He's in Switzerland. And after twenty years Mother thinks he is still too boring.'

'Does he know Baby Baharvand?'

'He must do. Bankers are those kind of people. Hob-nobby. I'll have to see whether he knows of any skeletons in the cupboard. Things that could stop him becoming the Ayatollah's finance minister.' She paused. 'Andy, this is all just so sudden. This is just crazy. There's not about to be another Iranian revolution is there?'

Western intelligence on Iran had slumped to this. No networks. Not much of anything. Andy sensed the tension in her voice. Although a veteran, Cath had only been on Iran for six months after nearly a decade on various African sections. She was scared of failure.

Andy was already a failure. He had no such worries. Iran, the country he truly loved, had eaten more out of him than he could ever admit. How could he be expected to know what would happen in that place? Iran puts fortune-tellers out of business. Just before the 1979 revolution, the Shah had been Jimmy Carter's island of stability. All he knew was that, if it did blow up, the same people would win and the same people would lose. The little tyrants would come out on top. Maybe they would be our friends, maybe not. The people Andy loved would be shat on again, from Washington and London deciding in their infinite wisdom that they know best. Troops will fire on crowds and scholars will be strangled in dingy stairwells. And he would only be flattering himself if he thought he could do anything about it.

'Well, there's one overdue. 1953, 1979. Has 2007 got a ring to it? I can never tell, Cath. We need to know so much more before we can work out whether this is big.'

'But you don't think he's just a paper tiger do you?'

'No.'

He remained silent and Cath sensed his need to let Iran drop for the day.

'Lomax says he is giving you one of the Westminster pads while you are over.'

'Indeed. Cyrus will be glad. On the third night, the guest begins to stink. I'll move over there tomorrow. You still in that huge place on the Thames?'

'No. Otto has moved into an even bigger place on the Thames. It's got an incredible view but there's just something that gives me the creeps about it. Oh, I don't know. Otto tries to fill it up at the weekend with his dinner parties and all his City friends. They all think I work in fisheries. Fancy, fisheries. They look down on me and flirt and think I should be impressed. Then at eleven they all go home and it's a bit empty. Lonely.'

She finished her cognac.

'Sorry, that's how you lose friends, isn't it? Look, I should run. We are probably going to be kept rather busy from now on.'

4.

Gossamer streaks of mist lingered over Chesapeake Bay. Overhead, the hollow, grey cloudbank had a luminous white heart where the Wednesday morning sun was straining to break through. With a sudden crack of their wings and a chorus of throaty quacks, dozens of scoters and eiders lifted through the mist, skimmed across the top of it for a few hundred yards and then arched towards the two men in the hide. Danny Valerio fired quickly and jerkily, as if trying to snatch the wildfowl out of the air. Fuck. Nothing. Fuck it. Arkady Fyodorovich Dolokhov waited, then swung the barrel round in a composed and unhurried sweep. Two more blasts cut through the damp morning air. This time, two birds buckled in flight and dropped into the estuary. Peggy, the black retriever, bounded happily and purposefully into the chill grey waters.

'Nice shooting, Arkady. Nice one, man.'

The Russian smiled.

'You're just too tense, Danny. Calm it down and you'll do great.'

Valerio cringed at any advice, particularly on shooting. He was one of those men who, like the Duke of Wellington, ought to have been a fine shot but was actually lousy. He boasted he lived by the gun and, in his most famous speech to the National

Rifle Association, had vowed that he was willing to die by the gun. They had lapped up that Valerio-classic at the 1999 Christmas dinner and Charlton Heston, still exuding the pious gravitas of El Cid, had squeezed the lawyer's shoulder with avuncular pride.

Valerio felt like a fraud. He found it infuriating that all the military men he idolised accepted him on his own terms. He was their legal hot-shot and they needed him to pull the strings and talk the talk. They loved his homespun values and were damn glad they had such a wily operator on their side. Valerio was a very impressive man, but not in the way he had dreamed of being. By his late thirties he had become one of the three most predatory sharks in the Defense Trade Advisory Group. There were often days when the big guns at Lockheed Martin and Raytheon wouldn't take a leak without clearing it with Valerio. Aerospace, missiles, small arms: he had his finger in all the pies. But he often wondered, if God came down and gave him the option, whether he wouldn't just give it all up to be able to shoot straight. OK, sure, perhaps he wouldn't be so influential in the defence of the American dream, but at least he could live without shame.

The remarkable thing was that he never gave up and kept putting himself through torture. He felt duty-bound to keep living the gun-toting fantasy. To Valerio's mind, you couldn't possibly invite a military attaché like Dolokhov, a man's man who'd fought the Panjshiri Mujahidin, out to a little Italian eatery with red-chequered tablecloths, the sort of place where a waiter with a pencil moustache would come round with a giant pepper mill. No, no, it had to be a duck or goose shoot.

Dolokhov, on the other hand, always sighed when he got his invitations from Valerio and just wished, for once, the phoney would take him to some little Italian place like everyone else.

'I'd better wear a flak jacket in case the cack-handed bastard shoots me by accident,' he joked to his secretary.

Valerio stared out over the water and passed Dolokhov his hip-flask. It was time to get down to business.

'I guess you guys have heard that the president held a big pow-wow on Monday night. Cheney. Condy. Pentagon. NSA.'

Dolokhov had heard something along those lines.

It was, of course, galling that Valerio had to be fed details of these meetings when, only two years ago, it was widely assumed that he would be in regular attendance. Valerio was the clear front-runner for National Security Advisor. But they found a little problem in the vetting process. Valerio's secretary was forced to reveal that Valerio wasn't quite the apple-pie hero that everyone had assumed. The secretary's testimony had started off saccharine enough. Mr Valerio might be right at the top of the food chain in the Washington jungle but he had a heart of gold. Often he would look down from his office window and see a vagrant, or someone less fortunate than ourselves, rummaging around in a garbage can or picking through trash that had piled up by the sidewalk. Mr Valerio would ring Al in security and get him to go and buy something. Not much, you understand, but, you know, a coffee, a donut, that sort of thing. Starbucks. Mr Valerio came from one of those tight-knit Italian families and you could never separate him from his sense of Christian duty. So far, so good. Here we had an NSA in the making.

There was, however, that small issue of the photographs. She hadn't really wanted to go into it but it was important that they should know. She had her sense of Christian duty too. She had two sets of photographs, showing Mr Valerio with 'his wife and two kids'. Two different wives, two different sets of kids, if you understand me. Yes, that's two wives and four kids. The men in the white mackintoshes looked at each other quizzically, then wry smiles spread above their chisel-jaws. No, they had understood. Valerio had played a quite brilliant game of musical chairs over the last eight years. The city wife didn't know about the country wife and the country wife didn't know about the city wife. Only the secretary knew because she was the one who had to change round the photographs according to who was visiting. This was the last thing the GOP needed. So Stephen Hadley became NSA.

Valerio thought there was no way that Dolokhov could have heard the bigamy yarn but the gregarious Russian had turned it into one of his favourite dinner-time anecdotes.

'Well, it seems there's some real shit going down in Iran.'

Dolokhov slid a couple of fresh cartridges into his shot-gun and snapped it shut. This was unusual. Iran was the real bone of contention between Moscow and Washington and everybody knew that you could never really have a confidential chat with Arkady Fyodorovich. Valerio knew full well that his shooting buddy was a senior officer in GRU, Russia's massive military intelligence apparatus, a unit that seemed to revel in its sinister reputation by flaunting a giant black bat on its insignia. That's why he wanted to talk to Dolokhov so urgently.

'Ah, really?' the Russian said absent-mindedly. 'I had taken my eye off Iran, to be honest with you.'

Dolokhov never took his eye off anything.

'Oh yeah, it's crazy stuff. There's going to be a coup attempt.'

Dolokhov frowned and rolled his head to one side in a look that suggested he didn't like people trying to pull his leg.

'You know Ayatollah Ali Baharvand?'

'Of course, sure I do Danny. The former nuclear negotiator.'

'Well, seems he's going to go for it. Inside job.'

The Russians know about inside jobs and Dolokhov had orchestrated one or two in his time. He quickly played through some of the permutations in his head. It wasn't inconceivable. Unlikely, but not impossible.

'How do we know this? Do you believe it?'

'Well, it's serious intel. If some big-time student protests start tonight, then it looks like the whole thing will be on course. At least, that would be in line with Baharvand's plans.'

Dolokhov whistled.

Valerio knew there was still time to abort. As it stood, the Russian military attaché could just transmit some interesting back-room banter back to high command and that would be that. One more step and Valerio was betraying every kind of confidence. One more step and he knew that the Russians would have to act.

But that's what he had always liked about the Russians: they were the sort of people who believed in action, not the liberal elephant-dance. America needed to learn from the Russians on that score. Orthodox Mother Russia – hell, he admired the depth of the old faith and how it survived that Commie bull – was the last bastion against all sorts of Islamist nuts. And so was America, but at least the Ruskies appreciated that the rules were changing. They were just realists. Valerio sometimes had to give some of the junior attorneys in his office a piece of his mind when they started to fret about the course Russia was taking. They might spend all day boo-hooing about human rights but the Russians, Valerio helpfully explained, were on the front line. People in the West had no conception of the dangers posed by radical Islam in Chechnya. Some jumped-up reporter like Anna Politkovskaya goes kicking up a fuss, then, yeah, she's going to walk into a bullet in her elevator. Litvinenko goes ratting, then, yeah, he gets a polonium brew in his tea-pot in London. The Russians simply recognise the enormity of the struggle and they know how to deal with little shits who get in the way. Valerio didn't grasp the intricacies of this Russian cloak-and-dagger stuff, but who cares? The big picture was clear enough. What do we get here in the States? A bunch of do-gooding assholes who don't know jack shit hollering that Guantanamo is out of line. Screw them. They are the ones who are out of line. Valerio had got to an age where he cursed at articles in the liberal press. While hand-wringing western journalists were stunned by irredentist Russia's latest brazen offensives, planting its flag under the Arctic ice-pack and holding Europe to ransom with gas exports, Valerio just lauded a race who could stick up for themselves and be proud about it. You wouldn't find the Russians getting all wishy-washy about protecting their interests.

Which was why Moscow might lend him a hand here and stop this mother-fucker Baharvand in his tracks.

'But this is the bit you need to get a load of, Arkady: the guy thinks that we are going to back him all the way. He's got a nuclear deal.'

Too late now. Valerio had accepted on the short trip from Washington that his words could prove treasonable.

Dolokhov was alarmed. It was incomprehensible how any nuclear deal could not involve the Russians who were building and supplying the lion's share of Tehran's rickety nuclear hardware. The Iranians had ambitious, if slow-moving, plans to expand the number and sophistication of their reactors over the next few decades. That meant big bucks for the Russians. Furthermore, if the Iranian programme was going anywhere, it was thanks to Russian fuel that would then be shipped back in a flimsy guarantee that it wouldn't be converted into weapons-grade material. Closer to the bone, some of Russia's best boffins were extending the range of Iran's missiles and ensuring they didn't just keel over on the launch-pad. Some of the missile nose-cones were so distinctive that the Israelis could recognise the old

Soviet maestros behind the handiwork. Any kind of nuclear deal that didn't involve Moscow was a peculiar kind of deal. Valerio must have got his wires a bit crossed.

Dolokhov blew a Canada Goose out of the sky. Valerio hadn't notice it swoop in from his right, but as soon as he saw the goose crumple mid-air, he worried whether that moratorium on hunting the autumn migrants had come back into force. We have laws in this country, Arkady.

'The idea,' Valerio continued, 'is that Iran regains the trust of the international community by verifiably freezing all of its atomic installations for ten years. Baharvand comes in, patches things up with us and the Europeans, and gets some real investment back in the economy. American investment, you understand. Big oil goes back home.'

'Mr Cheney will be glad,' Dolokhov said sardonically. 'Halliburton are still licking their wounds over Iran. If the mullahs start handing out good contracts, there is really serious money for the oil boys.'

'Fuck yeah, they are already creaming themselves.'

Valerio angrily aimed his gun at something that Dolokhov was pretty convinced didn't exist.

'Bush apparently sat there talking about the need for democratic reform and Condy chimed in with all sorts of positive remarks on this being our big opportunity to defuse the nuclear crisis without a war.'

Valerio lowered his weapon and looked towards Dolokhov.

'But Cheney, oh, he's a tricky customer. He got right behind Baharvand's logic. He already seemed to know quite a lot about him. Odd that, no? Oil investment in Iran was the way forward. Political restructuring – perestroika, Arkady – and commercial interaction together. We could get a real US ally in the Gulf again. Another Shah. Shah Baharvand.'

As Valerio forged ahead with his increasingly irritable account of the meeting, the full scale of the potential calamity for Russia became evident. The billions of dollars in potential earnings lost to the atomic industry and the missile engineers was bad enough. Dolokhov could already hear big fists thumping down on tables in the Kremlin. Big men would be bellowing. But throw in the oil and Putin himself would be baying for blood: American blood, Iranian blood, he wouldn't care. The whole thing would simply be a disaster. The Russian lads like LUKOIL had hung on in there, allowing themselves to be screwed over by the Persian Ali Babas, just to get a foot in the door, hoping that one day the Iranians would relax the rules for their friends and grant them one of the big upstream projects. Let's say an Azadegan or a Bangestan. And now this: the cowboys from Conoco and Exxon were just going to waltz in there, get the girl and ride off into the sunset. And worse than that: he knew how markets would react: this could well slice $30 straight off the oil price and take a big bite out of Russian revenue. Once oil started heading south, who knew where it would end up? Russia's stock-market would fall to pieces. A few puffs on the peace pipe with Tehran would quickly lead to all sorts of cloud-cuckoo-land projections from the Iranian oil ministry. Those swivel-eyed Persians would doubtless promise to ramp production up to eight million barrels per day. With US investment, the bastards might well do it. If what Valerio was saying had a kernel of truth to it, Moscow would be bouncing off the walls the second his telegram arrived.

But Dolokhov doused his rage. Think it through. Some rather obvious objections must have arisen at the meeting. After all, even General Electric and Halliburton had to pull out of Iran eventually, after years of conning the great American public by using foreign partners and offshore chicanery to pretend they weren't in bed with the mullahs. They knew the domestic opposition was just too strong. 'The War on Terror' meant harmonious business with Tehran wasn't an option. And then there was the question of Israel.

'But the Jewish lobby isn't going to sit by and let the oil-men go investing in a terrorist state, are they?'

'Oh, I was coming to that, Arkady. You are going to love this bit. Baharvand has thought this one through. He realises none of this works until there is a co-operative understanding with Israel and Iran promises to discipline its wayward offspring: Hezbollah.'

He pronounced it to rhyme with 'His dollar'.

'No way. I thought I'd heard everything.'

Some long-tailed ducks sped past the front of the hide. Eye-level. Dammit, I wasn't looking, Valerio thought. As if he had all the time in the world, Dolokhov fed in a shell and settled his breathing.

'Wo-ah, forget 'em Arkady, They're out of range. Those things really shift.'

One sharp crack and the last duck in the fly-by squadron dropped out of the sky.

'Jeez, man, you're on a mission today.'

Dolokhov was thinking about how quickly he would be able to get back to the embassy, that soulless white cube on Wisconsin Avenue, and start transmitting. It didn't sound as if there were time to lose.

'The Saudis aren't going to take kindly to this. You taking them out shooting too, Danny?'

Dolokhov wanted to see whether he really understood Valerio's motives. Lawyers were unscrupulous swines at the best of times, but the depth of Valerio's cynical deception now astounded even a hardened GRU veteran. He wondered which of the wizened reptiles at the Pentagon was hand in glove with Valerio over this. Who was his source on the inside of the White House meeting? It couldn't possibly be Fallon; he knew the old Admiral wouldn't countenance the use of force against Iran. It was probably General Byrd. He always figured that Byrd had an astronomical shareholding in Valerio's companies. He helped smooth talk the last $20-billion worth of missiles, jets and warships that the Saudis were suddenly convinced they needed. Plenty of people in Moscow quipped that Ahmadinejad was head of sales for the US arms industry. After that, came Byrd. He was the vacuum-cleaner salesman who'd be out there at bases in the desert, telling the princes, viziers and generals just how much state-of-the-art American gadgetry they would need for the day when the Iranians finally got round to lobbing rockets into Saudi petrochemical cities. The British managed to milk some deals out of them but it had to be Byrd and Valerio who were the big winners, right across the Gulf. Everywhere. When the Sheikh Your-moneys came to the States, Mr 'Family Values' Valerio was their pimp. Back in their tin-pot autocracies they might be locking up girls for getting raped but, all along the top corridors of Manhattan hotels, the weapons deals were sweetened by lines of coke and leggy blondes in bunny ears who'd suck off the emir of somewhere or other to keep the world safe for democracy. Arms was a fetid sub-kingdom and Valerio sat upon its throne.

'I'd put it a bit stronger than that. The Saudis are going to hate this. They are going to tip their toys all over the goddam floor. For years, they have been confident that they are our sweethearts in the Middle East. We are not meant to have eyes for anyone else. Particularly not their arch enemy. I mean, Arkady, you really have to pity the poor Saudis on this. They are the guardians of the great holy cities, Mecca and Medina, and now they have to watch the Shi'ites of Iran become the rallying point for the Islamic world. The Saudis just see the Iranians as heretics, they don't want their sacrilegious messianic messages flying round the globe.

'And so how are we going to treat our Saudi allies? We are going to make the mistakes of the fifties, sixties and seventies all over again and throw our lot in with the Iranians. We support Baharvand and it's the clearest possible sign that we don't think that Saudi Arabia is stable. We also give the message that we are perfectly happy for the Iranians to start overhauling their oil industry and dethroning Riyadh as the big noise on the block. Well, in fact, the only noise on the block. Who knows, maybe Iran will double its slice of the OPEC cake. Then where will we be?'

The strategy sounded eminently sensible to Dolokhov. It was painfully evident that the White House was being forced to invest too many of its chips with the House of Saud.

'We go and treat the Saudis like this, Arkady, when, even as we speak it's the Iranians who are planting the roadside bombs in Iraq that are killing our boys and kidnapping British sailors. Don't tell me it's a coincidence that Iraq is full of Revolutionary Guards while our boys are getting bogged down in an intractable slaughter.'

Valerio was becoming genuinely impassioned. Peggy the retriever considered him with some apprehension and Dolokhov reminded himself that effeminate suits like Valerio had never actually seen a war, although they had started enough of them. He might be about to do it again. But who were the Americans trying to kid? Everybody could see that the Shi'ites weren't killing that many Americans. It would be the Sunnis who were fighting like men possessed to get them out. And who would be using Sunnis to fight a proxy war with Iran? Well that, in one of history's marvellously circular ironies, would be the Saudis.

Could the Saudis really channel their efforts into fighting the Iranians without their money and weapons also going off into killing Americans? All the reports that crossed Dolokhov's desk, top gen from the SVR, suggested that such clean distinctions became impossible in the Iraqi maelstrom. Sunni brothers were heroes, whoever they were fighting.

Valerio packed up his shells and Dolokhov felt sorry for him. He wondered why he kept putting himself through the agony of sparing every wildfowl in Chesapeake Bay. The lawyer had allowed his anger to get the better of him. When Moscow took this bait, it would be pretty easy for the CIA to determine who had leaked. Valerio was being reckless and it was hardly worth risking your neck for this. That, Dolokhov mused, was the big difference between westerners and Russians. They both played dirty for big money but the Russians wanted the money because money has a value: because it can be converted into cars, yachts, girls and drugs. And after what they had been through, that was fair enough. But to these westerners, it's no longer about the things money can buy. It's just a form of competition, and the prize may as well be plastic tokens or split peas. Valerio already had his millions, his lifestyle and his families. What did he really care if the latest big deal went through? America gets more bombers, Israel gets more bunker-busters and Saudi Arabia gets more missiles. There are high-fives in the hotel rooms after the midnight deals are clinched and the promise of more meetings with presidents and kings. But what was Valerio's material gain? Nothing, really. He just had to keep on gambling because he had to be the best and the most competitive. Dolokhov couldn't see the point. Valerio had committed treason through vanity rather than greed. That was really stupid.

The leaden dawn had dissolved into bright sunlight which scattered through the maple trees as they walked back to the cars.

'I hope you have worked out a good story for what we talked about. So we both agree,' Dolokhov said.

Valerio was still very naive on intelligence matters.

'Let me recommend an interest for you,' Dolokhov continued. Like all men at the top, Valerio was a big liability. 'You wanted to know about Russian relations with Chavez, particularly on the arms front. Sukhoi jet fighters and all that. It sounds important but I think we all know really it's a distraction.'

Valerio wasn't convinced that Chavez was a distraction. He often had to tell the Washington elite that Venezuela was the next Cuban missile crisis and that the Iranians would deploy their nuclear missiles on the Caribbean coast. However, in this case, he saw Dolokhov's point.

'Sure. Venezuela. Good thinking Arkady.'

The Russian grinned and slapped Valerio on the shoulder.

'Watch your tail, cowboy.' The Slavonic slur loaded the phrase with menace.

On the ride back to the embassy, Dolokhov had already made up his mind. If Valerio's story held water, then this was a job for the Tajik. He was by far the best man for the job. Since he was already in Herat, snooping around for the latest gossip on the local warlord Ismail Khan, he could be deployed quickly. Although his mother tongue was Persian, nobody had any doubts that the Tajik was at heart a proud Russian. He loved the opera, reverently recited Pushkin and sang raucously in Russian when he was drunk, smashing his glass on the floor. After twelve years as a Spetsnaz commando, the Tajik was now reserved for plum missions or the really difficult ones. It seemed to Dolokhov that everyone back in Moscow would see things the way he did and that the assassination of Ayatollah Ali Baharvand would soon be considered the Tajik's crowning glory: after that, he could look forward to the easy life back in Moscow, entertaining impressionable, young cadets with stories of his adventures. Though somehow, Dolokhov doubted that was the Tajik's style.

Café Naderi, only a stone's throw from the British embassy, is redolent of a lost Tehran. It belongs to the same Tehran as the waiters in white gloves who used to serve champagne on the flight terrace at Mehrabad airport. Seb loved soaking up the atmosphere of the ebullient jazz age that was snuffed out by the revolution. There was, for example, something haughtily magnificent about that dingy party hotel up at Anzali on the Caspian, the one with the chocolate and orange zigzag wallpaper and the champagne buckets used as ashtrays. In its day, the dance floor must have witnessed decadence unrivalled until you reached Hong Kong. Café Naderi was the same. A ghost from another age, its bosky courtyard somehow escaped the ravages of concrete encroachment and provided a humble refuge for bohemians.

The Naderi was easily Seb's favourite haunt for a working lunch. Some of the snootier diplomats insisted on heading to the lifeless pastiches of European restaurants that you could find uptown, but Seb was a loyalist. The decor seemed to hail from the 1950s. Fat waiters clad in burgundy jackets, sporting proud moustaches, ambled between the tables, occasionally deigning to take an order. The old bar boasted a zinc worthy of Les Deux Magots and the stiff-backed wooden chairs reminded Seb of his school dining hall. A few of the Naderi crowd were genuine intellectuals. He noted a group of three, white-haired mathematics teachers who often used to take a window table and spend the afternoon polishing off syrupy Turkish coffees as they put the world to rights. But mainly the Naderi set were fun, studenty pseuds with slicked hair and paperback novels. Then you got diplomats, homosexuals – there was a bit of cross-over there – and the ubiquitous Australian back-packers.

Seb had finally plucked up the courage to ring Negar, Miss Sequins. As she was in the auto business he could easily put her on the work tab. She arrived late and he hardly recognised her. Meeting girls in Tehran always had that embarrassing 'I didn't recognise you with your clothes on' dimension to it, but there was something more than the hejab that had changed her appearance. Maybe it was just nerves about meeting a British diplomat in public. That was often a problem and Seb sympathised.

She flashed a smile at him, waved meekly and came over to the table. Ever the gentleman, Seb stood and pulled out the chair for her. He was careful not to shake her hand.

'Negar, so glad you could make it in the end. How are you?'

'Good. I'm good. Busy, of course.'

'Of course.'

'And how are you?'

'Very well. I've finally recovered from Leila's party.'

At last, Negar smiled properly from underneath her headscarf. That was better. There, she was pretty. Seb was beginning to wonder whether the vodka had got the better of him and that he could be losing his old mastery. No, she was divine. But something was preying on her mind. Her cheeks were ashen and she had deep black lines under her eyes.

They continued chatting about the trivia that govern middle-class life in Tehran: anecdotes about traffic, new films and the advent of the ski season up at Shemshak and Dizin. The waiter finally took their order. Two Chateaubriands. The Chateaubriands were almost obligatory at Café Naderi, served in sizzling griddle-pans with dollops of white sauce and wedges of fried potato. Even in oppressive mid-summer, the heavy steaks were somehow de rigueur.

Then, quite suddenly, Negar sobbed and tears began to well in her eyes.

'Sorry,' she mumbled and yanked a fistful of tissues out of her handbag. 'I'm so sorry,' she continued, mopping her eyes and smearing her mascara.

'No, not at all,' Seb said, valiantly mustering his most knight-errant expression. 'Is there anything I can do?'

She started as if to speak but the words caught in her throat. She waved the sodden, stained clump of tissues at him and bit her lip. She took a couple of deep breaths, then cleared her throat.

'I am sorry, so sorry. You must be thinking I am a silly girl.'

'No, not at all. I am a bit worried though. Are you sure there is nothing I can help with?'

'I don't know. I really don't, Seb. It's my brother, you see, he's vanished.'

Seb poured a couple of glasses from the bottle of Damavand mineral water which was on the table.

'God. What happened?'

Negar gulped down the water.

'We don't know. But you've got to understand: he's a student.'

'As in a politically active student?'

She just nodded and took a quick glance round the faces in the café. Everyone seemed pretty young and hip. No one seemed to be paying any attention.

'We haven't seen him since Sunday. He disappeared with his best friend, Karim. They have both been at it for years. They were there in 2003. We have almost got used to them running into trouble every now and again. The police sometimes kept them overnight down at the station. But then they just gave them warnings and sent them on their way. It's not as if he is a student leader or anything. He's vocal but he's not a real rabble-rouser.'

The Chateaubriands arrived and Seb decided to let her take things at her own pace: he sensed there was a lot more to come. She speared a potato before starting to carve the meat. Iranian girls were a phenomenon. They were so dainty, spent so much on cosmetics and tottered around in perilous high-heels. But these delicate creatures wolfed down their steaks and manly kebabs with a gusto that never ceased to astonish him. Although Negar had an avian physique and was clearly in some distress, she was still going to make quick work of the hissing steak before her.

'And have you had any official comment from anyone? Police, or worse, saying that they are holding them? There's no charge of any kind?'

'Nothing. As ever. Iran really doesn't work like that. You don't know these people.'

Such rebukes didn't sting. Seb was genuinely glad that he didn't understand the workings of the judiciary or the intelligence.

'So this morning, my father decides that he is going to go and visit Karim's family. Just to see whether they have managed to find anything out. He would rather not speak on the phone – they have almost certainly tapped us by now – so he drives there. They have one of the villas on those roads that cut down from the mountains and link into Niavaran high street.'

Seb knew the places: swanky villas where affluent people with satellite television lived. They had swimming pools, high walls and gardens densely ringed by fir trees. The people who lived there were the sort who invited diplomats to parties.

'When he got there, the gate was open and Karim's father was sweeping leaves from the drive. That was strange. The Afghan should have been doing that. Karim's father doesn't sweep his own drive. When he saw my father, he put down his rake and

100

just gestured that he should come in. He closed the gate and hugged him. "They have killed Karim," he said.'

'My God.'

'They had dumped his body there last night. You cannot believe these people. They are just killing people, Seb. We are sitting here and they are killing people. Apparently it was really bad. You could see that he had been tied up. There were bruises.'

She put her elbows on the table and crossed her wrists as if they were bound together. She no longer seemed to care who was watching.

'Then they cut his throat. It was like they had tried to cut his head off. My father saw this and all we can think about now is my brother.'

'Christ. And there's no one Karim's father can go to?'

'Of course not, there's no one. They are the ones who are committing these crimes. These are the people who are probably torturing my brother to death, right now, as we speak', she sobbed.

For a moment, Seb felt the impulsive diplomat's reaction. Steady, Maynard, here's some kind of honey-trap, a pretty slip of a thing trying to get you to use your influence. What's her game? Then he hated himself for even thinking it. He was the one who had invited her to lunch in the hope of luring her into one of his three bedrooms at Gholhak. She had agreed to come although she was worried that her brother's life was hanging by a thread. She didn't really seem to be asking for anything. And more to the point, why shouldn't she ask? Plenty of British diplomats have turned excuses for not doing anything into an art-form. Seb despaired that many of the lauded role-models were just pimps for the FTSE 100, treading water until they were offered seats on the board. He had always told himself he would be different and not mock that rather old-fashioned sense of mission. This was his opportunity to avoid premature fossilisation.

'We could always make enquiries for you. There are a handful of people who still listen to the Brits in the foreign ministry. They can pass messages on. The thing is, I wouldn't want to make things worse. Any suggestion that he is close to the Brits might just make life a whole lot more unpleasant.'

She shrugged and undaunted ploughed on with the steak.

'Life can hardly get more unpleasant as it is. Karim's family were rich people, far richer than us. They knew people and had good connections. Those sort of things don't seem to matter any more. These people will kill you. Some kind of publicity really couldn't hurt. If they think someone cares outside this bloody country, if they think it could become an international issue, they might just listen.'

The horror of it all made Seb nauseous. He thought about the insincerity of what he did. His memos often included a paragraph on worries about human rights but he always saw it as a minor distraction. Iran wasn't that bad when you saw it close up. But nobody in the embassy had seen it close up. Nobody in the embassy had seen their son's sallow corpse drained of blood and dumped in the driveway. This was happening every day, in cities and in the provinces. No one knew much and the killings simply rumbled on.

'I'll see what I can do. There are definitely possibilities.'

Negar smiled again.

'Thank you.'

'It really is the least I can do. I had rather got the impression that student politics was quietening down a bit at the moment.'

Negar frowned and shook her head.

'On the contrary. Seb, you've got to get out there. Go down to the university tonight. Or tomorrow. It's all about to flare up again. All the young people are talking about it. There is going to be another big push.'

'What, soon?'

'Today. Tomorrow. I don't know, but soon.'

'Jesus, you're right. The ambo keeps us locked away, writing crappy reports about stuff in the press. The press for God's sake. We're not some kind of cuttings agency. You're right, I will go down to the university and try to have a chat with some students.'

'Good, then you'll find out what is really happening here in Iran.'

Seb caught the waiter's attention and ordered another bottle of Damavand.

The ambassador read Maynard's telegram on impending student unrest with interest. But the whole thing looked a bit premature and it would probably be worth waiting to see whether the battered vestiges of the liberal press had anything on this before heaving such a grenade into the staid corridors of Whitehall. One source. Dodgy.

'Would it not do us credit to be ahead of the curve on this, ambassador? If we need to be more sure then I am keen to go down to the university and chat to some students.'

Ah, youthful and impetuous. Maynard was such a grammar schoolboy.

'Always best not to be too hasty, Maynard. We cannot be journalists and diplomats, my boy. Most movements of this nature tend to crystallise in the media before they boil over. Just take that as the voice of long experience.'

There was no arguing with the ostrich approach. Seb nodded and decided to broach the more important subject. The ambassador was looking out over the embassy gardens and admired the way the Afghans had managed to mow a rather fine patchwork effect across the lawns. Clever bastards, your Afghans.

'The girl who was the source for this telegram fears that her detained brother could face the same fate as the murdered student. She was wondering whether we could make inquiries. At least that might make the Iranians think twice about killing him.'

The ambassador chuckled. It was a strained and effeminate giggle.

'Really Maynard, one moment you want us to be journalists, getting out there and interviewing students. The next you want to turn us into Amnesty International, sticking up for someone we know nothing about. This is far too delicate a period in bilateral relations to risk such an inflammatory escalation.'

Seb reckoned it was a perfect time for the British to start making a nuisance of themselves. The Iranians were kidnapping British sailors and delivering uncompromising monologues on their nuclear work. It was surely time to stop being quite so diplomatic and start slapping the Iranians across the face a bit.

'And by the sounds of it, Maynard, we are too late. The Iranians have probably murdered her brother too. Out there, it's their world, Maynard. There are clear boundaries.' Don't let yourself get too wrapped up in it all.

After biting his lip and telling himself not to resign, Seb vowed to spite the ambassador and head down to the university that night, if only to save his own soul. The Iran Mandarins at the FCO would be at home watching the first blurry shots of the demonstrations on BBC News 24. It was a little rum that the embassy hadn't sensed any of this tension building up. But Iran was an awfully difficult country to try to gauge. The embassy, after all, had been convinced that Rafsanjani would trounce Ahmadinejad in the elections. They had his people round for tea. And now this unrest had passed underneath the radar. Oh well, the poor old ambassador had a very young team there. That

Maynard boy was on his first posting. His Persian probably wasn't good enough to see the clues in the newspapers.

Seb had a clear idea of what student demonstrations should look like: he'd seen enough photographs in books and on reformist websites. Well-heeled students, clean-shaven boys and girls in pink headscarves, would sit cross-legged in the streets and chant pro-democracy slogans. Cordons of police would stand by and journalists would mingle with the crowd. Finally police would break up the crowd, there would be some argy-bargy, a little fisticuffs and a number of students would be taken off in vans. Seb decided he would try to count how many were carted off, to see whether his eye-witness telegram gelled with the official reports.

But as he neared the central university campus, he felt nervous. For a moment he couldn't work out why, then he realised it was the deep, brooding darkness. Tehran normally burned off its energy resources like no other city he had been to. But all the street lights were off. They had browned the place out, the bastards. He was back in a medieval city. The few shops that defiantly remained open were using paraffin hurricane lanterns and even candles.

He heard the voices. They weren't the melodious choruses of 'Freedom, freedom, freedom' that he had been expecting. It was more visceral: a cacophony of roars, whistles and bawling, like spectators before the nastier football clashes, like a baying crowd at the Coliseum. Every few seconds there were sharp cracks – not loud enough to be bullets – but Seb could not work out what they were.

As he turned on to the main street that ran past the front railings of the university, he saw one street light still illuminated. It cast a jaundiced triangle of light over a ghoulish phalanx of riot police below. Fifty or so storm-troopers had formed into lines, linking their shields together. Seb realised he shouldn't be there. They looked like something straight out of a science-fiction film. Their helmets and padded khaki suits cast giant shadows down the tarmac. A few daring photographers, the same breed who spent the war darting from trench to trench, scurried around, taking shots of the assembled battalion. Flash-bulbs reflected off visors. The police beat their batons across their shields in a macabre drum roll and took a crunching step forward.

Seb wheeled round and thought that he should at least let Rice-Jenkyns know where he was. He pulled his mobile out of his trench-coat pocket and flicked through the contacts list. Strange, no signal. He would have to ask to use a landline. He retreated to an electrical hardware shop where the owner was reading a magazine under a storm latern.

'I am sorry. I have been caught out,' Seb began. 'I need to phone a colleague, very quickly, just thirty seconds. Could I please borrow your phone? I can give you a couple of toman to cover the cost.'

He pulled out two green notes and smiled at the shopkeeper.

The shopkeeper returned the smile and laid down the magazine. It was written in tight script, without pictures. Seb couldn't work out what it was about.

'I wouldn't take your money, my friend, you are welcome. The thing is, they have cut the phones again. The lights and the phones.'

'I see, do they always do that when the students demonstrate?'

'It is usual, yes. What country are you from?'

'Engelestan.'

'Aha, embassy?'

106

'Ha ha, yes. Is it that obvious?'

The shopkeeper just shrugged.

'You must do something about our government instead of supporting it. Why do you support them? The students are right. Our government are bastards.'

This, again, was not a personal attack. In the same way the British are thought to be running the world, they are also widely believed to be running Iran. Every mullah, Seb was often told, had 'Made in England' written under his beard. Iran's favourite television series, *My Uncle Napoleon*, had given the nation a catchphrase: 'This is the work of the British'. To most Iranians it was still a catchphrase that rang true.

'The student movement is certainly something that preoccupies us,' Seb lied, imagining the ambassador planning his next salmon fishing expedition to Connemara.

'I am glad. Then good luck.'

'Is there a safer place where I can just take a look at the students?'

The shopkeeper pointed dead opposite.

'You can hardly see it but it is there. There's an alley called Delshad. From the end you can see the front railings.'

Seb followed the noise of the tumult and those strange cracks. There was an open drain, a jub, at the end of the alley. It glistened in the light of the moon which had just emerged from a dense bank of autumn cloud. He followed that silver thread of shimmering water to the main drag.

The police had moved twenty yards nearer the university. But now he could see the students, and nothing could have been further from what he had imagined. There was only one placard hung on the railings: a long yellow sheet with 'andisheh zendani nemishe' written down it. Thought cannot be held prisoner.

The students were a shock. This wasn't the safe, peaceable

world he had imagined. The students were in balaclavas or had tied cloths across their faces. They knew what happened to you if, like Ahmad Batebi, you were unfortunate enough to get your photograph emblazoned across the front of *The Economist*. From the dozens ranged up against the railings, Seb could hardly judge the numbers but they may have been hundreds deep. They were like a cabal of jailed pirates clamouring for freedom.

Seb's eyes adjusted to the gloom and he could see that the street was strewn with a litter of short, square-cut debris. He couldn't work out what they were. Then he heard one of those sharp cracks on the wall above his head. Then a thud at his feet. Christ, they are shooting at me, he thought. No, wait. He picked up the object at his feet. It was half a brick, pulled up from the pavement and cracked in two by students with rock-hammers. The police had also put up with enough for tonight. There were a couple of pops as they fired tear gas cylinders.

Seb knew he couldn't afford to hang around any more. He became disorientated and turned off Delshad too early. Cursing his stupidity he saw how he could navigate his way back. He was in another side alley that cut across Delshad. If he took the next left, then he should reach the road where he had asked to use the phone.

He turned left and, a split second before he was blinded, realised he was not alone. Motorbike engines roared and there was an explosion of cyclopic headlights. So, these were the basij. They were clad entirely in black apart from the green head-bands of the martyrs. Originally the basij had formed the crack suicide divisions on the battlefields: they were now the attack-dogs of God knows who. No one knew which part of the Persian Hydra operated them, but everyone knew you didn't want to bump into them alone, particularly up a dark alley. Two of the rear-riders were wielding Kalashnikovs. Others had batons and chains.

'Kill the foreign spy,' one said with a chilling nonchalance.

The leader of the pack revved his bike.

'Who are you?'

'Diplomat,' Seb said. He couldn't disguise the fear that caught in his throat. Speak English, he told himself. This will turn really ugly if I speak Persian.

The group sighed in disppointment.

'Kill him anyway,' one rejoined.

The pack laughed.

'Get out of here. Run. You chose a quiet night: don't come back. This place is going to be a battlefield soon and some of our friends will not leave alive a single Zionist spy.'

They jeered as Seb retreated back up the alley. He'd just had a glimpse into the world on which he wrote his reports. And it scared him.

Andy was watching the woman on the bench. He hoped it was pity that drew him to her but it was probably something far less admirable and inordinately more compelling. He leant against the wall of the Embankment, smoking a Gauloise as he collected his thoughts. She wasn't aware of his presence as she cast occasional glances out over the fast-flowing, murky expanse of the Thames. In her mid-fifties and smartly dressed she had a bluestocking look with sensible shoes. At first he had thought to rebuke her for smoking with a baby in her lap. But as he got closer he saw that it wasn't a baby, just a rubber doll. Her face was lacquered in tears. There were so many possible explanations. Maybe it wasn't as obvious as it seemed. Things rarely are. He thought of Juliette and how she never wanted children. She probably knew the risk was too great: that we are all only a step from nursing a rubber doll on an autumn evening. In Andy's case, it was the life of his choice that had condemned him to leave no traces of his existence, not a miscarriage nor a cot death. And now he was too much of a coward to take the supreme risk and come in from the cold. He thought he should ring Juliette. Just to see how she was doing. But he felt the judder of his mobile in his breast pocket. It was Cath.

'Hi.'

The woman with the rubber doll looked up and swivelled on the bench. She shot him a venomous look, furious that her privacy had been invaded.

'Hi, Andy. I am watching the first footage on CNN and the BBC. There's a demo down at Tehran University. Baharvand was right about Wednesday. It's started.'

5.

WHEN THEY SAW the dogs, the people of Shiraz knew it was all going to end badly. Every tree and every lamp-post circling the barrel-towered citadel of Karimkhan bore a strange fruit: a dead mongrel, with a mullah's turban bound around its head. Although there was no Anglo-Saxon sympathy for the serene final rictus of the hanged strays, no one dared spit at these unclean creatures. The timorous crowd milled among the trees, hypnotised by the atrocity. Around each dog's neck a piece of roughly torn cardboard had been squeezed underneath the noose. Across the cards, the names of the most senior clerics in the land had been daubed in thick, deliberately clumsy brush-strokes. This was heresy but, despite their fears, the shambling crowd couldn't tear itself away and skulk off to their offices or the bazaar. There were machinations here that entranced them. Everyone knew times were tense but this monstrosity was simply unprecedented.

The night before, the notoriously liberal students of Shiraz had put on an even better show than their brothers in Tehran, thousands of them punching the air and waving placards as they demanded a right to genuine self-expression. Angered by the prominence given by CNN and Fox to the lame efforts of the students in Tehran, several Shiraz activists had submitted their grainy images to YouTube. The crowd now felt for those brave students: their own nephews and grandsons. Few of them could remember such a calculated affront to the theocracy. The authorities would already be planning a merciless retaliation.

But the crowd knew in its heart that the students could not have done this. Students would never have dared. Bookworms and medical students wouldn't be able to suborn the police and paramilitaries, ensuring that they wouldn't pass through the square for an agreed hour during the night. There were forces at work here but the crowd had learned not to ask too many questions. Questions in Iran only mean trouble. Don't ask.

At the Vauxhall Bridge ziggurat, Andy checked his e-mail and found 'Pepe', Anoush's industrious alter ego, had sent him some images of the dogs. One of the crowd must have snapped them surreptitiously with his mobile and forwarded them to his old friend. It was a foolhardy thing to have done. Iranian intelligence service can find it tricky to tap mobile calls as they need to know in advance who they want to listen in on. But they can sift through a back-catalogue of all text messages and images at their leisure, then pay a nocturnal visit to the sender, despite all those constitutional safeguards against eavesdropping. It was about time Pepe changed his numbers anyhow. Andy printed off a few of the dogs and enlarged the scrawny black bitch who was painted with a 'Baharvand' placard. He slotted them into a file and headed to the morning meeting.

Despite the modernity of the service's blast-proofed base camp, humming with hi-tech wizardry, its rooms somehow maintained that damp, institutional air of staid British officialdom. A clock, whose battery seemed to be dying, hung off kilter. The yellowing wall map suggested that the Soviet Union and Yugoslavia were both alive and kicking.

Cath had already started to brief Lomax. The Emperor nodded reassuringly and puffed away like a locomotive cresting a hill as she spoke. They smiled at Andy as he took his place at the end of the table.

'So, the student protests were backed up by demos from the unions in the copper complex at Sar Cheshmeh and zinc workers in Zanjan,' Cath continued. 'The numbers are still vague but Sar Cheshmeh is in Kerman and Baharvand has all sorts of involvement in the place. So that, at least, looks like he could be pulling some of the strings.'

'Good,' said Lomax. 'Now what about his promises on the ethnic minorities? Have we seen anything from them yet?'

Cath shook her head.

'Nothing so far but information from there will take longer to percolate through. The Iranians are ultra-touchy on that and have got good at suppressing it.'

'Sure.'

'We also seem to have a useful foot-soldier at the embassy. A junior, a third secretary, called Sebastian Maynard showed some initiative and went down to the Tehran demonstrations. He also had some good background on a murdered student. He always writes good memos but he seems to be rising to the occasion here.'

She slid a copy of Maynard's telegram down the table to Andy.

'He describes a stand-off between the students and the police. The basij kept their powder dry last night and waited in the backstreets.'

Andy scanned the memo and was impressed. The diplomatic service needed more Maynards.

Lomax laid down his pipe.

'So, it's still a "maybe"? The PM wants me to give him daily briefings from now on.'

'I think that's a fair assessment,' Cath said, poking her glasses on to the bridge of her nose.

Andy took out the photographs of the dead dogs.

'There's also this. It may be nothing but it's certainly inflammatory. Right round one of the main sights in Shiraz.'

'Heathen bloody savages,' said Lomax. 'How can you do that to a dog?'

'It seems there were dozens of them. You could read it as posturing by radical students but this is perversely offensive to Iranian eyes.'

'It's perversely bloody offensive to my eyes too. I never understood why your Muslims hate good, loyal bonzos so much.'

Dogs have never elicited much love from the Iranians. When the French government gave Iran some Alsatians to help sniff out contraband in yet another misguided attempt at rapprochement, a disgusted Iranian security officer hurled one of the creatures through an upper-storey window, almost triggering a diplomatic incident.

Lomax resolved that Lucy would get lots of special attention and long walks across rolling Oxfordshire farmland at the weekend.

Cath was already seeing the bigger picture.

'But what you're saying is that this could also be Baharvand ratcheting everything up, trying to catalyse some big face-off between protesters and the state?' she asked, holding the print-outs with distaste, pinching them as if her fingers were tweezers lifting a photograph out of developing fluid.

'It's more than possible. I certainly wouldn't put a thing like this past Baharvand. It's very daring, very audacious. It's the sort of gambit that Baharvand likes.'

'Aah, you can smell him again, can't you?' Lomax barked with satisfaction. The Scottish spy master liked instincts. He saw instincts as the greatest trait of the secret servant. It was the gut feelings of his fieldmen that he liked to quote to the prime minister.

Andy shrugged. 'I wouldn't say that.'

He was looking at Cath and wondering how she managed to give such a frisson to cardigans. Juliette avoided them, fearing that they made her look 'froumpy', a word she overused as she entered middle-age and, uncharacteristically, mispronounced.

'By the way, where did you decide to hide baby Baharvand?'

'Newcastle,' Cath said.

Lomax winced.

'Wooh, brisk this time of year. Better be careful; a pack of Geordies might finish him off before the Iranians get to him.'

Margot, Lomax's secretary, knocked politely and entered without waiting for a reply.

'It's all over the wires. I thought you should know. I've run them all off: Reuters, AP, AFP. There's been some bombings in Ahwaz. Government buildings mainly and a bank. No one has claimed responsibility yet but it looks like one of those Arab nationalist things.'

Andy could taste the humid air back in the south. He could hear the frantic, counter-productive shouting as they pulled the bleeding bodies out of the devastated masonry. The streets would be carpeted with rubble and broken glass.

'Thank you, Margot. You can leave us now,' Lomax said, perhaps too sternly.

He waited for her to go, then linked his hands and planted his elbows on the table.

'All those Arab groups have people in London. We can probably get a quick claim of responsibility,' said Cath, pulling out her mobile and skimming through the contacts.

Lomax nodded.

'I think our man Baharvand seems to be delivering the goods.'

Several hours before the Ahwaz bombings, an assassin had taken a four o'clock coach from Herat in Afghanistan and travelled west, crossing the Iranian border to the shrine city of Mashhad with an army of excited, garrulous Afghan migrant workers. At Mashhad's bus station the broad-shouldered killer remained smoking in the back corner of the coach while the Afghans clambered over each other, trying to excavate their possessions from the bundles of linen and crates of chickens crammed into the central aisle. When the bus had finally emptied, he flicked his cigarette out of the window, took his hold-all down from the overhead netting and crossed the forecourt to a cheap kebab restaurant with formica tables. The plastic-coated menus were slotted between the salt shakers and the sumac and the walls were covered in tasteless, ink-tinted photographs of chalets in the Swiss Alps. Why mountain people hankered after other people's mountains was a mystery to him. He ordered a chicken kebab and flicked through a copy of a government newspaper, *Kayhan*.

Valerio had been right that the Russians weren't the sort of people to sit on their hands in the face of such a crisis. And Dolokhov had been right. GRU high-command had sent the Tajik.

Nobody in the coach or at the restaurant had noticed anything remarkable about him. Naturally he had a slight Tajik accent but he could have been a naturalised Iranian, or an Afghan. He was olive skinned, almost Mediterranean in appearance, but that was also entirely unremarkable in the melting-pot of eastern Iran. Many travellers ventured that they had found lost Greeks with Nordic blue eyes and blond locks up in the passes of Afghanistan. Some said they were the descendants of Greeks punished by King Darius for the Ionian revolt and exiled to the furthest outposts of the Persian world. Other theories said they were Macedonian footsoldiers that Alexander had left behind. Ultimately, who cared? Mashhad was a pilgrim city and welcomed all good Muslims. The Tajik had a well-trimmed beard, a new suit and good money. He could do as he pleased.

The restaurant's television reception wasn't too good. The images were tobacco brown and occasionally lurched across the screen. But the sound was fine. The news was showing shots of bombings down in the south where most of the population were Arabs. So, this was all part of Baharvand's plan, was it? Ingenious. The Arabs were always ripe for revolt. They lived on the country's richest oil deposits but were kept in poverty by a Persian ruling class that was rumoured to favour relocating them from their ancestral lands. The Tajik watched for a while and drank a doogh, a salty yoghurt drink. It surprised him that state television dared to show a few snatches of Arab protesters facing off a cordon of Iranian police. That was an unusual thing to broadcast. Valerio hadn't mentioned to Dolokhov that Hossein Jafari was part of the plot. It was possible that Byrd had neglected that. The mercenary general never really understood the power of television.

The Tajik paid at the till and hailed a taxi to the Pars International Hotel. It was a typically Iranian name. Everything in this cock-sure country was 'Pars'. The phone company was Pars, detergents were Pars, gas fields were Pars. The Tajik had little time for such disdainful Iranian nationalism, forever revelling in the faded glories of the Persian homeland. Many Tajiks see themselves as the rightful lantern-bearers of the culture of Omar Khayyam and Ferdowsi, accusing the Iranians of becoming complacent and lazy, the spoiled offspring of a lavish oil economy. He had once heard an Iranian justify the nuclear programme by saying: with oil, we have to work very little; with nuclear power, we won't have to work at all. That more or less summed up the Tajik's view of Iranians. These people somehow convinced themselves that Cyrus the Great invented human rights and salt. Grandiose assertions.

As if to endorse his dismal appraisal of Iranians, the taxi driver overcharged him. Eager not to cause a scene and get himself remembered, the Tajik paid, thanked the driver courteously and presented himself to the concierge.

'I have a meeting with Mr Kryuchkov, a Russian gentleman. I would be very grateful if you could call his room and inform him that I have arrived.'

The Tajik's Persian had a starchy formality that ensured people snapped to attention. The concierge ran his finger down the room list, nodded when he came to 'Kryuchkov' and picked up the receiver.

The embassy man skipped down the stairs in a linen suit and crossed the lobby with a broad smile. Every hotel room where foreigners stay is infested with transmitters, so it would be foolhardy to talk over business upstairs. Kryuchkov, a youthful, sprightly army attaché, greeted the hit-man in Russian and shook his hand with more than a little reverence. Meeting the Tajik was something to tell the grandchildren about. Later though, after the Tajik had retired to his dacha to shoot bear and write verse.

The Tajik warmed to his colleague as they strolled round the lacklustre fountain in the hotel gardens. He was diligent and seemed to have done Moscow's bidding promptly and correctly. Many GRU men were getting slapdash these days. However, he could sense that Kryuchkov was not a reader or a man who would travel up to Saint Petersburg for a night at the Kirov. How he longed to be back on the banks of the frozen Neva. He was finding, as he got older, that the Central Asian cabin fever set in earlier and earlier. It was time to clear his debts with GRU and settle down. The Tajik was not an impatient man and was certainly not going to rush anything on a mission of this importance. However, it just seemed, with Kryuchkov, that there was little else to talk about other than the mechanics of the impending kill.

'So, you got me the Dragunov sniper rifle in Tehran?'

'No problem, sir, we have loads of the SVDs. It's in a metal casing welded to the underside of the car.'

'And the car itself?'

'As you requested, a battered, rusting blue Paykan. Twenty years old, sir.'

The Tajik had seen it in the hotel car park and had hoped that it was his. It was the sort of car that would pass unnoticed in Kerman and Baluchistan.

'Perfect.'

Kryuchkov handed him a key.

'Thanks.'

'It's an honour to work with you, sir.'

'Bah, enough.'

The Tajik hated lionisation from junior officers.

'There is one thing though, sir. Moscow would like me to do a report on where you are headed next. Basically they want to know how you are going to set up your escape route.'

'Naturally.'

Kryuchkov knew enough of the assassin's business to understand that it went far beyond the 'one shot, one kill' stuff of popular legend. The real art was the back-up, the knowledge of terrain, camouflage and escape-routes. With the squalling cross-winds across a stretch of Kermani desert, the Tajik would have to engineer a position where he could guarantee himself two shots. Maybe even a third. Perhaps he wouldn't even use the Dragunov. Plans always had a habit of suggesting themselves at the last minute in this line of work.

'The first step is to try and meet Commander Abdollah at his base. I got him on a sat phone last night and we have arranged a rendezvous.'

'Abdollah? Is he one of Rigi's men?'

Kryuchkov could be forgiven for asking. Abdollah was hardly a household name. The allegiances of the tribal commanders in the volatile, narcotics-ridden triangle that straddled the hinterland of Iran, Pakistan and Afghanistan were the Tajik's pet obsession. It was his contacts and reputation among these men that made him the most formidable player of the new Great Game.

'Abdollah is Abdollah's man and hopefully he's our man too. One day he seems to be with Rigi, the next day, I am not so sure.'

Abdolmalek Rigi was always a hot topic. Iran had spent two years accusing the Sunni warlord of every brutality in eastern Iran: a televised beheading, a bus-bombing and some road-side executions. Tehran labelled Rigi the top al Qaeda operative within the country. But the man himself responded by showing how canny he was, appearing on US television in a programme that suggested he could be backed by the CIA. Rigi was softly-spoken, charming and moderate, claiming he sought only to free Sunnis from the Shi'ite yoke. Furthermore, he was good-looking and only twenty-four years old. The western media had found a fitting successor to their earlier hero from the Afghan mujahidin, Ahmad Shah Massoud, the lion of the Panjshir, the kind of rebel that the living rooms of middle America could adopt.

Yet the Tajik had played this sordid game long enough to know that a warlord's profile could change overnight according to the whims of the great powers. One day, America would be happy for Rigi to be the internet-savvy religious moderate who sat under a palm tree pensively jotting down notes. In a few years' time, the White House would probably patch up some deal with Tehran and accept that Rigi was a dangerous fuel smuggler or drug runner. The Tajik had no time for such political games. To him, all that really mattered was that Baluchis like Abdollah and Rigi hated the Iranians, had more stomach for a shoot-out than poorly trained Revolutionary Guardsmen and accepted anyone's money. Money has no scent.

'So, you'll be heading out through Baluchistan?' Kryuchkov confirmed.

'Probably, though plans could change. I might have to change my plan at any moment. But I'll try to let the embassy know where I am going.'

'When do you rendezvous with Abdollah?'

'Saturday morning. But he chose a place right in the middle of the desert. A hell-hole. $40,000 has already been wired to that account in Stockholm, yes?'

Sweden was the chief fund-raising centre for the restive Baluchis. It was just as well, as Iranian intelligence would certainly have heard about a sum of that size landing in an account in fly-blown Zahedan or Zabol.

'Of course, sir, it was delivered in cash this morning.'

It seemed such a small price to pay for what was at stake.

'Good. Well, I know Abdollah's sat phone works, so hopefully he'll already know that it's arrived.'

'He's probably already spent it, sir.'

The Tajik laughed.

'I bet he has. Right, I had better set off. It's a good journey ahead.'

'Best of luck, sir.'

*

The asthmatic Paykan, Iran's stalwart national car, headed south from Mashhad on the Birjand road. Two hours clear of Mashhad, the Tajik pulled off the highway on to a track between two fields. The soil looked awful, full of grit and dusted with a sugaring of sand. He couldn't work out whether the fields were being left fallow or whether they had simply been forsaken. There was a large rock outcrop in the middle of the field to his right and the evening sun had crowned it with a halo. The Tajik stepped behind it. Some cigarette butts and a discarded Zam-Zam cola bottle suggested that it wasn't a completely forgotten spot. Within five minutes, he had changed into the costume of an Afghan, donning the shalwar kameez, Chitrali cap and bottle-green waistcoat. He then shaved off his moustache and put a square cut across the bottom of his beard. He made sure that the papers in his pocket were those of the Tajik carpet trader from Kabul. From now on, he would play up the eccentricities of his native brogue. His sister was his khohar rather than his khahar. Wolves would be gurg rather than gorg. On the eastern borders such a man would pass unnoticed, and make friends.

Only the previous morning, Dolokhov had telegraphed his urgent cables to Moscow. At sunset on Thursday, the hunter was loose. He flicked on his headlights and pushed on to Birjand. One last job.

The British Midland hostess sighed as 'fat, greasy man' in business class pushed his buzzer yet again. It was quite clear what he wanted. Well, that, of course, and another whisky.

As she approached him with an exasperated smile, Bernie lifted his latest empty miniature of Bells in his chipolata fingers and waved it at her. There always tended to be one of these losers on the Tehran flight.

'Another one, is it, sir?'

'Ah, be an angel. You must take the opportunity before you arrive in these dry countries, you know.'

She laughed politely. 'Fat, greasy man' already reeked of Scotch when he boarded the plane. His navy blue suit looked far too young and too Italian for his unsightly frame. His beer gut hung over his belt like a heap of snow about to belly-flop off some guttering.

'Must be quite a tough run for you young ladies, eh? Tehran.'

'How do you mean, sir?'

She couldn't quite place his accent.

'Well, you must want the Caribbean or the Med or something, eh? Get your bikini on at the other end. Have some fun with the boys.'

The hostess laughed again, rather sweetly, but kicked herself for doing so. Why did she always let these lecherous old fuckers feel like they were getting somewhere? She balanced herself over the top of the empty seat in front of the reprobate.

'Oh, I think I'm a little past that now, sir. My husband and I rather like Tuscany.'

Her husband only existed for men like Bernie Whelan.

'Ah, bet you do. Very cultured. Very arty, eh? Very nice.'

'Let me get you that whisky, sir.'

'Bloody good idea.'

Bernie had that journalists' sixth sense that told him he was about to land in the middle of a biggie. He could smell where this was all leading. When he got back to Reuters' frigid new HQ in Canary Wharf, there would be all sorts of herograms waiting on his desk. It would be pints aloft and 'please to be upstanding for big Bern' at the City Pride on Westferry Road. He would have conjured the Whelan magic yet again.

As a copy editor on the international desk, Bernie had read some of Wednesday's stories on the student demos. It looked like the same old blah and he wasn't that interested. But on Thursday morning, seven types of shit seemed to be hitting the fan: the unions had joined the students and bombs were going off all over the Arab territories, Iran's oil heartland in Khuzestan, but in any case there was often tension between the Arabs and Iran's Persian majority. Pegler, the resident international staffer in Tehran, had just jetted off on honeymoon to the Seychelles and the Middle East editor told Bernie he wanted Tehran backed up immediately, as this brewing storm could hardly be left to the local stringer, Shirkhan, no matter how good he might be. Although essentially a burned-out desk-jockey these days, Whelan realised that a jolly to Tehran might pay dividends. He still had a valid visa from his last visit and told the news editors that he'd get the evening flight. Well done, Bernie. Knew we could count on you.

Khosro was the sort of reporter on which Reuters was built: a tenacious, principled individualist who could find ways of digging up scoops without being arrested. Whelan, on the other hand, was the sort of hack who became a legend among the international press corps by bigfooting the copy of indispensable soldier ants such as Shirkhan and putting his own name at the top. Despite the mystique, being a foreign correspondent is actually remarkably easy.

Bernie was proud of his caustic, no-nonsense Irish wit and cut-through-the-crap approach to story writing. He always told his correspondents to keep things simple, tutted when their copy landed and added crass oversimplifications in his editing that showed he didn't really get the point. Bernie despised the new order of Reuters journalists, in their smart suits and silk ties, always on their mobiles. They were the kind of Oxbridge poofs who went to juice bars and said 'ciao'. Pegler was one of them. As far as Whelan was concerned, Pegler was so obsessed with not upsetting anyone that he couldn't write a story to save his life. Iran needed one of Whelan's tell-it-as-it-is classics.

He had unceremoniously downed his fifth miniature and had fallen asleep with his sagging chin planted on his chest. Dribbling a little with his in-flight magazine slumped to the ground, he was instantly transformed into a rather pitiable figure and the air-hostess, despite her earlier internal invective, covered him with a blanket.

While Whelan slumbered somewhere above Anatolia, Shirkhan was sniffing round the maze of Tehran back alleys where Seb Maynard had run into the basiji bikers the night before. Things looked set for a fierce street battle. Shirkhan, the lion king – a name as vainglorious in Persian as the English suggests – tended to rise to such occasions. A metallurgist by training, he had stumbled into journalism, like so many other Iranians, during the war, when lost international newsmen were desperate for charismatic locals who could hold their hands. Shirkhan had carried a bijou Pentax with him in the first offensives across the frontlines, taking gory and quite unpublishable shots that turned him into a by-word for physical courage. When younger journalists felt a giddy bout of nerves before doing a stint in Iraq or taking a flight on a Tupolev held together with string, Shirkhan would just ruffle their hair and say 'Natars', don't be afraid. Love him or hate him, Shirkhan was the father figure of the Iranian press corps.

Shirkhan had little appetite for Whelan's flying visit. Some of the Reuters internationals were weak, like Pegler. But at least his kind tended to be respectful and cautious. Shirkhan could push them about and he liked that. Pegler was a good kid and he would make sure Shirkhan got his bonus. Whelan was a different animal: an old style, colonial animal.

But Whelan's arrival was an annoyance Shirkhan would

contend with on Friday. Thursday night was poised to explode. He had spoken with a few student leaders that afternoon and their blood seemed to be up. About a quarter of an hour earlier he had seen that the students had ventured outside the university gates chanting 'Death to Ahmadinejad'. He didn't think he would get that past his censors at the Ministry of Culture and Islamic Guidance. He would have to phrase it as the journalistic chestnut: 'anti-government slogans'.

Shirkhan encountered the basij much as Seb had done, but they held no fears for him. 'Natars'. Shirkhan had seen the real basij back on the front lines, teenage heroes and idealists who threw themselves under tanks and ran across minefields. The basij of today were not cut from the same fabric. They got their kicks from beating up their own people. Furthermore, Shirkhan knew how to talk to them. He was not one of these fops whose parents had thought Tehran was a kind of Parisian playground back in the 1970s: Shirkhan's family were religious conservatives who had backed the revolution but then, like so many others, been betrayed by it.

'Peace be upon you brothers,' Shirkhan said to the pack of militants revving their bikes.

They invoked the names of the Shi'ite martyrs and Shirkhan followed suit. The thugs warmed to him and asked him what was new.

'So are you boys going to give the students a good hiding tonight?' He spoke with a thick south Tehran accent. They recognised him as one of their own, grinned and let heavy chains spill out from their gloved hands.

'God willing. Insha'allah,' they murmured.

'God be praised,' Shirkhan replied.

'Didn't you hear about the dogs?' chirped in one of the younger basij.

Shirkhan confessed that he hadn't.

'They hanged dogs dressed in turbans from trees in Shiraz. They had the names of our most revered leaders written across their chests.'

'Dear God, the devils.'

'Oh yeah, those students are going to take one hell of a kicking tonight. And that comes from the top. You understand?'

'God be praised.'

'God be praised,' they echoed.

'Well, I will leave you boys to continue God's work.'

'Good night, hajj agha. Look after yourself.'

This was worse than Shirkhan had assumed. He took a vantage point in a friend's flat opposite the university so he could watch the two unequally matched armies cross swords. He had brought the bureau's sat phone so he could ring copy real-time back to the night-filer in London. Phone lines were still cut around the university and mobile signals had been jammed. The electricity was off and Shirkhan's friend was making some tea with camping-gas.

The veteran reporter did not have long to wait. Only twenty minutes after he had taken his position, a battleline of riot police began to march towards the posse of buoyed-up, jeering students. It was so hard to tell numbers in the dark. Maybe five hundred students. Eighty or ninety cops. The students hurled thirty or forty Molotov cocktails. Most of them landed short and shattered in sharp bursts of flame ten yards from the advancing line. A few bounced on the tarmac and exploded against the wall of plastic shields. Shirkhan saw one of the policemen frantically clawing at flames that darted across his shoulders. Two of his comrades wrestled him to the ground and smothered the burning uniform.

Then came a barrage of stones. The thuds and cracks were

unmistakeable: the students had unleashed a rain of batons and broken bricks. The journalist felt sorry for both sides. His cousin was a policeman and he knew they didn't much care for this work either. They bore no festering hatred of the students. A handful of police were on the ground, concussed and cut by projectiles they couldn't see falling out of the blackness. Their line began to fall back and a large gap opened in the middle. There was now only one way that this could end.

He heard the roar of motorbike engines, dozens of them, firing up in side alleys. A chill terror silenced the students who tried to work out where the paramilitaries were lurking. The basijis bellowed and invoked the martyrs. With a rallying call of 'Allahu Akbar' they raced their bikes out into the main road and grouped for the spearhead attack. God, Shirkhan realised, there must be fifty of them, their bikes buzzing like furious hornets. The students faltered and some screamed that they should fall back behind the university gates or get back to the dormitories. Not that you could deter the basij. They would simply drill through dormitory walls. It was all too late. With a screeching of wheels, the basijis raced towards the students like an armoured cavalry charge hitting the undefended flank of an infantry column. Many of the basijis were wheeling heavy chains in their hands as they ploughed their bikes into the middle of the fray. Chains dragged across the tarmac and spurted showers of sparks like circular saws tearing into sheet metal.

Shirkhan had seen enough and rang the news desk in London to dictate an eyewitness account. He had seen the results of these one-sided battles before and had no desire to go poking around. The street would already be smeared with a tacky veneer of blood. Disconsolate girls would tell him that twenty or thirty polite, talented, young men had been carried off. In his experience, half of them would never reappear. As the paramilitaries said, their orders came 'from the top'. Whatever that meant. The basijis were the immortals. No one could ever hold such national heroes to account.

By Khosro Shirkhan
TEHRAN, Oct 25 (Reuters) – Islamic militiamen on motorbikes used chains to quell student protests at Tehran university on Thursday, breaking up the latest demonstration in a nationwide display of anti-government feeling that has also included trade unions and the Arab minority.

On Friday morning, Shirkhan arrived at the bureau early, ready for the trumpeted arrival of the London man. Unsurprisingly, Whelan wasn't there. Shirkhan flicked the radio on and kept half an ear on a camp interior ministry spokesman who was accusing the Great Satan of fomenting violent dissent among small, unrepresentative groups of renegades. Shirkhan yawned and made himself his Friday morning treat: an icy café frappé. He lit a cigarette and stared out across the Alborz mountains. The gleaming snowline had stealthily crept to within spitting distance of the city.

Whelan was still at the Simorgh hotel on Valiasr Street and had concluded, once again, that he was dying. The sauce never used to hit Big Bonking Bern so hard. Maybe it was the altitude. Tehran was pretty bloody high, wasn't it? He stood before the mirror in his boxer shorts and pulled down his lower lids to examine his bloodshot eyeballs. Hell, he looked rough. He gargled and washed the stale whisky taste out of his mouth. At least he hadn't chucked his guts up this time. He was beginning to fear he had a peptic ulcer. He wasn't exactly sure what a peptic ulcer was but the term somehow seemed to whisper its name every time he was staring down the porcelain throne. Can't hold your liquor. Can't keep your pecker up. What's become of you, man? He had a hot shower and ordered a cab from reception.

When he arrived at the bureau shortly after ten, Shirkhan was kneeling by the fax, deeply intrigued by the document juddering out of the machine with a high-pitched buzz. Whelan greeted him with an insouciance that suggested they met every day.

'All right, Sheer karn.'

'Welcome back to Tehran, Mr Whelan. I do hope you had a pleasant journey.'

'Yeah, great. A wee dram or two and I slept like a baby. Fighting fit now. How's our revolution coming along?'

'Well, there's something very interesting here,' Shirkhan said, tearing off the fax. 'It's a declaration from Ayatollah Ali Baharvand.'

'The nuclear negotiator?'

'Yes, yes. It's very difficult to translate as the Persian is rather fluid and ambiguous.'

Whelan looked sceptical as he took his place at Pegler's desk and fired up the computer. Although he spoke no foreign languages, or perhaps *because* he spoke no foreign languages, Whelan had no sympathy with the dilemma of translating nuances. As far as he was concerned, editors had to be tough with bureaux that dithered over the niceties of a subtle phrase. Persian and Japanese were notoriously problematic. But Whelan was always firm, maintaining that languages were simply made up of words and that the words must mean something.

'You see, it's not that dramatic when you just read it as it is, but there's just something about it. It has the feel of one of those statements from Grand Ayatollah Montazeri, the rebel cleric under house arrest.'

Whelan logged on. He already knew the fax was a damp squib.

'What does the thing actually say?'

'Well the first half sounds pretty conventional. Baharvand said the protesters should stop and that the authorities have no choice but to crack down on anything that could be considered as a danger to national security. He says there are certainly several foreign elements working within the country which means that the violence which we are seeing is a regrettable necessity.'

'The old boy seems to be trotting out the mullahs' party line pretty nicely then.'

'Sure, he is. But then at the end, it's all more vague. He talks about the glory of the Islamic revolution in 1979 and how proud he was to serve a movement that accommodated a popular cry of freedom. He says that he would always back any similar call today. He does not exclude the possibility that some within Iran could make such a call.'

'Yeah, well, that's all a bit mealy-mouthed, isn't it? He doesn't specifically come out and nail his colours to the mast, does he? He's not saying: I support these protests. In fact the only direct quote we have is more like him condemning the protests.'

'But this is the language problem. It's all about the tone. Although what you say is strictly true, the Persian makes him sound very sympathetic. This, to me, as a Persian, sounds very much like he is backing the protesters. It all ties in with his mood of late, like the *Time* magazine interview.'

Whelan didn't read *Time*. He grappled with *The Economist* from time to time because it told him what to think and furnished him with an armoury of condescending bons mots.

'Mmm, well, we can't trade in what we feel people might be saying. Afraid we only deal with hard facts.'

Shirkhan looked crestfallen.

'I wouldn't be surprised if people latch on to this. He could become a kind of figurehead for protesters.'

'Right, OK, if they do that, then maybe we can write something but as it is, we don't want to start chasing our own tails. More importantly, this Bavand guy isn't still a nuclear man, is he?'

Shirkhan stopped himself wincing at the pronunciation.

'No. And that backs up the idea that we're dealing with a man who is unhappy with the system.'

'Perhaps. But to put him in a story, he needs to matter. He doesn't hold any official position any more does he?'

'No, he doesn't.'

'Well, there you go then. There's no particular reason why we should get excited by him. Whatever he is or is not saying.'

'The thing you must always remember about Baharvand in Iran is that he has real influence. He's mixed up in everything.'

'In a way that we can write about? In a way, that we can prove?'

'Not really. But if we just say 'influential', that would cover it.'

'Look, Sheer karn, I know what you're trying to say about this Bavand geezer but he's yesterday's man. You have always got to remember that we are writing about Iran for the outsiders, the international markets. You guys here get a bit bogged down in all the internal minutiae. But that's the small fry. Our readers don't want that crap. Don't get distracted by Bavand. Just focus on the really big news.'

Shirkhan accepted that there was no reasoning with a man such as Whelan.

Tehran bureau had two stories to cope with that Friday and Bern was out of the office for both of them. Not that it stopped him putting his by-line on the stories. He had to let London know Big Bern was back out there on the front line.

132

The front line in this case had meant a two-hour lunch with the British ambassador. While Bern and the envoy were washing down a brace of partridges with a bottle of Château Margaux, Shirkhan was banging out a story from Friday prayers. Ayatollah Mesbah-Yazdi had levelled a scorching broadside against the protesters and vowed that they would choke to death on their own blood. It was vitriolic stuff and confirmed Iran's spot at the top of the news agenda. Only moments after Shirkhan had dashed off his copy on the prayer-leader's outburst, the state news agency reported that the Kurds had entered the fray. In Maragheh, they had staved in the windows of some banks and strung anti-government banners across the streets. The state news agency simply reported that there had been many arrests. Shirkhan rang the local police who said twenty or thirty people were in cells: he decided to send that as an urgent bulletin 'with bells'. With Turkey prowling around the Iraqi borders for a crack at the Kurds, any kind of Kurdish insurrection merited high-priority treatment. The reporter had never before seen such coherent insubordination from disparate groups across the country.

After sticky toffee pudding and a few coffees with the ambassador, the grizzled copy editor returned to the office and read Shirkhan's slick, accurate dispatches with an unimpressed, stonewall expression. Having just wrung Her Majesty's emissary dry of top-class intelligence, Whelan was now equipped to do what he did best. He hung his jacket on his chair, laid out the little column of cigarettes that would get him through the afternoon and banged away on the keys as if they had done him a grave offence.

Cath passed Andy the story just before their meeting with Max.

'Bernie Whelan? Jesus Christ, I thought Reuters had put that guy out to pasture years ago.'

By Bernard Whelan
TEHRAN, Oct 26 (Reuters) – Iran is a country
where people riot over changes in telephone codes.
Protests are not a sign that there's a revolution
afoot.

Andy skimmed through Whelan's rant. There seemed to be only one source. Probably the British ambassador. It was a tub-thumping, bombastic piece explaining that there was no central co-ordination between the groups involved in the Iranian sedition. Each of these groups had completely different agendas. The Kurds believed they, as Sunnis, were the object of discrimination, and they were unhappy because they were poor. The students were fighting for social freedoms that were a total non-issue out in rural Kurdistan. These groups were all just seizing on the momentum of other protests because they wanted to give a communal two fingers to the government. But, deep down, these revolutionary aspirations would never come to anything, Bern argued, because there was nothing fundamental tying these groups together. It was the same smug argument that the ambassador was putting in his memos. He quoted that thing about the telephone codes in every dispatch.

'Is it true about the phone codes?' Cath asked.

'Yeah,' Andy said with a short laugh. 'It was near Tabriz, I think. But the ambassador really never got the point. I'm not a psychologist but, if you ask me, these riots over postcodes or voting districts, or whatever, show Iran is just mightily fucked off. People hate their lives and they look for any excuse to get out and shout. At the moment, there's food on the shelves and high oil prices, so people might not want to risk bullets. But there's a lot of anger out there. It's dangerous. Baharvand knows this better than anyone. Your ambassador and Whelan might think Iranians are silly little people who let off steam every now and again. I don't, but they are all on anti-depressants.'

'Why do you think he completely ignored the Baharvand comments?'

'Easy. The guy's a moron.'

'You know him?'

'Sure, he was in Hungary a bit in the eighties. He was an idiot then.'

'Ah, yes, your mysterious past. You dark horse.'

'I don't think Baharvand'll mind too much. The BBC and CNN have included him.'

'So I saw. And crucially, I guess, if it is him pulling the strings, he'll love anyone who convinces us that there just can't be one central brain behind all this.'

Max had appeared at the shatter-proof perspex door of the office. He was agitated and wasted no time in venting his spleen.

'There's no way round it, the Pentagon have fucking shafted us. I'm sorry guys, I pretty much knew they would.'

Cath immediately looked concerned.

'You don't mean they are actually going to back Baharvand up on his co-ordinates?'

Max looked at her a little vacantly, then smiled, as if it suddenly dawned on him that things weren't quite as apocalyptic as he had been telling himself for the last seven hours.

'Oh, no, sorry, no, things aren't that bad but they are pretty damn bad. To tell you the truth, the co-ordinates had slipped my mind. There's no way in a million years they'll take that one up. The Pentagon are playing a far shittier game. Directly after the meeting with Bush, one of the generals goes to meet Danny Valerio.'

'Who he?' asked Andy.

'Arms lawyer. Real piece of shit. He represents all the weapons deals. He pimps his wares round the world largely on the assumption that Iran will murder us all in our beds unless we buy the latest whizz-bangs.'

'Gotcha.'

'Next morning Valerio goes shooting with Arkady Dolokhov, the Russian military attaché.'

'Not himself a saint,' said Cath.

'From then we make a little assumption: Valerio spills the beans on Baharvand. He doesn't want to lose the world's best ticket to arms sales and the Ruskies sure as hell don't want to lose all their nuke business in Iran.'

'A marriage made in heaven,' said Andy.

'Unfortunately so. Then we can pick up a second trail that we have been playing with for months.'

Max pulled a couple of large blow-ups out of his attaché case. They showed a tank of a man in a Chitrali cap, thick beard and sunglasses.

'I think I could find you about seventy million people who look a bit like him,' Andy joked. 'Most of them are a bit of a worry.'

'I know, I know,' Max confessed. 'This is our problem. This is from an intelligence sharing network we have set up with the Afghans. There are plenty of Afghan security guys who can smell a Russian. They still hate them. This guy is high on their suspect list but they cannot make anything stick. His accent is Tajik. But he might really be Kabul Tajik rather than Dushanbe Tajik. Loads of people reckon he's a drug-runner or a gun for hire. But we are also sure this guys checks in with the GRU guys in Kabul.'

'Do we know a name?' Cath asked.

'Take your pick. Rakhman. Akhmad. Mokhamed. About a

dozen more too. Everybody who knows him seems to have a different story about who he is and what his name is. What we know is that on Wednesday, Dolokhov had got on to the encryptor and was wiring Moscow like he had the devil behind him. That night, our man here, Rakhman, Akhmad or whoever the fuck he is, meets a GRU contact in Herat. Next morning, he's disappeared. The Afghans ask around at the official border crossings into Iran. Of course, they get the wall of silence. Even if they did notice the guy, what would be in it for them? Snitching never did you any good over there.'

'And this kind of man doesn't really look like he pays much attention to borders,' said Cath.

Max and Andy agreed.

Cath summed up.

'So, I know it's shaky but your worst-case scenario is that the Russians have thought there's no harm in pressing the panic button and sending in an assassin?'

'That's my fear,' Max said.

Andy leant back in his chair and expelled a great puff of air. Max shook his head sheepishly.

'I am so sorry. I really am. I mean I know it was your baby, with Baharvand coming to you,' he said, with a tone of contrition that would generally accompany breaking a priceless vase.

'Hardly your fault,' Andy said. 'And we really are still shadow-boxing here. We think Baharvand may be fomenting a revolution. And we think that a man who may be a Russian agent may be trying to kill him.'

Andy had gone through twenty-seven years of guilt because of Baharvand and was resolved that he would take no moral responsibility for what happened next. He would behave with professionalism, but it was up to the old cleric to shoulder the human burden of his plot. It was only when Cath began to speak that he realised he was neglecting his duty. He had spent so long working with Iran that he had inherited its fatalism.

Cath had a mischievous energy about her. Forty years ago, she was the girl in specs who always got picked last for netball. She was a trouble-maker and the others girls judged her to be half-mad and unfit for any sorority. But the boys were immediately attracted to her devilry and loved her with abandon, transforming her into an even more loathsome pariah at Cheltenham.

'Really, all we can do, is make a judgement based on the national interest. We cannot sit on the fence for ever. Let's get Lomax to find out if we think Baharvand is potentially our man. If this is in our interest, then we can cross the wires.'

Crossing the wires. One of the oldest tricks in the book. So old or so deeply buried in Chapter One that it was readily forgotten. It was almost like the captain telling his strike bowler to come in under-arm. Andy darted a grin at his erstwhile lover. It was a grin that acknowledged her superiority at the trade. Back on rainy afternoons in the 1980s when they shared grubby hotel rooms around Paddington, he often teased her for feeling awestruck by him. A flimsy second in Oriental Languages somehow trumped a first in French, he would tell her. French was just, well, too easy for a degree. She would hiss like a wildcat and throw a pillow across the room at him. In truth, neither of them really doubted that she was the one with the brain. He allowed his heart to lead him and kept screwing up, messily. Cath was the one who could see how to cross the wires on Russian military intelligence.

Max nodded and folded his hands across his belly.

'We don't have many options and that would be a gem if it worked.'

'And it might well do,' Andy said.

Cath was trying to hide her satisfaction but he could tell that she was glowing.

'Good. We will have to run it past Lomax, of course. But Andy, I think you should stand by to go to Vienna first thing tomorrow.'

She was well ahead of the game. Her mind must be burning up the motor. Andy began to piece together her plan.

By eight o'clock, Shirkhan was at home in his flat opposite the synagogue in Yusefabad, a relaxed mid-town district. Being an agency reporter in a country such as Iran is a thankless task. Things just tend to happen: whether they be plane crashes, earthquakes or assassinations. Your paymasters will ensure that you develop an unhealthy and alienating paranoia. Twenty-four hours a day, Shirkhan knew the buck stopped with him and that a disgruntled newsdesk would be bawling down the phone if he missed data projecting a poor wheat harvest or a crude pipeline springing a leak at Gachsaran. The reporter picked at some bread and cheese and distractedly filled in a cryptic crossword. He turned the television down low but never took his attention off it. It was just as well. At a quarter past eight he saw something wholly unprecedented. The voice-over remained unchanged. The announcer spoke of a Zionist, imperialist conspiracy against the Islamic Republic and the noble defenders of the revolution crushing some isolated but treasonable outrages. But the footage showed a completely different story. There were pictures of the basijis roaring their motorbikes into the protesters at Tehran university. And it was top quality film, not a grainy haze from a camcorder peeking out from behind a curtain. There were shots from Abadan and Sanandaj, showing streets thronged with restive crowds. There were picket lines around smelters, mines and lorry depots. Television was showing a nation boiling over with hatred for its government. Shirkhan jotted down the scenes he saw and ran his hand through his silver beard. What was this? Heads were bound to roll. Jafari would be furious. But then the announcer broke the propaganda record and read out Baharvand's communiqué. 'What the fuck?' he barked in English. He always reserved the coarse Anglo-Saxon tongue for his earthiest exclamations. He grabbed his overcoat, trotted down the stairs and hailed a cab for Parkway, the north Tehran flyover and roundabout where these dramas always play out.

Some editors believed Shirkhan's unbounded energy proved that he was simply that all-too-rare animal: a newshound. Whelan always quipped that the Iranian was just after more money. Neither argument really caught the measure of the man. Like all Iranians, he was an obsessive when it came to the destiny of his country. He couldn't really take holidays. He would mooch round Parisian cafés or lounge on a Turkish beach, but it wouldn't be long before he was slipping into an internet café to check-up on the latest stirrings back in Tehran. Shirkhan rushed to Parkway primarily because his homeland was his contrary mistress and he would follow her to her inevitable destruction. His obligations to the desk in London were very much an after-thought.

Shirkhan was correct yet again. The protests were coming alive. He slipped the driver a couple of toman on the southern junction with Valiasr and stepped out into the mêlée. It was a cold, crisp night. He rang the photographer and told him to get off his fat arse. Whelan wasn't answering his phone. The first cars were gathering and beeping their horns at each other, flirtatiously, like birds of paradise flashing their lustrous plumage. This was how protests begin in a police state. Iranians had become masters of protests that weren't really protests. The same rituals would follow a big success on the football pitch, such as qualifying for the World Cup. Young people, curious people, professional people. They all get in their cars and simply drive around, hoping that they will recognise a few kindred spirits. At first there are a few tentative poops on the horn. Those can always be explained away as a slip of the hand or as a warning to another driver. Then before long hundreds of cars are blasting away on their horns in a dizzying roar.

By nine o'clock Valiasr Street and Parkway were gridlocked. The exhaust-clogged air reverberated with honking klaxons. Many of the cars were now blasting Persian pop through open windows, their bonnets draped with the Iranian tricolour. In the Park-e Mellat beside the main road, thousands of people were gathering to stand and stare. People flashed smiles at each other. Some strangers shook hands. Lanterns hung from the trees and bright light spilled from the sweet-shops and juice-sellers along the broad boulevard. The normally sedate avenue, bordered by open jubs and colonnades of plane trees, had taken on a raucous carnival atmosphere.

The Javads, Iran's versions of Jack the Lad, saw these explosions of colour and discontent as an opportunity to show off their souped-up cars, flaunting their booming sound systems, fairy lights and reflective hub-caps.

A black-shirted Islamic militiaman gunned his motorbike through the crowd with a brooding grimace of disapproval. The revellers hissed at him and two girls threw flowers in his face. Seb was watching six girls dance the Babakaram, making eyes at each other as they gyrated their peachy behinds. He liked what he saw. Dozens of young men had gathered round the girls, clapping. They screamed and wolf-whistled when one of the girls pulled off her headscarf and leapt bare-headed on to the bonnet of a sports car.

'Ah, Mr Maynard, how are you?'

Seb hadn't seen Shirkhan sneak up on him.

'Heavens, Khosro, hi. You gave me quite a start. Lots of good things on display here, eh? I have never seen anything like it. I cannot believe I am in Iran.'

'Ha ha, my country has many wonders. But don't get too distracted by the ladies. Look around you. Listen. You hear what they are chanting?'

Seb couldn't quite make out the words among the blaring horns and the pulsating pop.

'Something about the people and freedom, but I'm afraid I cannot really hear,' he confessed.

'Hey, great, almost. They are saying "a popular cry of freedom". Do you remember?'

'Oh, of course, Baharvand's communiqué.'

'Exactly. Interesting, no? And look in some of the back windows of the cars. They've cut out photos of Baharvand from old newspapers, recycled his old presidential camapaign flyers. Some people have even done print-offs from Google images.'

'Wow, I never thought Baharvand would end up as a liberal hero.'

'Me neither, Seb.'

Lomax had used his meeting with the prime minister to sound out the government's mood towards Baharvand. Was he the only way to stop a war? If they were amenable to the pervading spirit behind crossing the wires, there was no reason why such busy world leaders should be burdened with the mechanics of Cath's plan. It was quite sufficient to ascertain that Brown was shocked by the idea of Russia conducting an extra-judicial killing.

A brilliant politician, Lomax got what he needed.

Back at the ziggurat, he told Cath and Andy they had the green light.

'The PM thinks a pre-emptive move by Russia would be entirely counter-productive, regardless of what Baharvand's final objective may be. So in that case, if this hit-man is real or a phantom, I reckon there is no harm in crossing the wires, just in case. As a safeguard to global stability.

'Andy get yourself over to Vienna. Then we can sit back and watch the biggest manhunt in Iranian history.'

Andy always knew this would happen. After years of fantasising about killing Ayatollah Ali Baharvand, he had to go and save his life.

6.

THEIR NEUROSES BUNDLED up in overcoats and pashmina scarves, the people of Vienna scurried down the embassy-lined streets that fan out from the Schwarzenbergplatz. Saeed Khalilzadeh, a nuclear physicist with the IAEA delegation, left the Iranian embassy at Jauresgasse, 9, and checked his watch. Half past two. He winced at the bitter wind that whipped down the street, pulled up his lapels and headed for the rendezvous.

Taking a digestif round the corner at Metternichgasse 6, Andy had concluded his part of the sting. The British ambassador's residence had resumed its unruffled, rococo elegance. On Friday night, the ambassador and his wife had small-talked their way through Austrian National Day. The Anglo-Austrian businessmen had tucked into the vol-au-vents and chinked their glasses of Steinriegel. There had been rapturous applause for the cake: a Union Jack and the Austrian red and white, spiked with sparklers. By nine o'clock it had all become rather animated. Curious passers-by wondered where the sound of muffled frivolity was coming from. It did rather jar with the measured restraint of Rumpelmayer's facade.

Andy leafed through the Saturday papers. He had run Piers Standish through the gameplan and had banged in a couple of bouncers to get his eye in. He needn't have worried. Standish seemed to have been born with inexhaustible reserves of duplicity and had already considered every problem that Khalilzadeh could throw at him.

The ambassador's wife was fascinated by having Andy about the place. After a little too much Riesling, the envoy had confided to his wife that they would have a 'friend' staying with them for the afternoon. It all seemed desperately exciting.

'Do you ski, Mr Trevarthen? If so, you really must come back and stay with us for a few days in the high season.'

'Ah, that's so kind of you, but I'm afraid I am a terrible skier. I think I would become somewhat of a figure of fun if I took to the slopes in Austria. Maybe even worse: a menace.'

'Oh well, I am sure you could just come for the Glühwein. I suppose it's something you ought to start young.'

'And you did?'

'Oh yes, Daddy was out here with the army so we were all skiing before we could walk.'

'Yeah, that's the only way, isn't it? It's too late for me now. I am sure I would break something.'

The ambassador's wife poured him another coffee and despaired at the grey skies.

'What filthy weather. Do you know Vienna at all?'

'Very little. I was a journalist across Eastern Europe back in the eighties so I passed through from time to time, but no, I certainly don't have an intimate knowledge of the place.'

In fact, Andy had been to Vienna more often than he could remember. It was frequently in that very room that the spooks and military attachés had jotted down the fruits of his latest excursion behind the wall. They drained every last drop out of him. A garrulous Czech squaddie on leave, drunkenly discussing tank exercises near the Austrian border, was enough for pages and pages of intelligence reports.

'Oh, how exciting. But you've been to the sights here?'

Andy said he would always revisit the Brueghel room at the Kunsthistorisches Museum. In Brueghel, Andy found a friend who shared his fascination with the details in life's fabric. As a lapsed Anglican, he often feared that a reverent appreciation of the details was the only point one's life had. But those were certainly not the sort of intimate sentiments you shared with an ambassador's wife. He simply said that he admired the Flemish master for his relish in observing the complexity and excitement of our daily lives. She looked unimpressed by this comment and confessed that she found Brueghel a somewhat sordid painter.

If only he'd known more about skiing.

Khalilzadeh saw Piers Standish in the far corner of the Café Hawelka. The British diplomat had colonised one of the highly-prized long tables beside the window. He had already ordered his coffee and was sipping from the glass of cold water that accompanied it. The scientist slung his overcoat on the stand beside the table and shook hands.

'I love these cafés. Very atmospheric,' he said in his accented but correct English.

'Wonderful, isn't it?' Standish said with his customary debonair charm. 'This place used to be one of the great hang-outs for writers and bohemians. You know, after the war, Herr Hawelka himself had to go out with a cart into the Vienna woods just to collect fuel to boil the coffee.'

Twenty-six years before, Khalilzadeh himself had arrived in Tehran as a refugee, fleeing the house-by-house fighting at Khorramshahr. He was always affected by the stories he heard from the older generation in Vienna.

The waiter appeared at the table.

'Ein Kaffee mit Sahne.'

The waiter nodded.

Khalilzadeh was the perfect candidate for a sting of this kind. Although a respected member of the IAEA delegation, he was there to back up the rhetoric with scientific credibility. He was not a political chameleon and entirely lacked Standish's guile. Although he was on good terms with the Briton after the weeks of back-room horse-trading they had attempted, Khalilzadeh had still tipped off his intelligence minder that a British diplomat had sought this urgent weekend meeting. Had he not done so, this cup of coffee could well have put him straight on the next flight back to Imam Khomeini. Khalilzadeh had told the Etela'at man that it couldn't be that important or Standish would not have chosen a public place. Oddly enough, public places are better, the Etela'at spook explained. If you are discovered in a secret location, you're done for. On the other hand, the chances of two diplomats bumping into each other and exchanging a few words at the Hawelka are relatively high.

Khalilzadeh was one of the few men who really understood what went on at the heart of the Iranian nuclear programme. He carried all of the programme's inherent contradictions in himself. He found the idea of atomic weapons abhorrent but if Pakistan, Russia and Israel all had them, well, why the hell shouldn't Iran?

But for now, that was hardly the point. The overriding objective was to ensure that the enrichment passed off successfully. And that wasn't easy, particularly with the president on their backs. They had to lie more to him than to Standish and his friends. The uranium hexafluoride feed gas was a disaster and eroded the centrifuges. Then, the cascades of centrifuges wouldn't work together in that vital synchronicity. Washington kept saying they could have enough for a bomb in 2009 or 2010. Fat chance. At the moment, the only objective on their desks was to get the uranium to the low level needed for the reactor at Bushehr. But clearly one day, the weaponisation people would knock on his door and ask for the next step. And when they did, he would probably do what they wanted. Those facilities at Natanz, deep underground, ringed by anti-aircraft batteries, had been built with only one thought in mind: arms. And why not? Those were the dark nights of the Imposed War with Iraq. Perhaps it was the only way to save the nation.

Standish kept the conversation procedural until the coffee arrived, then rushed in.

'Look, Saeed, I have something very important to tell you.'

He pushed his own empty coffee cup to the middle of the table. The Iranian nodded.

'As you know, we have been pretty vocal critics of the Iranian nuclear programme and we have never wavered in demanding this atomic work end immediately.'

Khalilzadeh rocked his head and smiled sympathetically. Obviously it was regrettable that Britain and its European allies should take such a position, but this game had been dragging on for a long while and everybody had more or less accepted its idiosyncratic rules.

Standish looked out of the window for a few seconds, as if readying himself to unburden a great secret.

'But there are certain standards, ethical standards, by which diplomacy should be conducted. I accept that we are in an open confrontation with Tehran but it is a confrontation that must remain either here in Vienna or at the Security Council in New York.'

Khalilzadeh wasn't sure where this was going. Had Standish got wind of impending military action?

'Of course.'

'The thing is, Saeed, in my dealings with the US delegations

.... well, dammit, the CIA .... I hear things I probably shouldn't. And there are limits to what I can accept.'

'The CIA,' Khalilzadeh mouthed, innocently. The scientist didn't want to be the man in the middle. There were far more influential people than Dr Khalilzadeh to leak such matters to. Why him? He guessed he wasn't followed as much as the others. He was just the boffin. Were the F/A-18 Hornets ranged up on the supercarrier decks? Had the Europeans stomached enough US warmongering this time?

'You see, Saeed, it's about all these demonstrations across Iran and your old boss, Baharvand. Basically, what we, the Brits, and I am sure the Iranians, have known for years is that the CIA has been propping up Abdolmalek Rigi and the Baluch.'

Standish actually doubted that, but there was an outside chance it could be true.

'Rigi is a terrorist. Rigi is a very evil man.'

'And also for years, the Baluch have been begging the CIA for help carrying off a really big strike, something that hits at the heart of the Iranian regime.'

'They killed many of our soldiers this year in a bomb attack against a bus. These are very dreadful men.'

Standish nodded.

'But they want something bigger. They want to kill a big politician, a very important person.'

'They want to assassinate Baharvand?'

Standish wriggled into his most furtive body language.

'Look, I know this is really fucked up but I think the CIA have gone absolutely mad. And for Christ's sake, you never met me, OK? I don't want you to mention this to anyone else in Vienna.'

'Of course.'

Khalilzadeh felt this was surreal. Leaks in cafés were meant

149

to reveal titbits on polonium detonator acceleration or details on P-2 centrifuge imports. But this insight into a Baluch plot was off the chart.

That was part of the charm of a good sting. If it's all too credible, it smells of a set-up. People are more likely to fall for something that verges on the implausible.

Khalilzadeh looked distraught. He had not touched his coffee. Baharvand had treated him well. Baharvand had always behaved like a good patriot but the sort of patriot who showed that he was willing to do business with the West. He was one of the few leading clerics not implicated in killing Kurdish dissidents in Berlin and he could travel freely. He had done so and forged strong alliances in the international community.

'I do not understand. Why? Why would they want to do such a thing to Ayatollah Baharvand?'

'I have only got snippets of this plan, Saeed. I don't really know. But I know that Rigi's been asking for CIA help to kill Baharvand for ages. Now the CIA wants them to go for it. And more than that, they are sending in their own man. Not an American, but a US-trained Afghan who can pass unnoticed out in Baluchistan and Kerman. God knows what he'll do. Maybe he'll work with the Baluch. Maybe he'll disguise himself as an Afghan labourer, doing the jobs the Iranians hate. Either way, his plan is to get in there and kill the Ayatollah.'

'When will this happen?' says Khalilzadeh, his voice trembling.

Standish had fine tuned his sense of indignation.

'I dunno. I dunno the details. I just know they are green-lighting something that's been on the books for months, or years, whatever. But it's pure, unadulterated madness, isn't it? We spend so long crafting diplomatic solutions and then the fucking Yanks just screw everything up for everyone. They have never understood the Middle East and now they are just charging around again, like bulls in a china shop.'

'But why? Why go for Baharvand? That is not logical. He has retired.'

'Don't ask me. Easy target?' Standish threw up his hands in a gesture that signalled the Americans were capable of incalculable idiocies.

Khalilzadeh stared at his coffee.

'I do not understand. I know the CIA hate our president but I thought they would try to be clever. Baharvand is no ally of the president. The CIA has an interest in exploiting camps within my country. It is not in America's interest to have Baharvand killed.'

Standish sighed and planted his palms down on the table, putting such downward pressure on them that Khalilzadeh thought he might be about to stand up.

'As I said, I have only heard bits of this, but we figure two things could be going through their thick heads. The first idea is that they see the whole country going up in demonstrations.'

Khalilzadeh nodded. There was no point arguing that the demonstrations were anything other than grounds for very serious concern.

'The Americans want to raise the stakes. There would be nothing like a high-profile assassination to raise those stakes, turn this into a real revolution and get what they want: regime change. If the Baluch can knock off an ayatollah or two, why can't the Kurds? Why can't the Arabs?'

Khalilzadeh continued to nod. It sounded credible. Iranians were reared on stories of foreign intervention dictating the 1953 coup and the 1979 revolution. In some cases the tales were exaggerated, in other cases they were absolutely spot on.

Standish was getting into his flow.

'And the Americans win, whichever way you look at it. If their man gets in and kills Baharvand now, then they have just killed a guy who seems to be supporting the demonstrators.'

Khalilzadeh had seen the Ayatollah's statement.

'But surely for the Americans, this is a reason to discourage the Baluch, not send in an assassin to help them?'

'Huh, maybe. But if they know one thing about the Iranians, they know the power of a martyr. Right, maybe they just want to fan a revolt. Maybe you are right and the Americans aren't being fucking cynical. But wouldn't it be great for a sympathetic cleric to die in the middle of this? As soon as Baharvand dies, the White House comes out and blames the Iranian government for killing him. Then all the Californian satellite networks say Baharvand has been killed by Tehran. What effect is that going to have? Then you have one hell of a figurehead for a popular rising. I dunno. Maybe that's bullshit. Jesus, I dunno why the CIA have suddenly got all interested in killing him. But they have. I know you really admired the guy when he did his stints here in Vienna. Do him a favour.'

With a look of consternation, Standish pushed a five euro note under his saucer.

'Wait five minutes before leaving. And don't try to contact me again,' he said.

The Iranian opened his mouth as if to speak but Standish had gone.

Back in Metternichgasse, Standish loosened his tie in the foyer of the ambassador's residence.

'How did it go?' Andy asked.

'Cakewalk.'

There was not much that could have gone wrong. Whatever personal reservations Khalilzadeh may have had about the validity of the intelligence, he had no choice but to pass it on to the spooks. And when the message arrived in Tehran, Alef Baa would also be boxed in. Despite the Iranian spymaster's painstaking, but frustrated, efforts to build a case against Baharvand, there was no question of sitting tight while a US-trained assassin was prowling through the mountains of Baluchistan.

Forty miles beyond Koh-e Siah, the Tajik had seen the sunlight reflecting off a Kalashnikov barrel half way up a cliff face, half a mile to his left, and hoped that it belonged to one of Abdollah's men. Even after all his years building alliances among these people, he never relaxed. There was always a chance that a man such as Abdollah had stolen a rival warlord's sister the night before and that marauding Baluch were on the warpath. There was always a chance that you would meet bandits who didn't care who you were. And finally, there was always the risk that the men sent by Abdollah to meet you would have heard, erroneously, that you were carrying thousands of dollars. In that case, they would slit your throat without compunction and head off to pledge their allegiance to a rival chieftain. The Tajik had learned there was no room to be complacent.

The road narrowed and ran between a gauntlet of cliffs and rocky outcrops. It was a perfect spot for a rendezvous as the Revolutionary Guards never dared take a route such as this any more. Over the last two years, thirty of their men had been killed in ambushes in this spot alone. Their convoys had been mortared in narrow defiles such as this, then Baluch marksmen, perched on the cliff faces, would strafe the vehicles and pick off the poorly trained, shabby recruits as they broke for cover. Anybody with friends and connections could ensure that they didn't get sent on the suicide mission into Baluchistan. It was hard to think of better country for ambushes and the Tajik's pistol lay on the passenger seat.

As the road curved round a sweeping bend, a Toyota 4x4 pulled sharply on to the sand-quilted tarmac one hundred yards in front of him. The back was packed with Baluch fighters, sunlight glinting off their weapons and the bullet belts wrapped across their chests. The Tajik slowed to a crawl and slipped the Paykan into second gear. He took the pistol in his right hand and steered with the left. At fifty yards, two of the fighters in the back waved green flags and the driver pulled off the road, gently steering across a barren patch of scrub. The Tajik left the road with a clunk and feared for a moment that his car could have lost a vital organ. But the ailing car regained its poise and drew up behind the Toyota. The Baluch waved enthusiastically and shouted their welcomes. The Tajik pocketed his pistol and got out of the car.

To men pinned down by their raking Kalashnikov fire, the Baluch are fearsome warriors, inspiring terror with their flowing robes, dark beards and turbans. But up close, they are shy and almost girlishly giggly. When you shake their hands, you see how young they are and are shocked by the juvenile scrawniness of their beards. Their voices are soft with an effeminate lilt. The eldest was the driver, but he could not have been older than twenty-seven or twenty-eight. The Tajik towered above his spindly frame.

'I am Ahmadi,' the driver said. 'Welcome.'

'Many thanks. I am honoured. You are all well, I trust.'

A chorus of 'Glory be to God' emanated from the fighters.

'Excellent.'

'Commander Abdollah is delighted that you are joining us,' Ahmadi rejoined cheerily, casting an eye over the clapped-out Paykan.

'We will, of course, need to conceal that. It won't make the journey up to the base.'

Ahmadi pointed out a long cave at the foot of the mountains where the Tajik could put the car.

'We've been using it for years. It's smoothed out.'

The Tajik didn't believe that he would get the Paykan right the way inside. To his surprise, he did, with yards to spare. As he waited for the hot metal underbelly of the Paykan to cool, he exchanged gossip and cigarettes with the Baluch before lying on his back and wiggling underneath the car. He felt for the metal tubing, unscrewed the cap and slipped out the Dragunov. Confident that he had all the parts, the Tajik took the black plastic sachets out into the daylight and spread them on the ground. Four of the Baluch gathered round with interest as he slit the bags with a penknife.

'Ah, Dragunov. Very fine weapon,' one of them said, like a wine buff passing comment on a Château d'Yquem that has just been set upon his table.

'God's blessing. I am impressed, you know your weapons.'

The Baluchi blushed at the praise. He could only have been eighteen or nineteen, but these boys had a compendious knowledge of arms. The Dragunov was issued to the Iranians too. And the Afghans had captured plenty off the Russians during the war. There was a good chance that Abdollah might have a few sniper rifles purloined from the arms bazaar back at his lair.

The Tajik tied the assembled Dragunov into a canvas sack and hitched it over his shoulder. He smiled at the Baluch.

'Right. Let's go and meet Commander Abdollah.'

Two of them had draped black sheets over the car and taken positions on the cliff face, twenty yards above the opening of the cave.

'They will stay here,' Ahmadi said. 'There shouldn't be any trouble, but just in case.'

The two men nestled into the cliff face waved farewell with their rifles.

The Tajik took a seat at the front of the Toyota beside Ahmadi and they thundered across the desert, the kids in the back whooping with excitement every time they hit a bump or sagged into a dip. It was a pitiless environment, entirely waterless and devoid of any grazing.

Ahmadi pointed to some barren crags twenty miles away.

'That's where we're going,' he said. 'Not long now.'

At the foot of the mountains, the Baluch led the way, climbing a steep shingle path in a fissure that cut up through the ochre rock. Although still in peak fitness, the Tajik felt his knees and lungs burn. Salty sweat was dripping into his eyes. The Baluch, scampering ahead, swung round and flashed innocent, childish grins at him.

'Steep, huh?'

The Tajik nodded and steadied himself on a sharp rock that jutted out into the path.

'How much longer?' he asked.

They rocked their heads.

'One hour,' one of them replied, lifting his forefinger like a sage on the point of issuing a prophecy.

Before long, the Tajik was scrambling properly, catching his balance with his hands as his legs pushed him ever upwards. Abdollah had found himself an impregnable redoubt.

After an hour's climbing, in which they had not only ascended but also cut round the side of the cliff, they reached a long valley. The Tajik had seen few areas so littered with natural cover. The higher slopes were carpeted with Herculean boulders, each large enough to conceal four or five men and he was

156

surprised that earthquakes had not sent them barrelling into the valley below. He noticed the reflected dazzle from binocular lenses and rifle barrels: Abdollah's men were keeping the new arrival under close surveillance. Towards the end of the valley, there must be some source of water as he could see patches of greenery, dotted with junipers and black cherries.

'Our home,' some of the Baluch said, with mock pride.

The sun blasted the valley. A high-pitched whistle reverberated round the Tajik's skull. He was dehydrated.

Twenty minutes later, a smaller valley opened up to the right. It was cooler and shaded. The Tajik scanned a rock face like Gruyère cheese, riddled with caves. Each cave was home to a posse of fighters. On the ledges in front of the caves dozens of men sat on rugs, conversing and sipping tea, their AK-47s lying beside them. They stood as he approached, planted their right hands across their hearts and bowed. A sharp series of whistles and calls summoned a tall warrior dressed entirely in black robes from the highest cave. The Tajik recognised his old comrade, Abdollah.

As ever, the warlord was laying great importance on styling himself as a fashion icon. He pulled off his sunglasses as he shook hands with the Tajik.

'Ray-Ban Aviators. Really expensive. Very stylish.'

He pinched his fore-finger and thumb together in the universal 'OK' sign.

The Tajik complimented him on his eye-wear and remembered Kryuchkov's quip on the ease with which Abdollah would fritter away $40,000.

'How are you, my old friend? God has willed that you are well?' he asked.

'Very well, God be praised. Come in, come in.'

Abdollah clicked his fingers at a teenage attendant and demanded some tea.

The inside of the cave had a peculiarly homely air, furnished with carpets, cushions and lanterns. The Tajik had spotted the small petrol-fuelled generator outside the cave but was surprised by how many electrical appliances Abdollah was running off it. The far end of the cave was walled off by two curtains. Through the gap between them, the Tajik could see that the warlord spent his nights in a rather luxuriant double-bed and wondered who on earth had to carry that into the valley.

It would, of course, have been deeply impolite to talk business. Abdollah seemed in high spirits, which was an encouraging indication that he had heard the cash had landed in Stockholm. He gave the Tajik a whirlwind tour of the cave, showing off the latest trinkets stripped from the corpses of the Revolutionary Guard: watches, knives and amber rings.

'You still working with Rigi?' the Tajik asked.

Abdollah sharply sucked in air through his teeth.

'Rigi is a good man,' he said deliberately. The Tajik took this as a sign that the two would soon come to blows. The Iranians would never dare to take the battle to Abdollah in this terrain, but Rigi might.

'Jundollah, the soldiers of God, have done much for the Baluch people but I am not sure about their current strategies.'

This was presumably a turf war over fuel smuggling rather an issue of great political or ethical dimensions.

'You must understand, my friend, that the Baluch Popular Liberation Jihad is the only way forward now. We are the new dawn for our people.'

The Tajik nodded. He had no idea that Abdollah was calling his troops the Popular Liberation Jihad.

'How long has the PLJ been in existence?' the Tajik enquired.

'Well, in this guise, only two months or so, but we are inheriting and incorporating the struggle of many smaller groups.'

They seemed to have money and resources. The Tajik wondered how many of the al Qaeda core had made it into this valley.

'May God bless your Jihad,' the Tajik said as the boy returned, carrying a tea tray.

'Ah, come, come,' said Abdollah, extravagantly throwing back the curtains and exposing the bed. 'You are my most esteemed guest and old friend. Come and make yourself comfortable.'

The Tajik praised the bed and sat by the headboard, cross-legged. There was a television and video-recorder at the foot of the bed. Abdollah squatted beside him. They sipped their tea and the boy waited in attendance.

'Get the video of the angel woman,' Abdollah barked.

The boy rummaged in a tattered cardboard box and pulled out a cassette.

'Hurry, put it on. I am a man in love.'

The video started: a pirate copy of a Cindy Crawford workout video with Urdu sub-titles. The Tajik's heart sank. Not here as well. These things had become status symbols among the Afghans years before. He had no idea that the supermodel was now casting her spell on the Baluch.

A bikini-clad Cindy was with her trainer on a beach. The Tajik settled against the bed-head and nodded enthusiastically. Abdollah sent the boy from the room and drew the curtains. The Tajik had long accepted this as part of his job. Men like Kryuchkov would be shocked at how much of his time in the mountains he had to spend complimenting fighters on their eclectic assemblages of insipid erotica.

Abdollah laid down his tea and pointed at the screen.

'She is a radiant woman is she not? A houri who has cast my heart in chains.'

The Tajik agreed.

159

'She is a strong woman. I will have her for my wife,' Abdollah continued.

'This is an old video. Perhaps she has already married,' the Tajik joked.

The Baluchi grinned.

'Honestly? Miss Cindy has betrayed me and married?'

'I don't know I'm afraid. She may have done.'

Abdollah sipped his tea and watched as the trainer flipped her over in a cartwheel.

'Mmm, delicious.' Abdollah roared with laughter. 'Not to worry. Her husband is a weak man. I will bring her here. Maybe it will not be like America to start with, so she will kick and scratch. But I will tame her.'

After the final credits, Abdollah enquired whether the Tajik would like to watch Cindy strut her stuff once again. The killer confessed that a man could have too much of a good thing.

Their fraternity confirmed by their lusty viewing, the Tajik knew it was safe to discuss the job in hand.

'I hope that there were no problems with the transfer.'

Abdollah shook his head.

'Perfect. Perfect.' Once again, he gave the 'OK' sign. It was becoming a grating habit.

'Once our business is concluded, a further $40,000 will be deposited.'

The Baluchi commander whisked his hand through the air as if conducting an invisible orchestra.

'Money is of little consequence between old friends,' he lied. 'Come, let us talk in earnest.'

He threw open the curtains and invited the Tajik to join him on the carpets in the front section of the cave. The bed was no place to discuss battle plans. He needed to be surrounded by his weapons and by the spoils of combat.

While they had been watching the video, night had fallen. The tea-boy had kindled a fire from brushwood on the ledge outside Abdollah's cave. He had also changed into a long, diaphanous shirt and ringed his eyes with kohl. The Tajik had already assumed that, given the unavailability of Cindy Crawford, or of any women, the tea-boy spent the hours of darkness as Abdollah's *peri*.

The two men settled themselves on Baluch rugs and Abdollah shouted to the boy that he should bring a qalyan, a water pipe, and opium. The Tajik was a collector of rugs and was unimpressed by Abdollah's. The finest Persian craftsmen make one deliberate error in their warp and weft, a flaw made in the humble understanding that perfection is an exlusively divine attribute. Even to attempt perfection is sacrilegious presumption. However, the weavers of Abdollah's rugs seemed to have taken thick-fingered mistakes beyond the bounds of piety.

'So, $80,000, it must be quite some mission you have in mind my friend.'

'I want to go to Anareh in Kerman and kill Ayatollah Baharvand.'

Abdollah melted once again into uproarious laughter.

'Hah, is that all? You are paying over the odds. We could go now if you like.'

Alef Baa thought it quite possible that there was no one left alive who knew his real name. He had been Alef Baa, the simple initials A.B., for so long that he feared he might one day forget his real name. When he chanted it to himself at home in bed, it seemed to echo, hollow and meaningless, in the darkness. Some people from other ministries assumed that the intelligence monikers simply represented one's initials. That sinister Mr Alef Baa could, for example, just be simple old Amir Babaie or Ahmad

Bahrami. People liked to try and humanise the old man. It was something about his spectral face, a skull with deep, sunken orbits, that made them want to flesh him out. But Alef Baa weren't even his real initials.

The ageing spy chief had cursed when he scanned the encrypted message from the embassy in Vienna. This was clearly Baharvand's work. The man was leading him a merry dance. Sergeant Ahmadian had been dumped in the qanat in Anareh and that lingerie-sniffing fool Amiri had bungled in London. Tehran now had no idea where baby Baharvand was, and such incompetence incensed Alef Baa. His problems were manifold. On the one hand, he knew his own organisation was awash with traitors loyal to Baharvand. Ahmadian's cover was probably blown before he even arrived in Anareh. On the other hand, the rest of his department was staffed by cattle. Why should he have to depend on men such as Amiri? The agent was a pervert whom he had to transfer to diplomatic duties because he raped a fourteen-year-old in the city of Qazvin and needed to get out of the country. Alef Baa hated the stolid, uncomprehending faces of his stooges. The older ones had all worked for SAVAK, the Shah's equally grotesque security service. He was not dealing with men of belief or ideology: simply strong arms, who, with two hours and a coil of rubber hosing, could beat a confession out of a horse. If Baharvand seized power, Alef Baa knew that the detritus who wandered down the corridors of the ministry, dutifully greeting him each morning, would happily torture their old boss.

He lit a Panjah-o-Haft, dropped the burning match into his ashtray and read through the despatch from Vienna one last time, hungrily scouring it for even the slightest excuse not to act. But there was no way out. Two junior officers had already initialled the transcript so there was no question of shredding and burning it. The Americans were trying to kill one of the country's most respected ayatollahs and they had to be stopped. The nation's military and intelligence infrastructure was already stretched by the demonstrations, but he would have to mobilise as many men as he could. In a sense, he thought resignedly, it was all rather intriguing. He couldn't penetrate the sequential logic that had led to this report from Vienna, which meant that he had locked horns with a worthy adversary. The disappearance of Baby Baharvand must tie in somewhere. He decided that he would go down south himself and oversee the capture or death of this reckless Yankee gunslinger. Maybe they could beat part of the story out of this hit-man. If he actually existed.

Andy Trevarthen and Alef Baa, two men who had spent years dreaming of Baharvand's fall from grace, had just formed a grudging but professional partnership dedicated to keeping the Machiavellian cleric alive.

Otto was still away in Zurich, making pots of money for his meek little wife in fisheries. Cath herself was glad that the satellite shots had come in and that she had an excuse not to return to the palatial emptiness that she was supposed to call home. It was almost midnight.

The defence man had pinned all the pictures to a white-board and ringed various bits and pieces of military hardware in red and blue. She consulted the grid references and satisfied herself that she knew where on this map this was all happening. A lot of Kerman. A lot of Sistan-Baluchistan. She found it hard to accept the fact that she would never visit the country that was devouring so much of her passion and energy. Although the place had broken Andy, she envied him his knowledge of the smells and tastes. Andy knew the cries and clatter of the container port outside his window, the pressure-cooker heat. Her

Iran was a frigid bubble composed of tapped conversations between lowly army officers and shots taken from outer space.

The officer entered with a couple of steaming mugs.

'Thought we could do with a coffee to keep us awake.'

'Oh, that's so thoughtful, but, did you …?'

She peered into the cups. 'I am so sorry but I can't have milk. I'm lactose intolerant.'

'Ah, right. I can go and make another if you—'

'No, no, let's just get on with it.'

Cath had politely refused more cups of milky tea and coffee than she cared to remember. Lactose intolerance was one of three virulent allergies that suddenly flared up when her father died and the stress knocked her already fragile teenage self-belief. It was the period of her life that forged her insecurity and ensured that she would always choose an industrious, reliable Otto as her partner rather than a foolish, reckless Andy. Like her father, Andy would get himself killed and break her. So, she never allowed herself to love him. Really love him. And she wasn't sure whether he loved her. To his credit, he never made the mistake of putting milk in her coffee, so maybe he did. Did he love Juliette? Could a man like that really love anybody?

'Generally, what we are talking about here is a massive mobilisation,' the ramrod-backed officer began, wafting his hand in the general vicinity of the blow-ups.

'At about 20.00 GMT, we started to pick up huge deployments of army, Revolutionary Guard and border police. We are talking men and we are talking convoys of trucks. We have no evidence of the movement of armour or of an increase in air sorties.'

'Aha.' Cath kicked off her shoes and rested her stocking feet on a chair, scribbling notes on to unlined foolscap on a clip-board. 'From where to where?'

He reeled off the names of bases, some of which lay deep in central Iran.

'And they are all converging on the south-east?' she asked.

'Yes. If we look at these shots around the Bam, Kerman and Anareh areas, there are roadblocks every five hundred yards. There are already huge traffic jams. Saturday is, of course, a working day in Iran.'

Thank you for that.

'And in Baluchistan?'

'The area is heavily fortfied already. It's criss-crossed with trenches and ramparts to stop the drug runners just charging across. And then installations such as this,' he tapped a photograph unnecessarily with a pointer, 'are little forts, desert fastnesses, rigged up with pretty powerful machine-gun placements. The idea is that they should be able to resist siege from Baluch assault. What we are seeing is that all the military placements of this nature are being backed up, and heavily. Convoys of trucks are driving into the forts. Our assessment would be that they are waiting until first light before fanning out and sending search parties across the area. They are scared enough by day. So anything by night would just be madness.'

'And in your experience, this would all fit with a manhunt? A really big manhunt?'

'That would seem most likely, yes.'

This guy was such a stuffed shirt. Cath never really understood the fixation with men in uniform. Military types always seemed infuriatingly incapable of independent thought. But having married a banker, and one famed for his prudent, slow-burning investment decisions, she accepted she was in no position to pontificate. She continued to jot down the reams of military jargon with the zeal of a *Guns & Ammo* reader.

Leaning her head against the juddering, tacky window of the

165

cab on the way home, she revelled in the triumphs that motivated her. Secretly revelling in secret triumphs. Why did she have to dote on Otto's insufferable friends when she had just mobilised the whole Iranian army? Few people saw Cath as intensely competitive but they didn't understand her. When she found out that she had the third-highest first, her reflex action was to find out the identity of the two who outscored her. She tracked their fortunes, almost neurotically, and was delighted that neither had come to anything. One had become a contrarian red-brick don whose articles were derided for pretension even in the vapid world of literary criticism. The other had married young, lived in the country and gave violin lessons. Neither of them had broken West African drug cartels or negotiated the release of hostages from rebels in the Nigerian Delta. Deep in her heart, she sought a victory over Andy. She was better than him. The bastard. The adorable bastard. Iran may have wrecked him but she had already shown that she could confound the enemy out there.

It was half one by the time she got back to the palace and tossed her keys on to a marble sideboard. She didn't switch on the lights as the electric glow of the metropolis spilled round the minimalist furnishings like the sheen of a full moon. She poured a glass of Talisker and slid open the door to the balcony, surveying St Paul's, the illuminated riverside façades and phosphorescent skyscrapers across the eddying flow of the Thames.

She thought of Andy across the river, stretched out in that poky Westminster flat, lying with his bare back on the twisted sheet, just like in the Carnegie B&B in Sussex Gardens. She wondered whether he had learned to believe in God yet. He hadn't then, which worried her and she told him off. How could he make any sense of this whole business if he didn't believe in that greater sense of purpose? When she asked him that, he shrugged and went off for a shower. When he came out, a grotty towel around his waist, she had clutched at straws. But don't you believe in something, something out there that's beyond all this? Not really, no. What about an afterlife? He said that he would find that out, probably sooner rather than later, so it wasn't worth worrying about now. Was that a joke? Andy had probably forgotten that episode, while she recalled it every other day.

She downed the single malt and wanted to hug someone, something. She thought of Molly, the beautiful, fat labrador they used to have when she was a girl. It made her so angry when people called Molly a he. Couldn't they see how pretty she was? Otto and Andy were a waste of her time and energy, she wanted Molly back. Molly always understood.

Many visitors assumed that the pollution wouldn't be so bad in winter, figuring that the heat of summer would exacerbate the smog. But it was the low, grey cloud cover of autumn and winter that turned Tehran into a choking bowl of exhaust fumes. They had closed the schools again.

That Sunday morning Bernie Whelan was revolted by the view from the bureau window.

'Christ, it's like mustard gas. Brown, yellow. Disgusting.'

Some mornings there was even a tinge of mucus green. The Alborz mountains were, almost incredibly, entirely obscured.

'Sure. The solution, of course, is to stop giving away free petrol, then we would really have overnight regime change,' Shirkhan joked.

Whelan didn't get it.

'So what's on the cards today, Sheer Karn?'

'This could be quite interesting. There's an official notification of a massive anti-drugs crackdown in the south-east.

167

Lots of roadblocks, raids into the territory of known traffickers. It's a response to the murder of a Revolutionary Guardsman a little while back. A guy called Ahmadian.'

Whelan looked unconvinced.

'Drugs make for worthy copy but the problem is that it's never new. All these stories from Afghanistan, Iran and Colombia are so bloody dull. Unwinnable drugs war drags on.'

'Sure, that would be true if it were a drugs story,' Shirkhan went on undeterred. 'But why would they be doing this now? This is clearly a sign that the regime is frightened. They are looking for any excuse to mobilise the army, Revolutionary Guards and other forces. It's a big show of force, a warning to those behind the civil unrest.'

Whelan thought about it for a while. Shirkhan could well be right but Whelan had no idea how to handle a story like this.

'So how would you phrase it?'

'Oh, I don't know, maybe something like "Iran begins huge military manoeuvres as civil unrest worsens".'

Whelan grimaced.

'Yeah, well, you can't really play those sort of games with a news agency. You are putting two and two together and making five. That's not our job. Basically, you are getting distracted again. Keep your focus on the big story. Forget about Bavand and forget about anti-drugs stuff. Let's keep this tight and give the punters what they really want to know.'

As ever, Bernie Whelan was vindicated. In two hours, Iran would be ablaze.

7.

STRANDED IN IRAN's central desert, Qom is the worst conceivable setting for a city: oppressively hot in summer and bitterly cold in winter. Drawn through flaking, chalky bedrock, the tap water tastes like a dose of Epsom salts.

Qom has two claims to fame. The first is sohan, a sickly, tooth-rotting biscuit laced with saffron and pistachio nuts. The second is that it is Iran's great seminary city, the Persian Oxford and Cambridge, a nesting ground for clerics, its twisting alleys filled with the turbans and swirling black capes of its scholars. As with the Oxford and Cambridge of the Middle Ages, all you can study is theology. But that isn't to say that Qom has a rarefied air of fusty medieval bookishness. The Islamic Republic's oil bonanza has ensured that this is a modern city, equipped with first-class computer rooms. Qom seems to produce as many CD-ROMs as venerable tomes these days. Only a village a century ago, Iran has transformed this fly-blown town into the world's pre-eminent centre of Shi'ite scholarship.

But Ayatollah Hashemian had far more on his mind than recondite scholarship.

Hashemian's office looked out on to the central courtyard of the Feyzieh, Qom's most prestigious seminary. That same overcast Sunday morning and he was leafing through a mountain of correspondence. Hashemian was one of those men whom western intelligence services figure must exist, but whom they never pin down. He shared Baharvand's sources of corrupt private income but none of his pragmatism. Occasionally, he plunged Tehran into trouble that it never anticipated. Israeli troops would lever open crates filled with Iranian rifles in Gaza and British troops in Basra would be killed by an Iranian roadside bomb. All these little gifts, trinkets of affection from Qom. The fact was that central government could do nothing to restrain Hashemian and maverick mullahs like him. They fight private wars, confident in the justice of their jihad. Using centuries-old networks of family and friends that run from Lebanon to Pakistan, they can wreak terror on the world.

But the papers on Hashemian's desk that morning did not concern another flamboyant foreign stratagem, but focussed on a recurring enemy within Qom itself. His agents were reporting that the Sufis, those ascetic disciples of Rumi, had found more places to congregate and celebrate their mystical rites, approaching God through poetry and dance.

'Heretical bastards!' he snapped, reading through the despatches.

It was clearly time for another crackdown, time for some more blood in the streets.

But Hashemian never got time to pass his orders on to his thugs. Two grenades scudded across the floor and cracked off the skirting board like billiard balls bouncing off the cushion. Crippled by polio, the white bearded cleric couldn't crane himself round to determine what had made those irritating noises behind him. The door slammed. That was curious. Hadn't it already been closed? Must be the wind.

*

Only a couple of minutes after weeping seminarians carried Hashemian's bloodied corpse down into the courtyard, a Tehran municipal judge threaded his car out of the tide of traffic that inched along Abbas Abad Avenue, right in the heart of the noisy, polluted capital. Darya-ye Noor Street was free of cars and he slipped the nippy Peugeot 206 into fourth for the first time since leaving the courtroom. It had been a slow morning, just a couple of petty criminals to send down. He did not have another appointment until mid-afternoon and he wanted to get home, to spend a few stolen moments with his three-day-old daughter. Distracted by his reveries on this beautiful new addition to his family, he had neglected to check his mirrors. The biker roared down the hill and drew level with the car. The judge sensed the shadow of the motorcyclist with annoyance and lifted his arm to gesture that the fool was driving recklessly.

A girl in a blue chiffon headscarf was taking a break from her tedious job at the Kayhanrah travel agency. All those places she would never be able to afford to go to. She was on her mobile to Mama when the gunman pumped three rounds through the Peugot's window. The car slammed into a plane tree beside the road and its front wheels slid into the open drain. The girl dropped her phone and sank to her knees. She could see that ghastly red smear across the windscreen. For thirty seconds, though it seemed much longer, she was silent. Then she screamed. She couldn't tell the police which way the biker went. It was all just too horrible.

And so it went on. By midday, twelve men were dead, mostly clerics and Revolutionary Guard commanders. Some had just switched the ignition and blown their cars to pieces. Photographers swarmed round the splayed metal. The editor-in-chief of the Kayhan daily, a man directly appointed by

Supreme Leader Ayatollah Ali Khamenei, had forgotten something and gone back to his house. Fumbling for a key on his doorstep a bullet burst through the nape of his neck.

On the Reuters desk, bombarded by urgent newsflashes from Tehran, they joked that countries would do well to deny Bernie Whelan visas. He'd done it again. Maybe we shouldn't allow him back into Britain, joked one wag. Everyone laughed and a quorum was reached for tea.

By Bernard Whelan
TEHRAN, Oct 28 (Reuters) – Tehran accused Osama bin Laden's al Qaeda network of sensationally hijacking Iran's growing civil unrest by assassinating twelve senior officials in the space of two hours on Sunday.

The co-ordinated murders come close on the heels of nationwide protests, often tens of thousands strong, in which students, unionists and members of religious and ethnic minorities have called for greater freedoms.

Shirkhan sunk his head into his hands when he read Whelan's story. The man was simply not listening. Yes, the interior ministry had said it thought al Qaeda could be behind the killings. And that was enough for Whelan. But the judiciary accused the old enemy from the revolutionary days, the People's Mujahidin. Judges sent Marxist rebels to the gallows and there would always be people out for revenge. If that were not enough, the foreign ministry spokesman said that the assassinations were clearly the work of foreign agents. He then spoke cryptically, and at length, about British forces in Basra arming and training Arab nationalist terrorists. For Whelan, a ministry proffering a tasty nugget was enough for a story. But that was to misunderstand the Hydra-headed nature of Iranian officialdom. There is no co-ordination between warring factions and departments, so they all dream up their own stories and many find themselves duty-bound to disagree with each other. When the final version emerges, it is not as if anyone will ultimately be held accountable. Truth is a fluid and ultimately inconsequential commodity in Tehran. Trying to explain such Persian subtleties to Whelan would be impossible so Shirkhan swallowed his pride and lit a cigarette.

And anyway, didn't Pegler always say you should never use words like 'sensational' and 'dramatic' because the killing of twelve men should speak for itself? Didn't Pegler say you should always lead your story with the news? Assassins killed twelve senior Iranian officials in two hours on Sunday and the interior ministry promptly blamed al Qaeda for the murders. Shirkhan looked across the bureau at the slug pounding the keys with infantile glee. The guy's a total fraud.

More worrying to Shirkhan was the fact that even he, with his keen nose for the moods of Iran's tenebrous netherworld, simply could not work out who was behind all this.

Downtown at the British embassy, Seb Maynard was having the same problem. The ambassador was becoming more tetchy every time another FCO bigwig interrupted his lazy Sunday afternoon to ask what was going on out there. A Revolutionary Guard colonel had been blown up in Manouchehri Street, right opposite the embassy. A black plume of smoke hung in the windless air and the street was a cacophony of shrieks, sirens and blaring horns. Seb wanted to go out and take a look, if only to check on his friends, the two elderly Jews who gave him discounts on their coffee-pots and fake antiques. But the ambassador expressly forbade it.

In fact his friends were shaken but alive. Solomon's forearm had been pierced by a shard of window-glass the size of a dagger. His brother rummaged for some bandaging but Solomon stuck his chin out defiantly.

'I am so old, I don't bleed any more, brother. I am a fossil.'

Seb knew rather better than Bernie Whelan that the Delphic utterances from the ministries made no sense, or at least could not be reconciled with each other. He rang journalists, consultants, analysts, history lecturers and know-it-all businessmen to see if any of them had any conception of what was going on. Some were pretty confident. Definitely al Qaeda. Or definitely the mujahidin. But they were all taken aback by the ambitious synchronization of the hits. That would have involved a lot of people, more than Iranian al Qaeda and mujahidin networks were thought to be able to muster. Seb studiously bound all the threads together but avoided any conclusion. How the hell could he know what was going on when he wasn't allowed beyond the lofty brick walls of the embassy? And even if he had escaped through the cat-flap, how would he have ever cut through the walls of silence around men such as Hashemian and Baharvand? These men are spiders who sit under leaves, far from their twitching webs.

His mobile buzzed on the corner of his desk. Officially speaking, he wasn't allowed to keep a mobile switched on in the embassy as they were feared to be favourite listening devices for the Iranian intelligence service. But Seb often forgot to turn it off. 'Negar' appeared on the glowing screen. He puffed out. This wasn't exactly a good time.

'Hi, Negar.'

'Joonam, my soul, chetoori, how are you? Look, I'll make this quick as I know you must be really busy with all these bombs but thank you so much. Thank you, thank you, thank you.'

'Erm, you're welcome but what exactly am I meant to have done?'

'My brother is back. My darling brother. We are all here and everyone is so happy. I don't know what you did but they let him go. Mum, Dad, everyone says thank you. Oh Seb, you really are a darling.' She smacked a kiss down the line.

This needed to be handled carefully. Beautiful women in your debt were generally agreed to be a good thing.

'Well, I'd love to claim responsibility of course. But I really can't. Naturally I raised the matter with the ambassador and asked that we relay our concern to the foreign ministry people. But I really don't know what happened after that.'

'Oh, that must have been what did it. I mean, what else could it have been?'

Luck.

'I don't know. But this hardly matters. All that matters is that he's out. You must all be so relieved.'

'Oh we are. It's just great. And you deserve a special treat Seb, you really do. I think I know what you might like.'

'Do you indeed?'

'Aha. What are you doing tonight?'

Damn these bombs. Damn the ambassador.

'I don't know. Not much, but the ambo's keeping us chained to our desks. I got here at seven this morning and I don't see us getting out until nine or ten. It depends where this all goes, I guess. What are you thinking?'

'Ring me when you are finished, then Seb gets his big reward.'

A nation in meltdown suddenly seemed delightfully irrelevant.

Oblivious to the mayhem in Tehran and Qom, the Tajik had spent the morning accustoming himself to the idiosyncrasies of his Dragunov rifle. He had sent the tea-boy 1,300 metres down the valley with instructions to tie small squares of cloth into the branches of a juniper tree. The teenager had been sceptical that such shots were possible, suggesting they were just big talk when the fighters boasted round the campfire. The Tajik laughed politely and said many US professionals felt comfortable taking a head-shot at 2,000 metres. The Dragunov's sight, though, would only allow for the drop of the bullet over 1,300.

'But it is still a fine weapon, sir.'

'Yes, my lad, I am too attached to it. It's never let me down yet.'

'El Hamdulillah.'

The Tajik stretched out in some scree, resting his shoulder against a smooth-sided rock. He puffed away at a cigarette as he waited for the boy to scamper down the valley, absent-mindedly tracking the little mountain goat in his sights, flitting between head-shots and the broad of his back. Abdollah's little helper did good time and strung up the first cloth as instructed. Although the wind was slight, the cloth was flapping fitfully. A satisfactory challenge. The boy wondered whether the Tajik could even see it. He then retreated fifty yards up the hillside and sat on his haunches among a pile of rocks.

The Tajik watched the cloth squalling about in the PSO-1 sight and emptied his lungs. He squeezed the trigger with the ball of his finger, exerting a calm, steady pressure. The rifle cracked and the cloth flew out of the tree. The tea-boy saw it floating in the breeze a dozen yards behind the juniper, dropping like a parachutist in distress. He waved his arms at the Tajik and whooped with excitement. The Tajik lit another cigarette and waited for the boy to rig up a second square of cloth. When he had done so, the assassin laid his half-smoked cigarette on a stone beside him. He exhaled his last lungful of smoke and eased the trigger back with the same constant pressure. At that very moment he saw the cloth whip up in the wind, leaping above the reticule. He knew that he had missed.

All told, he hit three times out of five. Those were odds he liked when it translated to hitting a man well over six feet tall.

The breathless boy clambered up to him as he was cleaning his weapon, running a rag through the barrel. He hugged his new hero, told him that he was a real warrior and that he could even become an honorary Baluch. The Tajik slapped the boy on the back and told him to lead the way back to Abdollah's caves.

Approaching the hideout, they could see that a large crowd had gathered on one of the broader ledges. The atmosphere was feverish, cut through with solemn recitatives of 'Allahu Akbar'. The Tajik slowed his pace and stretched his fingers round the pistol in his pocket. The boy, rushing ahead, had become excited by what he could see.

'Come, sir, come. It looks like they have captured some Revolutionary Guards again.'

The crowd on the ledge parted for the Tajik. Commander Abdollah looked even more magisterial in full turban and robes, wielding a glinting scimitar over the decapitated corpses of two Iranian soldiers. Flies were already swarming around the rivulets of congealing blood that ran across the ledge. The Baluch fighters chanted 'Allahu Akbar' once again to greet the Tajik. Knowing his role well, the hit-man punched the air and echoed their cry.

In his heart, the old, dull ache gnawed at him. If you are new to death, you feel revolted, sickened or scared by it. Those are ephemeral emotions which you can easily leave behind. His kind of man carried a far weightier melancholy around with him, a burden he would never shake off. He had stomached enough of this slaughter and swore, yet again, that this would be his last job.

In the old days, he used to worry. He used to worry whether

dead men had once appreciated the numinous tapestry hidden in the rocks, rivers and deadwood that surrounded them. But the Tajik no longer saw the dead as his responsibility.

When he was among these people, he felt that he could only be a Russian. A group of Afghans had once shared with him details of a torturing technique they used on Russian soldiers: it took the form of a trial. An asp was placed in a bottle and the neck of the bottle was rammed up the soldier's arse. The bottle was then warmed with a candle for a minute. If the snake sat tight, well, the soldier could go on his way with a kick for good luck. If God willed it that the snake shoot up the Russian's arse, then that was that. God had always willed it. They had roared with laughter but the Tajik had seethed with hidden rage, knowing then that he was, quite simply, a Russian. Back in Moscow, they might see him as one of these people, some kind of noble savage, but he wasn't. He could prove it to them by reciting Lermontov or humming melodies from Glinka. In his teenage years, he had suffered some kind of schizophrenia about his identity. But that was all gone. After killing Baharvand, the Tajik vowed that he never wanted to see these people and these God-forsaken mountains again.

'What a morning!' Abdollah shouted. 'Great happenings'.

The Tajik cast an eye over the corpses.

'You ran into a patrol?'

'Today we could take a pick of patrols. And they all had stories to tell. Your mission is truly blessed by the Almighty. Let us go up to the cave and discuss these matters over tea. But first I must wash and pray after sacrificing these sheep.'

Abdollah clicked his fingers at the teaboy who ran over to him.

'And so, is our guest a fine shot?' he asked, pinching the boy's cheek.

'He is the finest shot I have seen. He could shoot a wasp at night.'

'Bravo, bravo,' Abdollah said with a broad smile. 'He's going to have to be good as half the bloody Iranian army is out looking for him.'

The boy puffed his chest out.

'Only half?'

The Tajik knew that counsellors close to the warlord Ismail Khan in Herat had been about to rumble him back in Afghanistan. But this was impressively slick footwork. Ismail Khan, the Lion of Herat, a fellow ethnic Tajik, had swallowed the killer's story and had believed that the assassin was a merchant from Kabul. The two men rattled away together in Persian, working through the knotted tendrils of Afghan family trees to work out who their shared cousins must be. But the captains and viziers around Khan could smell a GRU man like a turd in a back alley. This man was clearly working for the Russians. The Afghans had sixth, seventh and eighth senses. Russian bombers had pulverised their world and they knew the methods of these flat-faced Slavic savages. The hit-man worked back through the trail. The CIA got suspicious when news of the Baharvand plot reached Dolokhov, the hood at the embassy in Washington. Then Ismail Khan's lieutenants sold some gen to the Yanks: a suspected GRU killer had disappeared off the radar. He was headed west, over the Iranian border to Mashhad. Damn, the CIA were getting good, at long last. The Tajik realised some cunning devil had crossed the wires on him.

This was definitely time to check in with Kryuchkov. He dug into his hold-all and pulled out the sat phone.

The military attaché had already filled an ashtray with cigarette butts. GRU high-command had also spent Saturday night poring over satellite images of massive troop movements within Iran. Iranian soldiers on the Russian payroll confirmed that a huge manhunt was under way, that a CIA gun-for-hire had been parachuted into Mashhad.

Kryuchkov snatched up the receiver as soon as it rang. Please, please, be him.

'Russian embassy. Good morning.'

Thank God. It's him. 'Ah, is that Mr Kryuchkov?'

'It is. How may I help?'

'It's Pechorin here, ringing in connection with the reception for Russian gas investors on Thursday. I fear I lost my invitation and I have forgotten at what time it starts?'

'Oh, no problem, the reception's at seven, I'm pretty sure it is.'

The Tajik was impressed by the embassy man's coolness.

'Seven. OK, got it. How are things at the embassy?'

'All right, all right. There's a bit of a kerfuffle with the local staff about knocking down some big nests built by the migrant storks.'

'Oh, yes, that's bad luck to the Iranians, isn't it?'

'Yes the lak-lak is a hajji, a pilgrim bird. You can't knock his nest down.'

'Ha, right. Good luck sorting that out. I'll see you on Thursday at seven then.'

'See you, Mr Pechorin. So long.'

The Tajik switched off the sat phone and appraised his situation. Seven. So the plot was blown. Six was the all-clear. Seven, the cat was out of the bag. That matched with what Abdollah was saying. The area was awash with Iranian soldiery. Any reference to birds meant that he was free to fly home and abort, but could go on if he could see a way through Iranian lines. A reference to flowers or the embassy gardens would have ended the mission there and then. He would be winging his way back to his snug dacha in the forest. The dacha and Laika.

The tea-boy brought a piping-hot glass of well-stewed tea and the Tajik stared down the valley, lost in internal debate.

An esurient trio of Griffon vultures had been circling for at least a quarter of an hour, waiting for the fighters to clear away from the lower ledge. Finally, they dropped through the hot, dry air, braking their descent with that imperious wingspan, and began to strip the carcasses of the two murdered soldiers.

Abdollah reappeared, brimming over with a frenetic energy.

'My, my. You are an honoured guest,' he said, excitedly rubbing his thighs as he settled on a carpet opposite the Tajik.

'Why did you not tell us straight off you were CIA? This is a great honour for us. We are proud to be part of this. It's been a great morning for all Iranians.'

'You defeated many Iranian troops then? Glory be to God.'

'El Hamdulillah, but ours were small victories compared with these CIA jobs. An ayatollah in Qom, Hashemian, judges, colonels. You guys are ripping the Iranians' trousers off and spanking them hard on the ass. And we'll make sure that Baharvand's death is our greatest glory. Baharvand will die like a mangy dog. Oh, this is so exciting.'

The Tajik would have plenty of time to work out this puzzle. All that was of immediate importance was that the Baluchi warlord still thought the assassination of Baharvand was a realistic prospect. Abdollah was presumably jealous of Rigi and assumed that his rival was the one being courted by the Americans. For some reason, he now assumed that Uncle Sam had shifted his affections. A successful first job could prove to be a nice little earner for Abdollah's militiamen.

'Of course, I know what the problem is,' Abdollah said with resolve, slapping his palms down gleefully into the dust. 'You still don't really know who we are, whose side we are really on. The CIA doesn't want to find itself fighting shoulder to shoulder with al Qaeda. I understand your concern. I will be honest with you, my friend. Of course there are al Qaeda here with us. Five or six of them, Wahhabi crazies. I don't like them and if you want, I can have them killed. Here and now.'

Abdollah pulled a pistol from his belt and cocked it. The Tajik held his tongue.

'But look, these nuts could prove useful to us. I don't like them any more than you do. They do not understand the true faith. But, by God, do they hate a Shi'ite heretic? At the moment, we are fighting the same war. We can dispense with them later. You go into battle with some Iranian troops and these Arab maniacs will fight like hashishin. It's quite a sight. But if we promise them a fast-track to paradise, then they can kill Baharvand for us. We strap seven tonnes of explosives round one of the Arabs. Boom. No Baharvand.'

'Suicide bombers are notoriously hit and miss. Get me in range. Then get me out.'

Abdollah shrugged.

'Very well, as you please. It will be an honour.'

'So what happened this morning? How did you catch the two soldiers?'

'Oh, the Iranians are sending these bastards all over our territory. They are like lambs wandering into the domain of the lion. Poor kids, they told us everything. They hoped that might save their lives. They are all looking for a certain American assassin. That would be you, my dangerous friend.'

'Do they know the target?'

'They have no idea. But our Baluch brothers in Anareh tell us there are roadblocks every few hundred yards. So somebody knows that you are after Baharvand.'

Those Baluch brothers in Kerman would presumably be the opium runners, men who would know everything hours before it happened. But they would be frustrated by the roadblocks, left with huge stashes in the cellars of their safe houses. Valuable Turkish clients would hardly be sympathetic to their excuses.

'So, how do you rate our chances of taking him out?'

'Very good. Don't worry, this is an easy job. Baharvand is making a huge mistake.'

'He is?'

'Sure. Our friends in Anareh say he's planning some kind of large political set piece, a rally on Tuesday night.'

'Why?'

Abdollah shrugged.

'Why is really not our problem. But what's obvious is that he is holding it in a place where he can bus in all the faithful to clap and cheer him: his miners, his estate workers, his schools and his factories. Everybody on the Baharvand payroll looks like they are going to be there. Of course, the security will be impenetrable. They are gathering the crowd five whole hours before he is due to speak, handing out bowls of stew to keep everyone happy. They are already setting up scaffolding twenty miles outside Anareh.'

'Can we get close and then out of there?'

'Sure we can, and the cover of night makes it perfect.'

Abdollah had whetted his appetite. He could already see the wiry cleric in the tritium glow of the telescopic night-sight.

'So, what would be the plan?'

'We don't move by road. We move by night across the desert and by day through the mountain passes, places only known to shepherds and the Baluch. The mountains reach the desert plain five miles short of where they are building the stage.'

'That's where I have to work alone. What's the terrain like?'

183

'Ah, that's the beauty of the thing, my friend. You don't need to give a damn about the terrain until you head back. You can use the qanat, the underground waterway that will take you to as close to Baharvand as you want to get. It runs from the mountains right into Anareh. I don't think you'll find any Revolutionary Guards down there. You crawl down the conduit until you are, say, one kilometre away. Or further if you like. Wait for nightfall, shoot the bastard, head back to the Jebal Barez under the cover of darkness. We'll spirit you away again.'

It sounded a bravura plan, the type of gambit that appealed both to the Baluch and the Tajik.

'Easy as that?'

'Ever so easy. On your way back, we can have some real fun. We can create diversions all over the mountains. My men can light fires at all sorts of misleading spots across the mountains. The Iranians will hear the cries of the Baluch in the valleys, the crackle of automatic gunfire and the thud of mortars. All leading those fools away from you. Oh, it'll be chaos up there. Real hot stuff. Wonderful.'

Abdollah was warming to his theme and his sense of mission. It was the sort of operation that made him glad to be alive.

'And how many men can you get for a mission of this kind?'

'Oh, sixty, eighty, a hundred. I can't imagine that anyone would want to be left out. It will be a glorious triumph. How my lads will long to tell their grandchildren of the night when Baharvand was killed!'

It was pouring in Brittany. The unremitting deluge pummelled the granite walls and lustrous grey slates of the farmhouse. The latch had ripped off one of the pastel blue shutters which clattered on its hinges in the gale. Juliette gave little thought to the gruff, humourless Atlantic that often clamoured for

184

attention like a spoiled child. One shouldn't give it the satisfaction.

Her latest man was in the hall, ringing his mum.

Juliette, the French country vet, had listened to the news of the assassinations in Iran while the kettle boiled. And after all those protests. No wonder Andy isn't coming back to Paris for a while, they must want him in London. Or Tehran, who knows? She didn't know whether she was meant to hate Iran or love it. It had been such a part of his life and she had inherited the fascination vicariously. Or maybe she wasn't fascinated so much by that bloody country but rather by why it had destroyed her husband and her marriage. In a sense, she consistently reminded Andy, it was worse to be married to a spy than actually to be one. He had colleagues with whom he could discuss all the agonies of his clandestine past. But how could she explain her own anguish to her friends without betraying secrets of state? Who could she ever tell? Could she settle down for a girly-chat with a Breton farmer's wife and confess that her husband often seemed cold and distant because of the men he'd killed or let die? Sometimes she wished Andy had just been a philanderer or an alcoholic. That would have made it so much easier. Being the sensitive and affable wife of a spy is hell on earth.

He'd hit her once, in his sleep. It was in the middle of some major operation and he'd been coiled like a rattle-snake for weeks. From time to time, he'd been twitching as he slept and mumbling deliriously. Turkish she thought. Maybe Persian. How should she know? Then he'd convulsed and smacked her hard across the face. She'd wittingly deceived herself into believing that he was one of these bureaucratic types, that he never used guns or hit people. But there was something about the way he'd hit her, so grimly professional. He'd jerked up and smacked her first with the fist then brought the elbow across to make sure. She rolled out of bed and blacked out.

She had heard these stories before. There was one about some French undercover hood who'd worked for months in Algeria, right at the worst of it. He was our man in the casbah, playing cat and mouse with the FLN. When he got back to Normandy, he went to stay with his brother and made the mistake of relaxing. He had a whisky and fell asleep one evening, slumped in front of the television set. His brother's five-year-old daughter came down, saw him there and attempted a practical joke. She crept up behind his armchair and put her small, cold hands across his eyes. 'Guess Who?' In one spasm, he had whipped up the empty whisky glass, smashed it and driven it straight into her face. For the rest of his life, he would have to look at the jagged, circular scar that disfigured his otherwise beautiful niece.

Juliette told Andy that story as they sat in the kitchen in the apartment in Paris. It was three o'clock in the morning. She spat blood into the sink and he pressed ice on to the deep, yellow bruise that was spreading across her cheek.

'God, it's going to look like a pony kicked me,' she said, examining herself in the mirror. Blood was spattered down the front of her nightgown.

Andy apologised for the millionth time. He was furious with himself to a degree that defied all reason. Juliette told him he was suffering from extreme nervous exhaustion and that if he were a horse, they'd have to shoot him.

At that point, she forgave him completely. He was a man wounded by a screwed-up world. She wanted to look after him, to mother him. Maybe she could even convince the man she loved to quit this infantile shadow-world. She did her duty, reacting to being knocked out with a string of laconic jokes about wife-beaters. But by dawn, she knew it wasn't going to work. She had lost him. She could live with a man who'd hit her. She couldn't live with a man who could never forgive himself. If he could have no sincere pride in himself, how could he ever truly love her?

She worried about what it was that he hated so much. Was it that his darling wife had been hurt? She began to doubt it. The fear was more that he had betrayed himself, that he had shown himself to be weak and subliminally vengeful. How could she be expected to care for him when he didn't give a damn about himself? It was impossible. It was finished.

She had blamed that bitch Cath Spedding, as well. That woman didn't just offer and accept love, she had made Andy believe that he had to be qualified for affection through knowledge, intelligence, bravery and Christ knows what, satisfying a woman's undeclared tick-list. How could she poison a man's mind like that? Andy believed he was a failure because he didn't live up to ridiculous standards that existed only in his mind, and in the mind of some twisted, venomous English *salope*. Why could he never let her go and understand a real woman? Juliette didn't care about Andy's failings. She just wanted him to love her. Somehow and perversely, he was just too critical of himself to do so.

Marko, the replacement squeeze, had finished talking on the phone. Juliette had spread a copy of *Le Monde* over the great oak table and was loyally reading the editorial on Iran. They had run a short profile of Baharvand. Andy had told her that his men were hanged in Abadan but he had never told her about the Ayatollah.

Marko started to dice onions and carrots. He drizzled oil into a Le Creuset casserole. She smiled at him and forged on with *Le Monde's* analysis of the Iranian crisis. It was a Gallic masterpiece, argued with consummate brilliance from an armchair. The narrative strands intermittently sank beneath the waves of aphorisms and political theory but essentially they agreed with the great Bernie Whelan. A real revolution was impossible, they argued, because too many people had too many vested interests in the status quo, the rule of the clerics. Popular democratic reform would simply be unwelcome to powerful people who had feathered their nests rather nicely in Iran's protectionist, uncompetitive economy. Juliette thought that made some sense. But didn't they just treat people so badly out there in Iran? Was it only the business classes who made revolutions?

Of course, she was right to be sceptical. If only that Parisian pundit could appreciate how alienated the business class felt after Ahmadinejad's internal coup. If only he had seen the passion with which Baby Baharvand had mapped out the counter-coup, led by men who felt there was no longer any way to rake in fat profits.

Le Monde would have been right back in 2005. The glitterati of Tehran threw parties in their tower-blocks, sipped cocktails and lounged by their pools. In public they may have griped about those 'damn mullahs' but, in fact, those same 'damn mullahs' had put them where they were. Clerics happily accepted jibes when the cheques kept rolling in. This affluent class, which spends half the year in California, has spawned a raft of conspiracy theories among the less fortunate classes that stare up at the marmoreal apartments of Zafaranieh and Fereshteh, Tehran's Chelsea and Hampstead. Most of the theories focus on the surreal world of opposition television, beamed in from planet California.

If you listen to the stories in the bazaar, the consensus is that Iranian opposition television is so bad that it must be a sham. Iranian businessmen set up these channels so they can pretend to Congressmen that they are anti-regime. In fact, the conspiracy theory goes, the channels are so atrocious that they must be given the green light by the government in Tehran. Poor south Tehranis are cajoled into thinking that it's better to stick with the Islamic Republic if this is the best the opposition can do. But the supremacy of these rich appeasers was under threat, creating the hidden catalyst behind Baharvand's revolution.

Yet the column inches, obsessed by the bubbling soup of Iran's economic and religious tensions, all missed the greater truth about successful coups: ultimately they hinge on accidents and human foibles. Coups succeed because one captain refuses to fire on a crowd or fail because a river bursts its banks and swamps the main road into the capital. Similarly, the success of Baharvand's coup would hinge on whether Jahangiri and his muqannis cleared a sump of floodwater out of the largest of the qanats running through to Anareh. If they did shift the blockage, the Tajik would be in place in time for a clean shot on Tuesday night.

Juliette pushed the newspaper to one side and watched Marko prepare lunch. The onions sizzled as he tossed them into the boiling oil. He raised his eyebrows excitedly. Such an easy man to love.

Cath rang Baby Baharvand, who grumbled about his exile to the benighted hinterland of Hadrian's Wall. A week without access to Fortnum & Mason was an agony beyond human endurance. An unsympathetic Cath suggested that he might be able to shed light on the assassinations.

'I thought you told us there was no list of senior figures to be liquidated?' she began.

'When it comes to the really big names, there isn't. But Iran, as Mr Trevarthen knows, is this kind of country. Generally, at the height of a coup, most military commanders will sit tight and wait to see which way the wind blows. They are sensible men and rational men. Certain lieutenants in the middle order will not be so prudent. That is regrettable but we need to take some kind of pre-emptive action. Let's say that we are just clearing the decks.'

'I am sorry, Mr Baharvand, but this is markedly different from what you told us. You did say that some bloodshed was inevitable but only because some people would resist the course of your uncle's take-over. What we are seeing now are targeted, calculated killings. How much more of this is yet to come?'

'That I would not be in a position to say. I agree with you that operations of this nature are unfortunate but I would ask you to understand our position here. I handed over a disc with vital co-ordinates on it. If those targets were eliminated, we would ultimately be able to reduce this kind of bloodshed.'

'I hardly think that it makes sense to saddle us with any of the blame, Mr Baharvand.'

'No, no, not at all. This is certainly not a question of blame. I think, though, that there is a need of some acceptance of practicalities on your part. These men were the strongest obstacles to my uncle seizing power – a transfer of power that is undeniably in your national interest. The methods may be more robust than you would like. But welcome to Iran, Madam.'

Welcome to Iran, Madam. Cath decided to add his name to her blacklist.

She was still bristling when Andy arrived at the ziggurat's ramshackle operations' room. It had come to resemble a crime-scene investigation tent. The walls were covered with maps and photographs, messily highlighted with pen and punctured with coloured pins. Four televisions had been rigged up to Persian channels and a ginger-haired woman, misleadingly named Bella, had come over from GCHQ to process the surfeit of information appearing on Iranian blogs.

'I wonder who they won't admit is dead,' Andy said, dropping his overcoat on to the back of a chair.

'How do you mean?'

'Well, I know that Baharvand has somehow got Jafari and state television on his side, but it's unusual for the Iranians to be so candid about an enemy being this successful within their borders. They would only admit twelve killings like this to give the appearance of honesty, to mask the fact that someone far higher up is dead.'

'Ooh. Really? You think so?'

'No, I am almost certainly being far-fetched. But it's possible. But there again, this will already have had an effect. The Tehran rumour mill will by now be convinced that Ahmadinejad and the leader are dead. They will have to show themselves pretty soon.'

'Right. That's a good point.'

She cast an eye at Iranian state television running continuously in the corner of the room.

'Oh my God, that's him, isn't it?'

Against a green backdrop, looking grandfatherly and scholarly, was the viper. The text-bar underneath read: an address to the nation by Ayatollah Ali Baharvand.

Since joining the Iran team six months before, Cath had made exceptional strides with Persian and was beginning to find her feet, reading leaked diplomatic documents, journal articles and transcripts of bugged conversations. But the fluidity of the spoken language and Baharvand's indulgent use of Koranic Arabisms cast her adrift. Andy turned up the volume and leant against a desk, jotting phrases on to an A4 pad beside him.

'What's he saying?' Cath asked.

Andy paused and waited for a moment to catch the flow. Persian is a difficult language to translate simultaneously because the main verb comes at the end of the sentence. By the time you render it into English, the speaker has galloped into the middle of the next phrase.

Andy, nevertheless, made a stab at it.

'The Islamic Republic of Iran has been cruelly stricken by many tragedies over the last week. These matters have caused grief not only within our country but have made the world weep with us. Innocent lives have been lost across Iran. By the grace of God and through the strength of Islam, we shall prevail and the Islamic Republic will vanquish all of its foes, domestic and foreign. The strength and the valour of the martyrs lies deep within us as a people and we can always draw upon the inherited spirit of Hossein when confronted with adversity.'

Baharvand continued in the same vein for almost ten minutes. He told of the dusty battlefield at Kerbala where Hossein was slain and interpreted choice Hadith of the prophet. Few viewers could have doubted that they were watching one of the founders of the republic defending its values and expressing regret about a crimson skein of murder unseen since the 1980s.

'I'm waiting for the punchline,' Cath joked, feigning a swoon over her desk.

But no one rushes a sermoner.

'I know that today's assassinations will lead many of you to fear that you are back in the old days, that you are back in the dark night of the Imposed War and the revolutionary chaos. But those were days when it seemed so difficult to defend an imperilled aspiration. Today, conversely, we are blessed. It is easy to defend the revolution by asking what made the revolution victorious. I am saddened when I see students, minorities and unions protesting because I believe in the unity of the Islamic Republic and the original vision that granted us victory. There will be no minorities and no fringes in a real Islamic Republic.

Within the framework of our constitution we can create a genuine and powerful government of national unity. A handful of fanatics from al Qaeda cannot destroy what we have built here in Iran. Let us join hands and fight the enemies of the state.'

Cath wondered whether the viper had said anything at all.

'So, what do you reckon? Sounds like he's sticking with the Islamic Republic for now.'

'He could never betray the revolution. That's his life. A government of national unity is brilliantly vague. It's typical Baharvand. It could win him friends but it could mean pretty much anything. I'd say he's just styling himself at the moment. He's the rock. He's the safe pair of hands who can steady the ship when it all turns to shit. Which it will.'

'Are you actually beginning to believe that he's going to do what he promised?'

'I have no idea. He's up to something but I am not sure what.'

'But just by being the person broadcast first, it's like you said, it will fan a feeling that he's the man to trust. The leader and president may as well be dead. But by stealing their thunder, isn't he endangering himself? Won't the intelligence go round and ask him what he's doing by running his own broadcasts?'

'Maybe, but I actually think not. You've got to remember how senior Baharvand is. To most viewers it would seem natural that he appear. Sure, a Grand Ayatollah like Montazeri can end up under house arrest despite once being Khomeini's adored heir apparent, but that sort of volte-face actually takes a long time. Within the intelligence now, they won't know where all the instructions are coming from. Baharvand is using speed to confound the Iranian command structure. Nobody will want to ask what's going on through fear that it has been sanctioned by someone more powerful than themselves.'

Cath stared at the IRIB screen which had switched to

innocuous shots of shimmering mountain streams and spring meadows filled with poppies. Iran looked such a beautiful country.

At dusk there were two almost simultaneous protests. Several thousand Kurds gathered on the banks of Lake Zarivar. In the capital, students brushed themselves down after their battering at the hands of the basij and regrouped outside the university's main gates. After facing down some fierce salvoes of invective, the police dispersed both groups without difficulty. Up on Lake Zarivar, some exuberant Revolutionary Guardsmen fired bursts of gunfire over the Kurds as they headed back to their villages.

The police had heard the slogans the demonstrators chanted a thousand times before. There was one new one though: for some reason, both groups had decided to call for a government of national unity.

Shortly past ten o'clock, a Revolutionary Guard colonel in Tabriz was found drowned in his bath. He was wearing full regalia. State media described his death as a tragic loss to the nation and gave a detailed account of his missions behind Iraqi lines. It was assumed that he'd been a comrade of Ahmadinejad's.

Andy arrived at 76 Beryl Road soon after eight o'clock. The neck of the Côtes du Rhône bottle poked out from the off-licence's brown paper bag.

Nazila was done up to the nines. Mother and daughter had exchanged sharp words. Najmeh had temporarily refused to attend any dinner party where a middle-aged matriarch wore silver strappy sandals. Anoush overheard the word 'sluttish' in the bilingual cross-fire. But Nazila had known Andy and Cyrus since before Najmeh was born, and she would wear whatever she damn well liked.

Andy complimented both women on their choice of garments. When his back was turned, Nazila poked her tongue out at her daughter. Anoush and Cyrus were standing at the far end of the kitchen, drinking a couple of beers. Cyrus had doubled up with laughter and was pawing Anoush's shoulder.

'What's the big joke then?' Andy enquired.

'Yes, tell, tell,' Najmeh chimed in.

'Ooh, it's about old Bobby K.'

Najmeh raised her eyebrows and shook her head to signal that the name meant nothing to her. Mother, examining the stews slowly reducing on the hob, cringed and said that her daughter really didn't need to know about such people.

Anoush laughed and handed Andy a beer.

'Bobby Kalantari,' Andy began, 'was this party-boy we all knew back in the seventies. He was a clever guy, a surgeon by training I seem to recall, but more of a lounge lizard by profession.'

'He sounds my kind o' guy. But must be getting on a bit I guess,' Najmeh enthused. Nazila raised her eyebrows. How little her daughter knew of the world and men like Bobby Kalantari.

'Well, he wouldn't be a great choice,' Andy confessed. 'You see Bobby was one of those fellows that things always happened to. He was famous for having the flashiest car in Tehran, a Lamborghini Miura. He used to race it down the highway to Karaj. Convinced that the revolution would only last a few months, he wrapped the Miura in plastic sheeting and buried it underground. Loads of the Shah's ministers did the same thing with their cars.'

'No way. That's surreal.'

'Anyhow, he buried it under a potting shed, or greenhouse, or something and goes to California. He comes back six years later and there's a twenty-five storey block of flats over his car.'

'Ha, ha. That's hilarious. But at least it's safe, I guess,' Najmeh added. 'So, Cyrus, what's he done now?'

'Well, he's moved back to Tehran full-time. He got himself a beautiful apartment in Niavaran and cars and some business partners and he's basically doing OK again. Then two months ago he went off to spend three weeks in Paris, leaving his trusted Afghan houseboy in charge of the flat. Now, this guy is an illiterate farm-worker from Herat, called Ahmad or something, but he's very smart. As soon as Bobby gets back from Paris, he keeps getting all these calls from young women looking for 'Mr Darius'. The first few calls, he just says it's the wrong number. But then it all dawns on him. As soon as he goes out, Ahmad the Afghan dresses up in his linen suit, goes out in his sports car and throws parties. He's been passing himself off as Bobby's son.'

Even Nazila dissolved into laughter.

'Did he sack him?'

Cyrus gave the big frog grin and shook his head.

'Not at all. He was really impressed by the guy's initiative.'

Anoush peered into the stews.

'I think we're ready, no?'

Nazila seated everyone at the table and laid out the steaming saucepans. First was the fesenjun, chicken drowned in a pomegranate and walnut sauce. Then, a ghormeh sabzi, succulent chunks of lamb with sauteed herbs.A knob of butter melted across the plate of fluffy, saffron rice. Everyone piped in with cries of enthusiam for the winter spread. Cyrus resignedly forgot his vegetarianism.

With a rallying cry of 'Nush-e jun', spoons cut in the rice and bottles of wine were uncorked.

'Well soon we'll be having wine again in Tehran. Oh, those places on Valiasr I used to go to before the revolution. They'll all be re-opened,' Anoush said.

'Here's to that,' said Cyrus, raising his glass.

'Dream on Dad,' Najmeh corrected. 'If anything happens in Iran, they'll just replace one group of nutters with another, that's what always happens. Don't give us all that 'the 1970s were great' bullshit. They were great for boozy naval officers.'

'Absolutely,' Andy said. 'Tehran in the 1970s was a bit like Portsmouth.'

But nothing could distract Anoush from his reveries.

'And the casinos. The casinos. You've got to understand we were on our way to becoming one of the most powerful nations on earth. Six million barrels per day. We could have been like France, we still could be.'

This was a subject on which Cyrus strongly disagreed with his old friend.

'I don't know where all this stuff is going but Iran will sure as hell never become a democracy.'

'Why not?' Nazila protested, laying down her spoon. 'What's the difference between the French and the Iranians? We have the human talent, we have more natural resources. Maybe our time is coming.'

'You just cannot take away the centuries of servitude,' Cyrus said. 'Iran is like an abused child. The people may claim to hate their tyrants, but deep down they need and love them. And it's not just the ayatollahs. It was Cyrus the Great, it was Shah Abbas, it was Reza Shah. We need big despots kicking us around.'

Baharvand was Putin. The survivor from the inside. The patriarch.

'Oh, that's horrible talk and you know it. You just like saying things to sound controversial, Cyrus. You shouldn't do it in front of Najmeh. She'll start repeating it all.'

Najmeh had indeed registered the 'abused child' metaphor. She loved it and would wheel it out several times in arguments with her parents.

Nazila regrouped. She had great respect for Iran's Jews, Esther's children, but they didn't see the country fairly, she felt. She had seen those extraordinary sepia photographs of Cyrus's ancestors. There were the Hakims, the doctors of the Qajar royal court, with their heavy beards and fezes. There was his great-aunt who dressed as a male dandy. Somehow, Cyrus's people lived their own incredible lives and Nazila worried they never quite saw her country straight.

'There is, of course, a little something in what you say about Iranians needing the whip hand from time to time. But that's only because of the centuries in which we have been victims of other people's history: Arabs and their Islam, the Russians, the British, the Americans. It just needs time to evolve into a real democracy.'

'About three thousand years,' Cyrus retorted. 'The reliance on big leaders means we have no history of middle management. Everybody has passed the buck for millennia. Nobody can decide about anything. The country just doesn't work. It never did.'

'The casinos used to work,' Anoush volunteered, trying to steer the conversation away from politics. But Nazila wasn't to be distracted.

'But with the level of education being preserved, real change is always possible.'

Cyrus nodded at this.

'That's partly true,' he said. 'But the quality of Iranian education is something of a myth. Iran certainly feeds the brain drain by churning out some of the best doctors and engineers in the world. The problem is that the non-scientific education system has been almost entirely bulldozed. Students in literature and the liberal arts just spew out pro-regime dogma. There's no academic rigour any more.'

'Sounds like Britain,' Andy moaned, reaching for a second helping of ghormeh sabzi.

'Oh you old fuddy-duddy,' Najmeh shrieked. 'I happen to be quite brilliant, thank you very much.'

Andy lifted his spoon in a sign of surrender.

Tehran was used to bottling up its emotions and life on the street seemed normal, if subdued. Seb had agreed to meet Negar at a fruit-juice seller on Shariati Street, close to the embassy compound at Gholhak. She had a pretty, if quiet, friend in tow: Parastou. Seb bought them both banana milk shakes and dared to hope that his treat might be imminent.

Lomax had cut short his weekend in Oxfordshire. He was shocked by the sight of Gordon Brown, hunched over his desk in shirt-sleeves. He'd never seen a prime minister looking so haggard. The heavy-jowled minister's son from Kirkcaldy greeted the security chief with an indecipherable grunt, barely looking up from the snow of papers littering his desk. Blair had bequeathed his chancellor a poisoned chalice and the venom was already spreading. Only four months in and Brown was already the unimaginative leader who had to rip off Tory policies. Brown was the lily-liver who didn't dare go to the nation for a general election. He was under the gun over Iraq and the EU constitution. The last thing he needed was yet another crisis boiling over in the Middle East but it looked ominously like he was going to get one.

Lomax waited to be addressed. For all the jesting back at the ziggurat that he was just another one of the Scottish mafia running Britain, there was no instant sympathy on Brown's part. Brown had nothing but unmitigated contempt for his white-tie world and Lomax feared that he was viewed as some kind of Tory prick by the son of the manse. Real Scots didn't go to Eton and Balliol.

'Just got off the phone with Bush,' Brown mouthed, chewing the words with undisguised hostility.

Lomax noted that it was 'Bush', not, heaven forfend, George.

'Looks like Ayatollah Baharvand has landed us in one fuck of a mess.'

'Yes, prime minister.'

'No, Callum, a real, real fucking mess. Bush believes the story that Baharvand's nephew gave SIS. They are convinced that the Ayatollah has the momentum now. This is the last great chance to stop Iran getting the bomb, they tell me. This is the last opportunity we have before we start World War Fucking Three.'

'Are the Israelis leaning on them?'

Brown shrugged.

'Dunno. But I do know they are considering something fucking dumb.'

'Prime minister?'

Brown leaned back in his chair and gently chopped his hand across the desk, stressing each strand of his argument.

'They see this as a once-in-a-lifetime opportunity to strike key Iranian installations with missiles, launched from submarines. They are keen for some Royal Navy solidarity if you see what I am getting at. Shoulder to shoulder again.'

Lomax ran his teeth across his bottom lip. God damn it. Fucking Yanks.

'Essentially, Callum, they think there is a high chance we are going to see divisions of the Revolutionary Guard splinter, then throw their fire-power at each other in the next few days.'

'That's certainly possible,' Lomax concurred.

'In the fog of war, coalition submarines will take out major nuclear sites and strategic targets that would help Baharvand.'

'From the co-ordinates given to us.'

'Exactly, from those co-ordinates. You said no one trusted Baharvand enough to help him like this. Looks like the Americans do, Callum. God knows I want to tell them to fuck off but I'm boxed in.'

'At present, our security evaluation is that we really don't know what Baharvand's up to. Today's assassinations were almost certainly his handiwork and went totally against the grain of what he said he'd do. Unless the Americans, or more likely the Israelis, have some other source of intelligence, we really can have no confidence in this man's motives.'

'Yeah, well, I'm not sure they give a shit about his motives. This is just their opportunity to send Iran back to the stone age.'

8.

IN THE ELEVEN days since Baharvand spirited away his family, Hossein Jafari had lived at a tangent to his own life. He felt like a beetle trapped inside an inverted glass. A thick but invisible bubble separated him from the nation in tumult. He was the impassive lightning-rod of a revolution.

Colonel Nouriani, Baharvand's military chief, had been pleased with Jafari's early efforts. Clearly, in the early days of the propaganda campaign, it was impossible to give prominence to those press conferences in which Bush and Sarkozy had robustly supported the student protests. Still, Jafari found a solution. He gave generous air-time to prolix Iranian officials lambasting the French and Americans as fools or liars. The West, they argued, failed to detect the hand of seditious rabble rousers, al Qaeda and the mujahidin in these unrepresentative demonstrations. Yet, within those parts of the news dedicated to this stock rhetoric from the government, Jafari spliced in twenty seconds of footage of Bush and Sarkozy. Just to show how foolish western leaders were. Naturally, such unprecedented images gave a huge psychological fillip to the crowds who now gathered each night in cities across Iran. Some students even waved posters of Sarkozy. Le héros.

Iranian viewers were swamped with more images of unrest

than they had ever seen before. They now knew their nation stood on the brink. Petrol stations blazed, streets were littered with broken glass and the corpses of murdered clerics were covered with plastic sheeting. It was all true. It must be, they saw it all on state television. Every time protesters gathered, they drew thousands of eager bystanders to their flame, men and women who wondered whether this could really be it. The big one. Most importantly, Jafari had repeated both Baharvand's communiqué and his address to the nation at regular intervals. But Monday would be the most important morning in the seizure of power. The smooth flow of broadcasts from the state networks would make or break Baharvand.

Nouriani arrived at 7.42, leading a khaki cortege of fifteen trucks and three armoured personnel carriers off Valiasr boulevard, down a side street and then into the news compound. Thirty Revolutionary Guardsmen fanned out around the grounds, lurking in the woods above the boating lake in the Park-e Mellat, where, each afternoon, courting couples larked around in ungainly, swan-shaped pedalos. A batch of about forty troops lingered outside, silent and focussed, smoking cigarettes and pacing on the spot to ward off the morning chill. Curious passers-by pointed at the flurry of peaked caps and bayonets. One young man with a goatee raised his mobile to take a quick photograph. Two guardsmen shouted at him and confiscated his phone.

Nouriani jogged to the second floor of the news building, flanked by troopers who relished the crack of their combat boots on the marble-lined staircase. The officer entered Jafari's office without knocking.

'We're ready,' he said, without betraying any timbre of excitement. He handed over a cassette. 'Broadcast this now. Radio and television will then keep it running, on a loop. Every twenty minutes or so.'

Jafari took the cassette with an acquiescent nod. He was a dead man anyway. If only he could think of a way to save his family.

There was no eight o'clock news. Instead viewers were presented with Colonel Mohsen Nouriani, an unknown guardsman, but a man with that dogged air of old-world sincerity that won instant admirers. Turning points often depend on the tone of a man's voice.

'In the name of God, the compassionate and the merciful, it is with great sadness that I must announce that we are passing through a period of national emergency. For the protection of the nation, key installations such as ministries, oilfields, airports, government buildings, television and radio will be placed under the immediate command of the Revolutionary Guards. Unfortunately we fear that rebels will try to use Web pages and satellite TV to disseminate destabilising propaganda. For the next forty-eight hours, we are temporarily shutting down the country's internet servers and jamming satellite transmission. There will be a curfew effective from 10 p.m. each evening.

'We would ask that the Iranian people remain calm but vigilant. This is in no sense an imposition of military rule in reaction to protests calling for greater political and social freedoms. Iran will never clamp down on the legitimate right to protest. Before 10 p.m. all legal protests will be permissible.'

Nouriani took a deep breath and looked directly into the lens.

'It is also with grave regret that I must announce that the latest wave of protests and assassinations has exposed a very small number of Revolutionary Guardsmen and regular army who are not loyal to the principles and ideals of the Islamic Republic. I, Colonel Mohsen Nouriani, have been personally charged with ensuring that these disloyal factions do not obstruct our defence of vital infrastructure. It is possible that we will witness short military operations as we extinguish these rebel elements. We ask the people of Iran to remain calm. God will grant us a quick and total victory.'

Nouriani remained inside the newsroom to watch the first transmission on the bank of screens. He showed no flicker of tension, his hands clasped behind his back.

'Good, now keep it rolling,' he said, and squeezed Jafari's shoulder. 'We're almost there, brother.'

Jafari figured he would have to pick out some wildlife documentaries and slapstick cartoons to fill in the airtime between broadcasts. Possibly some Miss Marple later.

Employees at the broadcast studios rushed out to the stairwell, shouting 'Good luck' and applauding Nouriani as he marched out of the building.

Nouriani looked at his watch. Seven minutes past eight. The airports and the ministries should be secure. It was eight minutes until the first air-strikes.

'Right, move out and block Valiasr. Signal to Khosravi that he should bring in the reinforcements.'

Soldiers double-timed out of the news compound, down the hill to the wide boulevard where they cleared the morning crowds. Nouriani's armoured personnel carriers stuttered on to the street and a handful of guardsmen used them as gun rests, fixing fleeing pedestrians in the cross-hairs. Troops emptied the bakeries, nut-sellers and greengrocers across the road, kicking through the back doors and forcing their way up on to the roofs.

Jafari, still numb to the world around him, stared from his window, trying to see what was happening on the main boulevard, discerning movements through the skeletal autumn branches of the stately plane trees. He watched soldiers on the rooftops signalling back to a cohort drawn up around a mosque, right beside Valiasr. Two of the guardsmen had television cameras.

Ripples juddered across the tea in his glass. His secretary yelled 'Earthquake' and several of the technicians ran for the door. But Jafari could see that the troops outside were unmoved by the tremors. Nouriani checked his watch yet again, almost neurotically. Seven Zulfaqar-2 tanks swung down Valiasr from Parkway. Two stopped to defend the top of the road, two halted outside the studios' main gates and three rumbled on to block the next junction. Iranian tricolours fluttered proudly from the sand-coloured warhorses.

In a sudden thunderclap, the MiG-29s, the backbone of Iran's air force, consumed the sky with the roar of their engines. They were so low you could make out the green and red roundels under the cockpit. The nose-cones drooped like the snouts of gun dogs. At first, Jafari thought there were just two of them, but then he saw the soldiers pointing towards three more silver arrows racing across the dull, white horizon. Twenty seconds later, three explosions shook central Tehran. Jafari stepped back from the window as it rattled in its frame.His ribcage tightened. An acrid, livid pall of smoke gushed from the defences of central Tehran. Terrified motorists abandoned the morning traffic jams and flung themselves into ditches at the side of the road. Anti-aircraft sirens, not heard since the war, howled through the crisp October morning.

Bernie Whelan woke, groggy and confused. He switched on the television to see if he could work out was going on. But every channel was showing David Attenborough crawling inside the great minaret of a termite nest.

Nouriani nodded with approval at the sound of the blasts. It was all going according to plan.

The Tehran traffic, awful at the best of times, was now

impassable. In some places, drivers were as irritable as ever, blasting their horns and demanding that magical forces cut a swathe through the congestion ahead. On the highways where motorists had witnessed the air-strikes, there was a dazed silence. Tehranis picked themselves up from the grassy embankments and flower beds at the roadsides, hastily brushing the grime from their shirts and coats. Raven-black plumes of smoke wafted from fuel depots and arms dumps, shrouding glitzy, neon advertising hoardings promoting flat-screen televisions and fitted kitchens. The first ambulances wailed but the medics couldn't cut through the tangled caravan of driverless cars.

It was like the old cliché: 'Tehran's just a big car park'.

At 8.27, units of the Revolutionary Guards loyal to President Ahmadinejad launched their counter-attack. But their trucks were also snared in the creeping lava-flow of traffic. Furious, they returned to base and loaded into Chinooks.

Nouriani gave Sergeant Khosravi a knowing glance when he heard the sharp drum of rotor blades pulse round the deep basin of central Tehran. He knew they'd have to use the Chinooks. The twin-rotored choppers hovered over Parkway and the loyalists poured out, abseiling on to a flyover. It was the only place he had figured they could set down any forces hoping to retake state television.

Khosravi was wearing a head-set, liaising with the MiG-29 commander.

'Ready,' he said, cutting downwards with his forefinger.

Nouriani green-lighted the attack.

The Chinooks pulled up from the Parkway interchange, gained altitude, and began to chug north towards the Alborz mountains. They pulled apart and flew parallel to the snow-covered peaks, one breaking west, the other east. Two incandescent flashes ripped through the sky. The helicopter to

Nouriani's left exploded. A fireball hung in the air over northern Tehran, then the two halves plunged through the canopy of the concrete jungle. The tail smashed into an exclusive apartment block.

The helicopter that had headed west banked sharply but couldn't escape. It disintegrated in the second blast. Effulgent, twisted metal rained down on the Sadr expressway.

There was an ear-bursting bellow as two MiG-29s swept in a low bow-bend across the sky, white vapour trails streaking off their wing tips. The pilots fired the afterburners and the twin tailplanes were swallowed by the glare of the sun.

As soon as the loyalist soldiers had taken up position, they sprayed wayward bursts of gunfire over the parapet of the flyover. The two Zulfaqar-2 tanks to the north of the state television compound unleashed a barrage at the poorly built structure. When the fog of rubble and dust cleared, the carriageway was strewn with the corpses of troops. Some had lost their legs. Shrapnel had paralysed others, slicing through their spinal cords. Barely men, the teenagers flailed helplessly in pools of mingled blood.

Nouriani's cameraman on the roof of the Shater Abbas restaurant, a popular kebab joint on the corner of Parkway and Valiasr, signalled that he had got it all. Marksmen beside him picked off the handful of survivors who were still taking optimistic pot-shots at Nouriani's tanks. A handful of Ahmadinejad's men walked towards the tanks with their hands raised. The man leading the surrendering troupe had tied a white rag to his rifle barrel.

The battle, if we can call it that, had lasted less than two minutes.

Jafari ran from the news compound and stared down Valiasr in disgust. Smoke and the rank, hot-steel stench of spent munitions hung in the air to the north. It was never meant to be like this. He cast his mind back to those pictures of Yeltsin on the tank. There would be people on the streets, but surely the army would shy away from firing a shot. What was wrong with this damn country? How did we form this inexorable bond with death?

At 9.30, Jerry was saved from Tom's clutches by a fresh broadcast from Colonel Nouriani.

'In the name of God, the compassionate and the merciful. The Revolutionary Guards Corps of the Islamic Republic of Iran is proud to announce to our people that it has fought off an attack from destabilising minorities within its own ranks. At 08.53 hours this morning, rebel guardsmen attempted to seize control of the state broadcasting networks. Naturally, our official elements of the Guards and air force were armed with tanks and MiG-29 fighters, far superior to the paltry firepower at the disposal of the rebels. We were easily able to defeat their two detachments in Chinooks. We have no doubt that these rebel elements were operating in the interests of foreign powers.'

Television showed that harrowing footage shot from the roof of the Shater Abbas restaurant: missiles blowing two Chinooks out of the sky and tanks overwhelming infantrymen with a rapid flurry of shells. Viewers were aghast at the familiarity of the locations. Places where they would stop for a bite: Yek Ta for a tongue sandwich or Super Estar for a burger were now on the sidelines of a battlefield.

Mothers turned away from the screen in revulsion when they saw the boys on the flyover.

'No, that's something they should not show. The children. The poor children.'

The men told them to shut up. This was important.

Iranians huddled around radios in furniture shops, news

kiosks and taxi agencies. Crowds had piled into cafés to watch the television. Grumpy proprietors shouted that everyone had to buy a coffee or leave. They were ignored.

The viper appeared in his first broadcast of the day. Silence.

'In the name of God, the compassionate and the merciful.'

The viper appeared calm, almost conceited. The ghost of a smile brightened his deeply-lined face.

'This is a black morning for Iran. Never did I imagine that such disloyalty was possible within the Islamic Republic. The scenes we have just witnessed sadden me greatly. In this period of national crisis, our estimable supreme leader, Ayatollah Ali Khamenei, has granted me the unparalleled honour of bringing together the forces of national solidarity. I have little doubt that Colonel Nouriani and our brave Revolutionary Guards will soon eradicate any renegade forces within the military. However, what we need more than military action is a resounding popular statement to hold the nation together. A gesture that will make our international enemies quake, as well as al Qaeda and the mujahidin here within our borders. Whoever you are, whether student, Kurd or unionist. This is the time to link arms and defend the republic. What I pledge now is sweeping social and economic reform. But such changes are meaningless if we cannot hold the nation together. Let us make a call now. Let us call for reforms and unity, for "One Iran".'

Across the nation, these were the messages seen by most Revolutionary Guard commanders. Half of them believed the messages were sincere. Half now recognised this was a coup by Baharvand. In either case, the worst policy would be action. This was the time to confine the men to barracks and wait. Let's see which side gains the upper hand, they thought. There's little point in getting hanged for being on the wrong side for three days.

Asian oil traders were quoting front-month contracts over $96. Most international airlines had promptly diverted flight paths out of Iranian airspace.

Nouriani had only moments to enjoy his victory in central Tehran. Moments later, he got a desperate call down the crackling, jungle telephone. His commander at Imam Khomeini International Airport needed instant back-up, screaming that he was outgunned by a column of loyalist tanks. Across the static-heavy line, the colonel could hear the scream and thunder of a tank battle. He promised to scramble a strike force of MiGs from Doshan Tappeh.

In the minutes before the MiGs swept in, the airport that Tehran had wanted to rival Dubai, was devastated. The gutted fuselage of a Turkish Airlines Airbus was lying crumpled on the tarmac, resting on its broken wing, like a wounded bird.

The main departures terminal took five direct hits in the bombardment. Three stranded Alitalia hostesses were killed when a roof collapsed. There was hardly a pane of glass left in the building.

But by half past ten, without air support against the agile Russian jets, the loyalist column was in flames. Militarily, they had very little left to throw against Baharvand.

In the presidential office, President Ahmadinejad was incensed by Baharvand's military supremacy. How long had the old Ayatollah been buying the loyalty of the military? Hunkered down with the president, Defence Minister Najjar was hardly helping matters.

'What the hell are you telling me? That I can't trust any pilots? I try to take state broadcasting back off Baharvand, I try to take the airport back – the airport named after our beloved

Imam – and now you tell me that Baharvand's got all the MiGs?'

Outside, they could hear the crackle of small-arms fire.

Najjar was guarded in the face of the president's rage.

'Not all, but many of the fighter squadrons seem to be with him.'

'Many? What does many actually mean?'

'We don't know.'

Ahmadinejad dragged his hands down his face, as if washing it.

'O God. O God. O God. How did it come to this again?'

Iran had been forced to execute its fighter pilots before. Back in 1979, few strands of the military had been as westernised as the air force. They were swaggering world-beaters who trained in Texas and proudly paraded all their latest, shiny presents from the United States. When the revolution came, they had a plan. Khomeini could be taken out in one fell swoop, sending the bombers over Jamaran village, where the Imam had his humble abode on the flanks of the Alborz. The plot was betrayed. The pilots were executed. With those pilots alive and flying their sorties, Iran could probably have won a quick victory against Iraq.

Petrified by that plot, the Islamic Republic had spent nearly thirty years toiling to ensure that all pilots were regime loyalists.

'Then what do we do? What can we do?' Ahmadinejad asked, petulantly.

He was getting desperate. He had always craved martyrdom but not like this. He had always fantasised about a death defending the Shi'ites from the infidels and the hypocrites. He didn't want to die in a mucky internal scrap where he couldn't determine who had betrayed whom. If only I had died behind enemy lines in Iraq, he mused, wistfully.

Najjar pursed his lips.

'We still have two loyal southern bases. We can order Hellfire.'
Ahmadinejad looked up. His squinted at Najjar through the fierce, narrow slits of his eyes. He grinned. Hellfire was what every western government most feared. Hellfire could force ceasefire negotiations.

The supertanker captain handed control of the bridge to his first officer, stepped out into the midday sunshine and leant over the rail. His ship had taken its slot in the Strait of Hormuz and would be clear of the crowded chokepoint by one o'clock. This place was worse than rush-hour downtown. One fifth of the world's oil trade pushed into a twenty-one mile defile.

He stared into the bright blue water. It was greased with an oily purple film that dazzled rainbow-like in the sun. Gulls, four hundred metres away at the carrier's prow, cawed in dogfights, scrapping over some scrawny carrion that had been dropped on the deck. As a young seaman thirty years earlier, he had known the Persian Gulf as a living sea, brimming with sharks. There was still a pearl fishing industry back in those days. Now there was nothing. Sprawling desalination plants had killed off what little life remained. Man cared little for his environment and the Persian Gulf had become a symbol of that.

The skipper turned back and looked through the side-door of the bridge. His officers were pointing alarmed at dots appearing on the radar. He stepped back inside and peered across their shoulders. Whatever those specks were, they were moving in damn fast. He leaned over for his binoculars.

Then came the shattering roar. Operation Hellfire had begun. The world's oil trade was under attack.

The officers whipped their heads up as the carrier two miles to port, burst into flame. Its hull was enveloped in thick black smoke.

'Fucking hell. What the fuck was that?,' yelled the first officer. 'There must be over one million barrels of crude in her. Look, her ribs have broken. She's going straight down. Fucking fuck.'

'What the hell blew that?' screamed another.

The captain pulled the alarm.

'Reverse propellers and hold her steady. Ready the lifeboats. We'll go over to take off survivors.'

Almost directly at eye-level, two Sukhoi 24s raced across their bows. The ashen bridge officers saw a couple of missiles away. Seconds later, a pillar of sea water spurted upwards. The second missile struck home and a blast ripped through a second ship. The fire seemed contained to its centre. Men ran for the lifeboats as their haemorrhaged tanker spewed out a black cloud from the midships.

'Were those Iranian planes? Fucking bastards,' the first officer asked.

'Yeah,' the captain replied. 'They had the red, white and green tricolour on the tail. It's finally happened after all those years of us just talking about it. They have decided to block the Strait of Hormuz.'

Frantic oil traders pushed the price of a barrel over $110 in the next five minutes.

Seb's morning had started as well as any morning could. At six, he was enjoying breakfast in bed with not one, but two beautiful young women. The girls sat cross-legged, eating muesli and prunes. They had rummaged around in his wardrobe and found a couple of gentlemen's shirts they liked. Long, old fashioned cuts from Thomas Pink.

The girls eyed him up, hungrily. Again.

'Do we make you nervous, Sebastiaan joon?' Parastou asked.

Seb admitted they did.

'Ow, you are so, mazloum. How do you say mazloum in English?'

'Innocent,' Negar said. 'Yes, he is. Running the world but very innocent.'

She leant over and kissed him on the head.

'Innocent imperialist.'

Seb was very happy to be innocent. But did this sort of thing happen all the time in Iran? God, he loved this country.

'There's normally a bit of a fuss if a diplomat has to explain that he has an Iranian girlfriend. Two might cause an incident.'

The girls laughed.

'That's easily explained,' Negar said, planting her foot on his chest and bowling him over. 'We are not your girlfriends. You are our boyfriend.'

'That's a convenient way of putting it.'

'Erm, hello! That's how it is. It's that way round. You bring us breakfast, mazloum.'

At seven, the embassy staff were shocked, and slightly irritated, by Seb's perkiness.

By two o'clock, all memories of breakfast in bed had evaporated. The FCO had made a snap decision and recommended that all British subjects should be evacuated. The Brits clubbed together with the other EU embassies and made an overwhelming case for Mehrabad airport in central Tehran to be re-opened for emergency evacuation flights by the flag-carriers. Since Imam Khomeini International had been knocked out by the tank barrage, it was more or less impossible to deny the request. Seb spent most of the day locked in meandering phone calls with confused aviation officials whose chains of command had disintegrated.

*

215

The minister took his seat at the end of the table and opened his file. He was flanked by the Chief of the Defence Staff and the First Sea Lord. Lomax's haughty nature and his immaculate tailoring made sure that he cut an imposing figure. Cath and Andy looked unprepossessing among all the uniforms, medals and braid that surrounded the Whitehall table.

'Well, it's a full-blown shooting war now,' said the minister, clumsily priming his voice with an unwelcome machismo. 'It has been confirmed that the Strait of Hormuz is now closed to shipping. We have vowed our commitment to re-opening the channel and have expressed our grave concern.'

Grave concern. Expressed to whom?

'Last night, President Bush spoke to the PM and told him that, in light of intelligence received by western services, US forces were considering clandestine support operations to facilitate regime change, backing up Ayatollah Ali Baharvand. This ayatollah has promised to disband Iranian nuclear work and recognise Israel. Bush sees Baharvand as our last hope of preventing what he calls World War Three. Sweeping, I know, but there may yet be method in his madness. At the moment, I am advised, it is very difficult to know which parts of the Iranian military are loyalists and which are with Baharvand. However, what we do know is that the planes that attacked the tankers today were launched from, from, sorry, Jock, where was it?'

Sir Jock Stirrup, Chief of the Defence Staff, scanned his papers.

'They were Sukhoi 24s launched from Fars.'

'Right, yes, Fars province. Now, those planes took off from one of the airstrips that Baharvand said we should neutralise when he handed over co-ordinates of potential obstacles to his coup. Is that not the case?'

'It is indeed,' Lomax agreed, with unnecessarily dramatic aplomb.

'So the planes that blocked Hormuz are regime loyalists? We are sure about that?'

'We would agree with that appraisal. In our estimation, this smells of desperation. They are trying to force Baharvand to sue for terms,' Lomax said.

The table murmured, as if the notion had not occurred to them.

The minister took a breath.

'After this attack in Hormuz, President Bush now sees military intervention by western forces deployed in the Gulf as both inevitable and potentially highly advantageous. If Iran is going to block the world's main oil thoroughfare then a response has become a prerequisite. After emergency meetings, the Royal Navy has pledged that one of its Trafalgar Class submarines will join a US assault tonight. These strikes will take advantage of the chaos within Iran both to support Baharvand and eliminate various nuclear facilities which the Iranians have continued to run in defiance of international law. We have picked sites that could only have a military application. The US will employ both submarines and high-altitude bombers in tonight's missions.'

Andy was surprised by how calmly everyone was taking this news. But since the military had been training with mock-ups of Iran missions for years, it must have seemed like an extended training exercise. That was the trick of dogged soldiery, wasn't it?

The minister was still rambling in fluent officialese.

'Our intelligence services have been extremely active during Ayatollah Baharvand's coup and we have a strong line of communication to this claimant to the purple. It's what our friends here call the "jungle telephone". His nephew is in hiding in this country. But not even I know where he is. Nobody tells me anything.'

Nervous laughter stuttered round the table.

'The nephew insists that his uncle can pin responsibility for tonight's strategically vital raids on domestic forces, rogue elements inside the Iranian military. Everything we have discussed is totally deniable. It never happened. US and UK forces never engaged in any assault on Iran during the night of Monday 29th October and Tuesday 30th October. From a legal perspective, this is not a war. We are simply launching a proportionate defence of shipping lanes. The number of submarine officers who know the target will be kept to a bare minimum. Most of the crew will be led to believe it's an Iraq mission. I am sure that is not a point I will have to labour in this room.'

The discussion melted into strategy. Andy glared at the Top Secret documents in front of him. There were basic typographical mistakes in the target names. For Christ's sake, if you are going to kill people, you should at least have the common decency to check the spelling of their airfields' home villages.

Two of the twelve targets counted as a proportionate defence of shipping lanes. Maybe three. The word 'proportionate' seemed to overlap with 'illegal'.

Andy felt no animosity to those around him. They were professionals. To a small extent he blamed the prime minister who didn't have to agree to this. But oil was nearing $120 per barrel and there was little that his much vaunted fiscal prudence could do now to save the economy. Some tinkering with interest rates wouldn't do the trick. No, Brown was just a servant to the markets like every other leader. Seated impishly above all the generals and politicians, he saw the devious cleric, the hanging judge. You've engineered all this and the chances are that the West

218

is going to fete you as a hero by tomorrow evening. You'll say all the right things. You always do. Oil will turn tail and plunge to $80. Everyone will forgive you your sins.

Descending in the lift after the meeting, Lomax told Andy and Cath to go and get some rest. He wanted them to do a night shift from seven o'clock.

'It's going to be a hellish night. We'll need full reports every hour.'

'Sure,' said Andy.

As they stepped into the fresh air, Cath tugged at Andy's sleeve.

'Come round to my place. Please.'

'The empty palace?'

'Just for coffee.'

As they crossed the Thames, Andy talked animatedly about some hiking trip down to Fars province one spring in the late 1970s. Probably 1978. The citrus groves, sparkling brooks, meadows of long grass and bright carpets of wild flowers seemed so remote from the damp, greyness enfolding London. Andy recalled the kindness and the good humour of the farmers who had put him up each night, welcoming him with that profound Islamic reverence for the sanctity of the guest. He recalled the imposing stone reliefs of the Sassanian kings cut into the valleys. You could see the Roman Emperor Valerian, humbled before the might of Shapur I.

Cath dug her hands into her greatcoat and imagined the scenes. There was nothing mawkish about the way Andy told the stories. She knew it was the impending strikes that had triggered this nostalgia, but there was no note of sadness or protest. And strangely it was almost as if Andy were not talking about himself. It always struck her that he very rarely appeared in his own stories. He could lovingly describe a goatherd and tell you about that man's fears and hopes. But Andy himself was always invisible in his tales.

He described the Palace of Ardeshir, site of the first recorded squinch.

'What the hell's a squinch?'

'It's a way of getting a dome to sit on a square building.'

'And the Persians did actually invent that? It's not another one of the things they claim to have invented.'

'Oh no, the squinch is utterly Persian. Made in Iran.'

'Hadn't the Romans done that? What about the Pantheon? Oh, I see. That's a dome on a circular building. And with a hole in the top. What does it look like? It sounds like a sort of amphibian. A squinch.'

'It splays out from the corner, making the right kind of base for a dome.'

He pushed his fingers out in an unhelpful exegesis.

Cath smiled. It consistently amused her that, despite their natural suspicion of each other, Andy and Otto would probably have got on very well. As it was, on the rare occasions they met, they would treat each other with prickly courtesy and strained bonhomie. In fact, both were men who savoured life's clutter. They could have spent hours talking about cloud formations, where salmon breed and how, of all things, you get a dome to sit on a square building. She figured she must attract that kind of man. It was probably the spectacles that made her look sympathetic.

Cath unlocked the flat and tossed her beret and coat over an armchair.

'Gosh, it's cavernous. It's an amazing place.'

It was also freezing and infused with the misery of a wet afternoon.

'Come on, I'll make some coffee.'

She traversed the expanse of open pine floor to the marbled kitchen surfaces. She took down a bag of ground coffee and spooned it into the pot. Andy picked up the bag.

'Ethiopian Fairtrade.'

We drink Fairtrade coffee and acquiesce in illegal missile strikes. What a breed we are. During the 1980s, Andy and Cath had easily convinced themselves of the need for the netherworld. There were things that were too morally ambiguous for public debate. Andy's Cold War had been fought in that darkness but he still knew where the light was. Since 2001, things had been spiralling out of control. In the Cold War, there was an understanding underpinning the espionage, like a rope that a diver takes with him into the murkiest nooks of a submerged cave. You were fighting opposite numbers of a similar rank and education. Most captured spies of Andy's seniority got back home in one piece, if a little worse for wear. Only the locals died like flies and were dumped in unmarked graves, sprinkled with slaked lime.

But this Islamic enemy had created a deadly, pre-emptive paranoia. These wild men in the hills would never let you out alive, so the rules were different. There was no safety rope. Illegal night-strikes were the only way to fight such forces.

Andy had often drawn a parallel with the fin de siècle anarchists. By the time King Umberto was finally assassinated by an anarchist in 1900, after surviving a knifeman in 1897, it had seemed clear that anarchism would destroy our civilisation. In fact, wars that would rip the world apart were indeed imminent, but they had nothing to do with the anarchists. Andy knew World War Three would come one day or other. It had to. But it would probably have very little to do with those bearded anarchists holed up at Tora Bora.

And did the secret services of the late nineteenth century

break all the rules to defeat the anarchists? Did they just dump suspects into the Tiber? Probably. Almost certainly. There was no point in being too self-loathing about the wars we wage.

Cath knelt down in front of the fridge and sniffed the milk.

'Oh, God, I am sorry Andy. I've let it turn. You see, when Otto's away, I just forget about milk.'

'Ah, you and your allergies. Don't worry. Black's fine.'

They turned a couple of canvas chairs to look out over the Thames. Bookends.

At two o'clock, Andy announced that he was going to sleep for a few hours, unlaced his shoes and lay down on the sofa. His old flame brought him a blanket and by ten past two, he appeared to be asleep. How does he do that? And after coffee. That's an art. She knew from his keen eyes that he still wanted her. But that self-pitying side of him foolishly accepted that he had lost out to a more deserving man.

She lay in the downcast afternoon gloom, unable to sleep in her cold, wrought-iron bed. She flicked through a magazine but it wouldn't do; she was an insomniac at the best of times. She swept up a blanket and went through to the main room. She read as Andy slept. She felt that she hadn't much enjoyed being his lover but had preferred the excitement leading up to their fling. She remembered that freezing night when he had, quite suddenly, hugged her outside a pub, without knowing or caring where their lives were going. She craved another hug now and was greedy for a kiss. But she knew, despite her mastery of deception, that the one man she could never deceive was Otto. Fool that he was, Andy would never deceive him either.

They arrived early at the ziggurat's operations' room and got up to speed. It had been a slow afternoon.

Baharvand was still firmly in control of the air and the

airwaves. However, it looked like the Supreme Leader and Ahmadinejad were still hanging on. There'd been no coup de grâce. Fighting had subsided although there were still a couple of running gunbattles in central Tehran, one close to Pasteur Street, the central thoroughfare of government. The transatlantic consensus was that Baharvand had flexed his muscles, called in all his friends and terrified the leadership. Baby Baharvand insisted that the government had approached his uncle and were attempting to sue for terms. No one could confirm this. The Strait of Hormuz raid had blindsided the old cleric. He had never imagined that his enemies would stoop so low.

'But he's still winning, just,' Cath concluded.

'The viper always wins,' Andy retorted, slipping the rubber band off his Top Secret dossiers.

Fucking hell, firing times. The first in three hours seven minutes. There would be a full crew of satellite imaging people working to see whether the targets had been hit. Max and Avi were expected at three o'clock to share their own appraisals.

On Iranian state television, David Attenborough was perched on the side of an inflatable. Behind him, the broad tail-fin of a Humpback plunged into the water.

The control room of HMS Torbay was bathed in red light and the Tomahawks were away, inperfect synchronicity with the cousins. The crewmen were quiet and unmoved, studying the banks of screens. The weapons had reached their cruising speed of 550 miles per hour. The captain thanked his men and congratulated them on the smoothness of the launch. He hated those Hollywood films that portrayed submariners punching the air, embracing and shouting after a kill. Nobody liked to be called a murderer. Some people had said it after Kosovo. One of his wife's closest friends suddenly refused to speak to her. There was duty, that was all. If you couldn't accept it, you were free to leave. Film-makers needed to understand two things. Firstly, a sub gives you a sense of the fragility of life. You don't cheer when you hear a ship's hull rip apart in the water above you. No one wants to die out there. And secondly, perhaps more importantly, you don't so much as drop a spanner or a fork at battle stations. Who knows who's listening for you, hunting you in the deep. An Iranian Kilo-class submarine could be lurking a mile to starboard, waiting for any careless outburst of noise to pinpoint your position. Coming into port you can fly a Jolly Roger. But at moments such as this, you keep your mind focussed on the icy technicalities of killing.

Andy whipped the envelopes out of the geek's hand the second he entered the room. The images were unambiguous. Runways looked like the surface of the moon. Nuclear facilities which, one week ago, the West had known nothing about were shown exploding over a series of freeze-frames.

'Which one's that?' asked Cath.

Andy scanned the accompanying print-off.

'That is apparently what Baharvand tells us is the Pourian atomic research laboratory. Destroyed in the proportionate defence of shipping lanes. Along with anyone who happened to be working there.'

'I know. I know. You know Lomax protested to the prime minister, don't you?'

For all his swagger, Callum could produce a few surprises.

'I didn't, no. I'm glad.'

Iranian television switched from its rolling cartoons and propaganda to a building blazing orange in the pitch-blackness. Five fire-engines filled the courtyard with the throb of their lights. People in night-gowns ran through the streets, bawling and crying. The building had an institutional air, characterless and tall, dotted with small, square windows.

'Where is this?' Cath asked.

Andy said he had no idea. The street looked narrow and built up. It felt, his instincts told him, like a city. Six of the targets had been urban.

The cameraman had zoomed in on a woman in the full black chador. She had slumped to her knees, disconsolate and screaming. In the confusion, it was impossible to work out what was happening.

'What the hell is that building?' Cath asked.

She laid out all of the target photographs on the desk. Three had a courtyard at the front, as they could see on the screen, glowing pink and yellow in the flickering glare of the inferno. It could either be one of the nuclear laboratories or one of two bases of the Revolutionary Guards intelligence service, perhaps the most virulent and insidious strong-arms in the country.

Cath studied the images again and pushed the one she favoured over to Andy.

'Rev Guard Intel. Shiraz,' she said.

Andy gave a cursory look at the photograph.

'They look a bit more wild than a group of people should be when the Stasi have just been taken out.'

'They are shocked. It's not every night you get bombed, Andy.'

'Maybe.'

Andy was being cold and distant towards her.

The woman in the chador started speaking to the camera. Cath could follow all of it apart from one word. The woman was sobbing. How could they do it? She was demanding to know why the firemen weren't working harder. There was no time to be lost, she said.

Cath felt the cold catch in her throat. Andy had dropped his head into his hand, no longer watching the screen.

'Andy, tell me, for Christ's sake. Tell me. What's "parvareshgah"?'

'It's an orphanage.'

9.

FOR AT LEAST a hundred yards, retreating up the snaking blackness of the qanat, the water had swollen to chest height. But here, in the faint dusting of sunlight beneath the access shaft, the current lapped up to their beards. They were fifty yards below ground. This was work only for men with an unwavering belief in the benevolence of a compassionate Creator, al Rahman, al Rahim. The conduit's flow into Anareh had slackened to a dismal trickle.

Jahangiri the foreman could feel the cause of the blockage as he stretched his arm up. There was a rustle as he disturbed his fellow troglodytes, a couple of bats hanging in the jagged cavity.

'Oh, God, the whole roof has dropped out here. There's a huge hole. Little wonder there's a blockage again. It's dammed it.'

Abbas the Blind could already sense the dimensions of the collapse from the fast-flowing surface water around his neck. It was being squeezed through a narrow aperture above the submerged rubble, flowing over it like a lethargic waterfall. Tuesday promised to be a nerve-racking slog. The muqannis would take shifts, two by two, painstakingly scraping up the fallen debris into wicker baskets which would then be hauled up on the gasping, cross-strutted windlass.

If you just smash a hole through such a blockage or if it gives way, the rush of water will sweep you half way down into the village. That's how you drown or break your skull, as you're bandied around like flotsam in the tunnel. You had better hope the lads are holding on to your safety rope and that you can somehow grope your way back to the shaft, half-swimming, half-clutching against the torrent pouring against you. If that weren't enough, remember that collapsed roof in your prayers, lest another tonne of rock crash down while you are scraping around underneath.

The foreman and his stout, sightless companion were both men of few words. For an hour they worked in silence, yanking on the rope each time they filled a basket. They worked hard and fast, catching their breath face-up in the small air pocket, then pushing themselves under the water again. Their lungs burned and their backs ached. For the last ten minutes the lactic acid built up around their joints. They craved chai and cigarettes back in the dry sunlight above.

Jahangiri pinched the light on his Casio. The watch-face glowed: 07:58.

'Let's get out. I'm cramping up. I am too old for all this.'

Abbas slapped the last handfuls of stone and mud into the basket.

Back at the surface, Jahangiri threw off his wet overalls and towelled himself down, still caked in grey sediment. Rezaie and Hosseini descended into the waterway. Abbas gripped the ropes, waiting for a yank.

The foreman settled himself on a rock and lit a Homa. About a mile away, across the desert scrub, Baharvand's people were putting the final touches to the Ayatollah's stage. They had masked the scaffolding with green sheets and yellow banners. Flags and nationalist slogans fluttered in the morning breeze. To the right of the platform Revolutionary Guardsmen had erected field kitchens, where, that afternoon, they would boil ash reshteh, noodle stew, for the bussed-in legions of sycophants and yes-men. Coils of barbed wire encircled the whole area at a radius of three hundred yards from the dais where the viper would be delivering his speech. Thirty or forty sentries were doing their rounds, patrolling the outside of the wire. A couple of armoured personnel carriers had parked beside the stage. A television crew, burdened by miles of cable that never seemed sufficient, bickered among themselves.

At a quarter past eight, a white jeep pulled up at the first check-point beyond the wire. After the driver had exchanged a few words with the Guardsmen, the vehicle headed straight for Jahangiri, who sighed and stubbed out his cigarette in the sand. He buttoned his shirt, trotted towards the approaching dust-cloud and flagged the motorist down, eighty yards from the access shaft.

The driver was a spectral apparition in a black suit. The gorilla beside him was wearing a bomber jacket and caressed a machine gun.

'Salaam, brother. May you not be weary,' Jahangiri said to the driver. He was respectful, correctly assuming that the two men were intelligence agents.

'Blessings be upon you,' replied the spymaster, Alef Baa, immediately identifying a true man of the faith.

'I am very sorry for any disturbance, gentlemen, but we've got dangerous repair work going on down in the qanat. Could you please stop the car?'

Alef Baa killed the engine.

'Thank you so much. Part of the channel's roof caved in. It's blocked the flow into Anareh. I have men down there and I'm worried that the vibrations from your car could loosen more debris above their heads.'

The two officers from Tehran were impressed by the old man, his shirt smeared with grime and his leather boots cracked. Alef Baa stepped down from the jeep, but signalled that his simian strong-arm should stay put. He shook the foreman firmly by the hand and invited him to show him the access shaft. He figured that this must be the same team of muqannis who dredged up his man, Sergeant Ahmadian.

'My God, how deep is that?' Alef Baa asked, squinting as he tried to make some sense of the shadows at the bottom. He was kneeling by the main airway, steadying himself in the dirt with both hands.

'Fifty yards. That's disturbed water you can see flickering down there. My boys are round to the right, digging out the blockage.'

'That's heroes' work.'

'We just play our part.'

'May you not be weary.'

'Blessings be upon you.'

Alef Baa looked out across the rugged sierra of the Jebal Barez. Imagining himself an assassin at every point he stood, the thought flashed through his mind that a terrorist could lie hidden in the qanat, particularly one approaching from those peaks.

'My job, as you have probably guessed, is one of appraising security for Ayatollah Baharvand.'

Jahangiri nodded.

'Have you seen any new faces out here over the last few days? Anyone suspicious?'

'We are the only people working along the qanat. From time to time, we see a goatherd, but generally, it's just us.'

'Forgive my ignorance about such matters, but could someone lie hidden in a qanat?'

Jahangiri was fed up with all this official interest in his beloved water channel. First somebody flings a corpse into the water, now someone asks whether terrorists hide out down there. Enough was enough.

'No, the only people you find down the qanat are me and my boys. Everybody else is too scared. I have never, in all my years, chanced upon a stranger in a qanat. What's more, if one of your terrorists came this way, he'd drown. A hundred metres back that way up to the mountains, the water would come up to his chest. Right below us here it's blocked entirely. There's no way through.'

'How long will it take you to clear it?'

Jahangiri shrugged.

'Two days. Three, maybe.'

Alef Baa smiled and concluded that he probably shouldn't let his paranoia seep into the netherworld of the qanat. He dusted off his hands with a clap.

'Very well. Many thanks, brother. May God help you in your work.'

'And in yours, brother.'

The ghoulish spymaster returned to the jeep and waved. He gingerly reversed for a few dozen yards, wheeled round and sped back to Anareh. He doubted there was a US assassin out there. That supposed leak from Vienna was either an elaborate ploy by Baharvand or an infantile prank from Britain, the villainous Old Fox.

Hosseini may have been youthful and impetuous at the surface but underground, in the gloomy vein of the qanat, he was as cautious as his elder colleagues. What happened was an accident; certainly not carelessness on the young man's part. For five minutes, he had picked at a large stone that was welded into the top of the rubble, the eroding ridge where the water was cascading over. He dug his fingertips and nails into the gritty mud holding it in place but it was wedged fast. It was like pulling a tooth with twisted roots. Then, suddenly, it lifted, as if a magnetic current holding it in place had been flicked off.

'Hah, just like that. Got the big one.'

Rezaie congratulated him.

'Pass it over.'

Rezaie gently laid the offending rock in the basket.

At first, the water picked up speed and the two men felt the current exerting more weight against them.

'Heh, something's up,' said Hosseini.

'It's giving way. Just see whether you can ...'

He never completed his sentence. In a reflex, the two men glued themselves like limpets to rocks jutting out of the wall. For thirty seconds they were rammed back and submerged by the onslaught of floodwater. Rezaie swallowed a lungful.

Perfect silence. Then Jahangiri and Abbas shouted down the access shaft.

'Lads, lads, what happened?'

Gasping for breath, Rezaie and Hosseini relaxed their grip on the walls of the qanat. The water had an easy flow. It was only just above waist deep. Rezaie choked and vomited up his gulps of water.

'We've cleared the blockage, Hajji,' Rezaie called up the shaft.

Wading past that same spot, ten hours later, the Tajik would never suspect that there had been a problem.

The world's newspapermen and broadcast channels were waiting for Bernie Whelan to work out what was going on inside Iran. As soon as Reuters came up with the official line, then they could simply copy that. It was a situation in life that Big Bern adored. That's what he loved about the wire. You could sit down with a screaming hangover and a packet of Malborough Lights and bang out the first version of history. All the parasites in cosmetic journalism would swarm round your story and suck out your interpretation, your turns of phrase and your quotes. Of course, some of his colleagues were dismayed to see all their hard work just lifted and pasted into *The Guardian* under the byline of some lazybones in London. But Whelan savoured that culture of dependency. The world's journalists were wet-nosed dogs who would eat from his hand and obey his every command. It was an elegant symbiosis. It had only one minor flaw: Bernie Whelan's judgement. He had been misleading the world for decades.

Shirkhan translated Ayatollah Baharvand's morning address as the portly Irishman opposite him slurped on a creamy, granulated coffee. At vital moments, Whelan thumped out a newsflash, then took another manly glug from his cup.

He had never doubted himself and his interpretation of events. The editors at *Le Monde* congratulated themselves too. They'd nailed it. The coup had failed. Baharvand was now saying so. Shirkhan had got so locked into the internal politics that he hadn't seen Baharvand for what he really was: a regime loyalist who would snuff out a botched putsch from splinter groups of the military. It needed the cool head of Bernie Whelan, the old maestro, to come in and see what was really going on. He'd cut through the crap again.

'It's a strange thing though,' Shirkhan mused. 'If it's all calmed down and everything is under control, as Baharvand tells us, where are the supreme leader, Khamenei, and the president, Ahmadinejad?'

Whelan shrugged and cracked on with his story.

'It's still fever pitch out there on the streets, Shirkhan. I guess Baharvand will stay on as the front-man for a couple of days while the leader and the president are safe in their bunkers somewhere. Just in case ...'

'But that's the point: they wouldn't cower in a bunker like Mr Bush. As president, Khamenei was out on the front lines in his fatigues. Ahmadinejad's an old soldier. Martyrdom is something he would embrace rather than fear. They are not men who would hide away when the battle begins. We should be seeing them on our screens.'

Whelan grunted and complained that he was trying to concentrate on polishing his masterpiece.

By Bernard Whelan
TEHRAN, Oct 30 (Reuters) – Iran said on Tuesday it had crushed a military rising that briefly closed the world's main oil nexus and killed more than 300 people, including forty-three orphans and three Italian air hostesses.

Ayatollah Ali Baharvand said overnight air force attacks had crushed resistance from rebels, destroying the runways used for Monday's strikes against oil tankers in the Strait of Hormuz. He vowed that emergency rule would end 'within hours'.

'The rebel threat is now entirely vanquished,' the senior cleric said in an address to state television.

'Tragically, in a futile and unhuman final gamble, the rebels shelled an orphanage in Shiraz.'

Whelan's story settled the nerves of the oil market and a barrel slid back under $90. Market-moving stuff. That's what Reuters likes. Well done, Bernie Whelan. Power to your pen, Old Sport.

*

Seb took a short walk from the embassy to Ferdowsi Square, mingling with the youthful, bubbly crowd that was gathering around the statue of the national poet, the bard of Tus. He had heard on the grapevine that these gatherings were springing up nationwide, even up in drizzly, northern villages along the Caspian. Gratified that the revolution had failed, just as he said it would, the ambassador loosed young Maynard's chain a little and allowed the whelp to take a five-minute stroll up the road.

Young people squatted around barren flower beds in the middle of the roundabout, lighting candles and chatting. They had posters of Baharvand mounted on canes which they harpooned into the soil. Where did they get those from? For a few moments they sang choruses from songs he didn't recognise, possibly pre-revolutionary anthems. They chanted 'Reforms and unity', 'Government of national unity' and 'One Iran'. They were all familiar slogans from Baharvand's televised addresses.

One dignified old gentleman caught Seb's eyes. He was wearing a pink bow-tie and a green tweed jacket. He had horn-rimmed spectacles and a pendulous, tapered silver moustache of the kind favoured by monarchists.

Seb introduced himself. The gentleman switched into French when he realised that he was addressing a diplomat. Seb felt awkward asking what was afoot, and scanned the crowd for signs of the basij or the security apparatus. All clear. The old man looked at him with an air of confidentiality. He gave the walrus a twirl.

'Well, to be honest with you, mon ami, it's all a little bizarre,' he confided. For a moment, he floundered as if he felt unable to explain the complexity of the situation. 'Look. You know Ferdowsi?' he asked, pointing at the statue.

Seb knew how to make friends in Iran.

'Of course I know the greatest of all poets. I have been up to his tomb in Khorasan.'

The gentleman purred with approval.

'Wonderful. Wonderful. And have you read his poems?'

'Parts of the *The Book of Kings*, yes.'

'Well, back at the time of the revolution, I was a literature teacher. I taught Persian and French. These kids weren't even born then, but I remember. Mon dieu, I remember those men in black trying to revise the syllabus, telling us what we could and could not read. You know, they tried to ban Ferdowsi?'

'No. That's impossible. Ferdowsi is a keystone of the nation. That's ridiculous. It would be like banning Shakespeare.'

'So we all thought, but the mullahs didn't see it like that. Oh no. Ferdowsi represented the dark age of stories from before the Islamic era. We could not have non-Muslim heroes. They demanded a complete revision of the literature syllabus.'

'There must have been uproar.'

'Of course there was, and the clerics backed down. In the end. But that's the bizarre thing. I remember all those arguments, those education committee meetings. And I remember the determined, clever mullah, there in his turban, banging the table and demanding that Ferdowsi be burned.'

When he mentioned the cleric, the gentlemen whirled his forefinger over his head, as if describing the shape of a Mr Whippy ice cream. It was the universal code for a turban. An akhond. A sermoner.

'Who was that?'

'That iconoclast there! That Nazi! The book-burner is now on those posters. Ayatollah Ali Baharvand. Life plays strange tricks on you, doesn't it? I could never bring myself to vote for him in a presidential election. And now here we all are, underneath a statue of Ferdowsi, and we are meant to suppose that he is the saviour of the nation. What a heap of merde.'

The crowd chanted: 'One Iran. One Iran. One Iran'.

'So it looks like our man has won,' said Lomax, untying the maroon ribbon that bound his files together.

'It certainly looks that way,' Cath agreed. She was tired and rubbed her weary eyes.

'What's the word from Baby Baharvand?'

Andy, who had just got off the phone to the Ayatollah's nephew, joined his hands as if in prayer. The phone call had ended with raised voices and sharp words, but Andy collected himself and started off methodically.

'He's happy. He's confident. His uncle certainly seems to be on a roll. Ayatollah Baharvand is now negotiating with the leadership. He reckons that the government is cornered, with little choice but unconditional surrender. All Baharvand's men are waiting in the wings. He has his cadre of air force commanders, oil men, ex-ministers and ambassadors ready to form an emergency government, while he lays the ground for elections. Hopefully those will be in January.'

Lomax nodded. January had been the earliest anyone could realistically hope for.

'So, this new government would have lots of familiar faces? All the crooked Charlies who had their noses put out of joint by Ahmadinejad and his Revolutionary Guards?'

'Oh, yeah, sure. It'll be the usual suspects, all right. These are men who will have been out of the picture only for the last two or three years.'

'I understand. And how the hell does he defend this fucking orphanage fiasco?'

Lomax was simmering. Andy shook his head and leant back in his chair.

'Baby swears blind that those were the co-ordinates of Revolutionary Guard intelligence in Shiraz. One moment he tries to hint that the Tomahawk may have gone astray. The next moment he accuses the Revolutionary Guard of using the orphans as a human shield. He can't have it both ways.'

'No, he bloody well can't. The oily bastard. So how does Baharvand play it?'

The clock, its battery long flagging, finally expired. Clack.

'For now, he's got something to throw at the so-called rebels. Those are the vermin who bombed the orphanage and blew up the oil tankers, he'll say. When he gets round to accusing the previous regime of treason, then I am pretty sure that he will conjure up some evidence that will link them to both attacks.'

Cath interrupted.

'What do we know of these impending treason charges? Are there any details?'

'Again, it's vague. But basically Baharvand is going to tap into one of the most nationalistic, primal fears that Iranians have. It sounds like he is going to accuse senior government figures of collusion with Arab governments.'

'Anything in it?'

'Relatively little. But it will cause nationwide outrage as it is widely held to be true. It will be a popular witch-hunt. Everyone has heard a story or two: there's a knock on the door in the middle of the night and a blacked-out 4x4 is waiting in the street. The guys inside all wear balaclavas and don't speak Persian. Yet another good honest Iranian disappears after an encounter with ultra-religious Arab vigilantes. The story goes that the mullahs have to use their Arab henchmen for really twisted shit, because an Iranian torturer might baulk at harming his own countrymen.'

'Ah, if only,' sighed Lomax. 'Now, just back-peddling a bit, to the part of this story that's really got my wick: this bloody orphanage ...'

'If you want my opinion and if I know Baharvand, he's engineered this firstly to tarnish the so-called rebels, then to tarnish us. His men will have sifted through the rubble with a fine toothcomb, photographing the fragments of exploded Tomahawk. As we move forward, whenever he wants to put pressure on us and the Yanks, there will always be 'the incident of the orphange'. Wouldn't it be a pity if that were to leak out?'

'Christ,' said Cath. 'Is he really that cloak and dagger? Couldn't this just be a tragic but genuine misidentification of a building? I know you don't trust him an inch but, God, aren't you taking his Machiavellian side a little far?'

'I hope I am. But all we are doing with Baharvand is hoping and guessing. We've helped him seize power, but for what? We have no guarantees that he's really going to end the nuclear work.'

Lomax disagreed.

'Baharvand did recommend the destruction of two sites that were used for military applications of nuclear technology. Those are corroborated sites. Or let's say rather: we knew they were military labs four years ago. If he were committed to the bomb, he'd hardly recommend that we pound them to smithereens, eh?'

Andy conceded the hit.

'I guess not. Maybe you're right, Callum. Maybe I am too suspicious of the guy. We might not like his methods. He may liquidate opponents without telling us and get us to bomb orphanages, but he could well be the only chance we have to stop a full-blown war.'

'I think that's very much the sort of moral compromise that

the PM has been prepared for. It's pretty ugly. But life tends to be.'

In Central Africa, Cath had met commanders brutalised by genocide and conflict, whose hearts were filled with bile. They were men who could have massacred orphans of another tribe or race. They could unleash their bloodlust at will, channelling the pain that permeated their whole lives. They were subsumed by violence and it became part of them. But never before had she dealt with a man who had meticulously thought through the comparative merits of getting someone else to destroy an orphanage for him. She doubted that the sage old Ayatollah could really be such a man. Andy had allowed decades of rage to fester inside him, and still could not be trusted to think clearly.

'The PM's right, of course,' Andy conceded. 'The MPs who sit in our parliamentary committees have never really understood the true nature of political reform or revolution. They fret about the froth on top: students, feminists, Bahais, homosexuals and Christian-converts. But such people are never going to constitute a real force for change. Tragically. Baharvand *is* pretty much our last chance.'

Alone in his Westminster digs, boiling a can of soup or amassing a binful of empties, Andy had been pondering the shared traits of successful revolutionaries. Even though the centuries teach us only that revolutions come from Pyms and Cromwells, why do we still always look elsewhere, on the smiling peripheries of failed states for hopes of change? It was obvious that only a Baharvand could be a Cromwell. The West's pre-occupation with Iran's students and women was comparable to seventeenth-century Spain opening a dialogue with the Levellers, Ranters and Diggers, the mad but often noble fringes of the English revolution. Useless allies.

Andy had long been obsessed by the ferocity of the Civil War.

The geography of Royalist bastions had surrounded his childhood. One summer's day in Lostwithiel, his father had sketched out the big picture, and had told his son to decide whose side he would have been on. Forty-seven years later, Andy still couldn't decide whether he was a Roundhead or a Cavalier.

What really motivated England's parliamentarians? Did they really want profound social change? No. They wanted to protect their faith, their own land-owning interests and their trade in the West Indies. So later, when groups of real reformists appeared, radicals calling for everything from universal male suffrage to pantheism, they were crushed, brutally. England got the major-generals and another tyrant. Only a rich, powerful class – Baharvand and his friends – could ever be muscular enough to remove a tyranny. Why do we never learn this? Why do we always get distracted by the romantic also-rans? And now Baharvand had won. Give him a few months and he'll be one more despised despot. He'll probably close the theatres and concert halls.

Lomax was also wondering whether Baharvand was going to prove yet another septic ally.

'So, with all his talk of social freedoms, his courtship of the religious and ethnic minorities and the students: you reckon he's been playing the winsome troubadour? This is all a sop to our namby-pamby, bleeding-heart western idealism?'

'It could well be. But there again, playing up to our sugary western sensibilities could fill his Swiss bank accounts. The reason that he may very well quantifiably do what he promised is that we will invest. Iran will become rich again, very quickly.

'Baharvand can keep the Islamic Republic alive by executing twenty or thirty big chiefs, all on concocted treason charges. If the IAEA is satisfied that uranium enrichment has halted and if Israel likes the wording of its peace deal, then we are on track to turn Iran into a firm ally. The country is, as Baby Baharvand says, a goldmine. Its young people are savvy, liberal and online. I am sure that EU clause on rapprochement being contingent upon advances in human rights will soon be a distant memory.'

Despite all her years in the service, Cath still hated to hear such cynicism. And from Andy, of all people. When did he become so openly jaded? Of course there were times when big money could trump humanitarian concerns. Sure, it happened. In Saudi Arabia, Central Asia, China and Indonesia. But that was a crass oversimplification of British foreign policy. There were plenty of humanitarian schemes across the world which Britain was running or bankrolling. There were foreign policy issues on which Britain had taken a moral stand. It was so easy and glib to parade one's weary cynicism. She wanted to say something about economic perestroika kindling better diplomatic relations. An active embassy could work with theatre groups, women's rights activists and refugees. But, as ever, she kept it bottled up. It felt like it would be such a naively optimistic thing to say. So she thought she would run through the transcripts instead.

'We've intercepted a huge amount of military air traffic in the last few days. The most salient parts are translated and are filed under 6B.'

Lomax slipped out the relevant file.

'Aha, I guess they got careless with all the pressure.'

'That's it. They forgot to switch codes on numerous occasions. There's a lot of confusion out there. Quite normal in the circumstances. The transcripts generally concur with the idea that there isn't some big counter-attack in the offing. There's no discussion of anything along those lines from the military wire taps. And satellite imaging shows no considerable or untoward military regrouping either.'

'Right.'

'Intriguingly though, there is a lot going on near Anareh. We have two senior officers, that's on page 34, discussing arrangements for Baharvand's speech tonight.'

She pulled out several photographs of the hard-scrabble patch where Baharvand was setting up his stage. The straight line of the qanat was clearly visible down the side of the photograph. The three spies ignored it, focussing on the armoured cars and rolls of barbed wire.

'Heavens. What razzmatazz. Is Baharvand getting ticker-tape too?' Lomax asked.

'It's certainly an impending set-piece of some kind.'

'Security looks like it's going to be tight,' Andy added. 'He's not even going to Tehran. He's holding it where he trusts every butcher, baker and candlestick maker.'

'If our Russian really is out there, he's got his work cut out now.'

On Iranian state television, David Attenborough had crouched beside an enormous toadstool. Andy couldn't remember whether Persian distinguished a toadstool from a mushroom, or whether they were both just gharch.

Instructed to return at three o'clock, Andy went back to Westminster to bed down for a few hours. There was a half-eaten slice of toast on the table. He poured the cold dregs of tea down the sink, walked through to the bathroom and pulled the light toggle. He tossed his shirt at the shower-rail. It hung there perilously for a few moments, then slumped to the floor. He was losing his touch. He splashed his face with cold water. He was greying faster than ever now. Always such a lean young man, he was now more slack and fleshy. He remembered the naivety of those summers down from Oxford when he would muck in with the Godolphin XI out at St Ives. He had an effortless poise and agility that set him apart from the middle-aged publicans and fishermen who made up the rest of the team. Back in his callow youth, he figured that he would remain lithely aloof forever, that he would never turn into one of those earthy, solid men who were winded by dashing up a few flights of stairs. He was there now, he thought, as he ran a towel round the back of his neck. He was certainly no longer irresistible.

He sat on the end of his bed and lit a Gauloise. Quite suddenly, it struck him. He could no longer blame Baharvand. It just wouldn't wash any more. He had dreamily worked through the bombing of the orphanage, flying on auto-pilot. Over the last few days, he had stopped himself worrying about anything. It's Baharvand who's doing all this, he said. It's all him. It's not my fault.

What a load of self-deluding shit. Of course, it's my fucking fault.

Andy relapsed. Once again, he was a cog in a destructive machine. He took those co-ordinates from Baby Baharvand, didn't he? He was the point-man whom Iranian defectors could trust. But after that, nobody cared about his judgement or his reservations. Men in Washington who knew nothing of Baharvand, or Iran, would make snap decisions. As would the prime minister. Andy was pointless: a humble courier who wanted to ensure that he received a comfortable pension. What kind of half-life was he living?

Defeated, he crashed down on his back and stretched out for his alarm clock. He set it for two o'clock.

The Tajik never doubted himself at moments such as these. Between missions, he was a haunted man. Was he out of trim? Did too many people know him? Had he made too many enemies? Had he made too many mistakes? Would it all catch up with him, morally and physically?

244

But as soon as he had the Dragunov slung over his shoulder and his mind was focussed on the kill, then he was transformed into one of the immortals. He was unkillable.

He had passed the afternoon belly-down on a ridge, studying the course of the qanat as it curved past Baharvand's impromptu stage. He had covered the binoculars with gauze to stifle any dazzle. Two Baluchis dozed beside him, steeling themselves for their impending dash through the mountains. He counted the number of access shafts that he would have to pass before he was a kilometre from the Ayatollah.

When Abdollah first proposed using the qanat, the Tajik had seen himself as Harry Lime, running through the echoing sewers of Vienna. He saw himself picked out by the light every time he passed underneath one of the bore holes. But, of course, it would be night. If he were lucky he would see the stars above the shafts. More likely, there would be a low curtain of October cloud. He would have to feel for the access shafts with his hands, tasting the kiss of fresh air.

At shortly past six o'clock, he bade farewell to the two Baluchis who had accompanied him since morning. Abdollah and his men, bristling with Kalashnikovs and Stinger missiles, were six miles away, setting up mortars and a blazing cocktail of pyrotechnics. The Tajik could imagine their febrile excitement.

The guerillas wished him good luck and lowered him into the waterway. After all his years in Afghanistan and Iran, where the state of a community's qanat or a kariz often dominated dinner-time conversation, he felt these waterways were old friends. But he had never been down one before.

The Tajik accustomed himself to the chill by taking short, sharp breaths. Then he forged on. It was easier to make out the access shafts than he had feared. For a few moments he allowed himself to relax. He swore, for the hundreth time in the last few days, that Baharvand would be the last man he would kill. After tonight, it would just be wolves, deer and game birds that fell prey to his steady hand. He would retreat to his dacha one hundred miles outside Smolensk and savour the stillness of the pine forest. He would have his Rostropovich CDs and his beloved gun dog, Laika. One more shot and all this will be behind us. He imagined good, loyal Laika beside him now, blind to danger and loving only her master, unconcernedly splashing through the water. Laika would stretch out on the river bank as her master grilled fish over charcoal. The two of them would doze off outside in high-summer. Just one more shot and we're there, Laika. Come on, girl.

Massoumeh's heart was heavy with pride. For two days, she hadn't felt the sting of the immovable mujahidin bullet that had been biting into her rib for the last twenty-five years. At last, her husband, her Ali, was about to become everything that he had been destined for. It was written.

She had helped him draft the speech. Its balance and decorum would satisfy everyone, at home and abroad. The choice phrases were hers. Of course, it was deeply regrettable – she liked 'deeply regrettable' – that Ayatollah Baharvand should have to take over the reins for an emergency period, but that was only necessary to preserve the Islamic Republic. In January there would be elections but this time unrestricted by the Guardian Council. Anyone would be eligible to stand. Ali would vow to create a far healthier economic climate, a climate that encouraged investment and created jobs. Wages would increase. It was time for Iran to take its deserved place as the regional superpower.

It was also, naturally, a source of deep regret that a handful of senior officials would have to face treason charges. But that was all behind us now. More pertinently, those officials had weakened Iran by not agreeing a temporary suspension of uranium enrichment. The West doesn't want us to give up our nuclear work and we never will. We will just stop for a short period, on our terms, to show goodwill. Then we can forge a real place for ourselves in the world. Too many of the clerics have turned us into the leper, the pariah of the international community by pursuing interests that did not serve the needs of the Iranian people. Now was the time to focus on the home front. Ali would listen to the rich and the poor, Persian and non-Persian, Shi'ite and non-Shi'ite. He would forge 'One Iran' that would once again take its rightful place on the international stage.

Massoumeh surveyed the crowd from her vantage point at the end of the stage. She had known so many of the faces over the last thirty years. There were the miners and the estate workers. Over there were the military top-brass on the Baharvand payroll, and all their men. On that side were the car-workers from the German and Korean plants in Bam that Ali had invited into the country. The tubby ones were the party faithful from the Association of the Combatant Clergy. The gaggle of kids were all from the Baharvand schools. They had received their parcels, an envelope of cash and a bowl of noodle stew. The camera panned across happy faces. They would lap up this speech. They would probably continually interrupt with their enthusiastic applause and cheers. They bloody well should do. That's what they were bloody well paid to do.

So this must be the one, the Tajik calculated. Cradling the SVD across his chest, he levered himself into the narrow chimney-stack. He pressed his boots into the far side and buckled up, catching his weight on his shoulders. He let his arms hang below him and pressed his palms into the rock behind him. He was a thickset, muscular man and pushing himself up would be a challenge. But he had entered that invincible mind-set that told him he was the best, that he would come out a winner. It must be about forty yards up. Foot by foot, he forced himself up the access shaft. He stopped every couple of minutes and took the weight on his shoulders, granting a moment's repose to his aching ligaments.

At the surface, it was pitch black. The Tajik found that there was a deep moon-crater surrounding the access shaft. Perfect. He was 1,100 metres from the stage. From his canvas knapsack, he extracted his binoculars and peered over the parapet of the crater. There was a dull murmur of voices from the crowd behind the barbed wire. The troop levels were what Dolokhov always used to call 'acceptable'. The crowd lay in darkness but the stage itself gave out a sharply defined luminosity, with a narrow corona of light pollution spilling out into the night sky. He slipped on the telescopic tritium PSO-1 night-sight. He could hardly imagine a cleaner shot. Come on Laika. One last big effort, then we are going home.

Miss Jane Marple had found the body in the library for the third time in the last two days. 'Oh dear,' she sighed with dowdy, Anglo-Saxon reserve.

Quite suddenly, the transmission ended and state television's cameras panned around the adoring home crowd in Anareh. 'One Iran', 'One Iran'. A commentator announced that Ayatollah Ali Baharvand would shortly deliver an address to the nation.

In the Reuters bureau, Shirkhan whipped to attention and stubbed out his cigarette in the heavy glass ashtray beside him. He set up a fresh screen on his terminal and wrote in the relevant news codes, ready for instant transmission. He rang Whelan, but the old boozer had disappeared again, presumably relinquishing his mobile at the embassy lodge before the ambassador uncorked a few Pauillacs.

In the ziggurat, Lomax had come down to the operations room. 'Should have brought popcorn!' he barked. Andy volunteered that there were some humbugs on the filing cabinet. Cath was already making notes before the viper had begun.

'Keen that girl,' said Lomax. 'She'll go far.'

In Gholhak, the British embassy's residential compound, Negar had huddled up on Seb's sofa, holding her knees to her chin. Parastou, tragically, had other commitments.

'Seb, he's on. It's the latest announcement.'

The young diplomat ran in from the kitchen, still carrying the knife with which he'd been dicing onions.

The viper took his place at the lectern. The crowd roared. He smiled and raised his hands to quell their enthusiasm.

'Please, please.'

The crowd dutifully obeyed their Ayatollah.

'In the name of God, the compassionate and the merciful.'

The atmosphere was electric. Millions hung on his every word. He stooped closer to the microphone, at which the Tajik had been aiming for the last ten minutes.

Staring at the stage, Baharvand was simply a vivid white speck. Squinting down the telescope, the cleric's chest ballooned into view. The Tajik ran the sight up to the point where the viper's tunic ran into the skin of his throat. The cross-wind was negligible. He aligned the cross-hair and made his instinctive compensation for the drop of the bullet, using the dots running down the centre of the reticule.

Never hesitate, Laika. Once you've got it, never think: this is too easy. Trust your instincts. Take your man down.

He emptied his lungs and held for a couple of seconds. He squeezed the trigger.

The flanks of the Jebal Barez dissolved into flame.

10.

An insistent rain washed the quayside while trawlermen unloaded their hauls: cod, whiting and sole neatly packed on to ice. The stark electric light spilling from the double-doors of the fisheries depot cast a sheen across the waterfront. The warm glow of port-holes threw reflected streaks between rusting bollards. Here and there red and green Christmas lights failed to inject any jollity into the cold, steely blue of five a.m. Andy tugged his overcoat tighter and pulled up his lapels. He'd never much cared for Plymouth. He lit a Gauloise.

Half way down the quayside, an excited group of fishermen in yellow sou'westers had gathered at the stern of one of the newly arrived fishing boats. As he neared, Andy saw the monster that had stoked up such animation. Stretched out on the dock was a giant squid. From the tips of its tentacles to the arrow of its tail it must have been twelve feet long.

'That's a lot of calamari, Eddy. You'll get squid rings like tyres off that bitch,' guffawed one of the fishermen.

One of his companions suggested that the aquarium would pay good money for a specimen of that size. Although the giants could grow up to forty feet, it was rare to haul one up in such good nick.

Someone took a photograph. The flash bulb burst off the puddles surrounding the dead squid.

'Bah, it's just come out as white lump. Shit. I'll try again.'

Andy stepped a few paces closer to the cadaver. Its deep, dark eye was filled with an ineffable melancholy. It too was a shadow-dweller. He must have been a monarch in the ocean-depths, but he cut a pitiable figure on the surface, anaemic and wounded. Andy knew they were two of a kind, he and the squid. There were plenty of extraordinary creatures in the world. There were just some that you weren't meant to see. Some whose existence was meant to remain secret.

He threw the Gauloise into the harbour, like a dart.

Thirty yards on, he found *Le Dinan*. A bedraggled Breton flag flapped against the stays of the fishing boat. The Plymouth fishermen had all spotted the stranger, but there was no love lost with the Bretons. Nobody had gone round to offer Monsieur le Capitaine a tea and a bacon sarnie.

A drowned rat stood upon the deck.

'Morning, sir.'

'Rossiter, morning. How's our guest?'

Andy stepped on to the trawler and shook hands with the tough guy.

'He's not what you'd call a mariner, sir.'

'No, not famed for their sea legs, the Iranians. Had a rough crossing did he?'

'You know those cartoons where people go absolutely bright green? I thought that was a joke.'

'Hah, right, OK, let's take a look at him.'

Rossiter slid out the hatch-boards and Andy stepped down into the fuel-rich fug below. Lafarge, the French heavy, was cleaning his pistol. He had a knuckle-cruncher of a handshake.

The Iranian was now yellow rather than green.

'So Dr Asgharian. Welcome to England.'

The defence apparatchik smiled to hear his native language

252

for the first time after a month on the run. In France, he had pretended to be a Greek.

'I hear you suffered a little from seasickness. I do hope you are feeling better now.'

'Yes, yes, sure. These gentlemen here have been most kind. Most attentive. But it will be good to get back on to dry land.'

'All in good time, sir. I am sure that we won't have to keep you on *Le Dinan* too long.'

'I wish to claim asylum now. For me and my family.'

No time wasting.

'That's not really my province I fear, Dr Asgharian. That would be a matter for the Home Office. But I suppose that we may well be able to help you in your application, as long as we can reach some kind of understanding.'

Andy hung his sodden overcoat on the edge of the cabin table. Dawn was beginning to lighten the portholes.

'Any chance of a brew, Lafarge?'

'Of course, sir.'

The muscles filled the kettle and lit the stove.

Asgharian was a weedy looking individual who would have passed for an accountant or clerk. As a civil servant, he seemed to have survived the first round of purges after the assassination of Baharvand.

Early November had been carnage. Not that any of it got into the newspapers. The leader and Ahmadinejad were suddenly back on the box. Bernie Whelan was vindicated again. There you go, Shirkhan, they were just lying low in their bunker.

Baharvand, the official line went, had been murdered by one of the defeated rebels. A young mining engineer was hanged. Several witnesses saw him shoot Baharvand from the crowd, twenty yards from the lectern. Baharvand was proclaimed a national hero and his funeral attracted nearly two hundred thousand mourners.

All the SIS could do was watch as people vanished. Jafari and Nouriani disappeared off the face of the globe and became non-people. Polite secretaries in their offices apologised, explaining that there must be some confusion: no-one of that name ever worked here. The air force flew markedly fewer sorties as its ranks were purged again. Academics and former politicians went straight to jail. The border provinces were put under curfew and separatist leaders were rounded up.

Western intelligence services were swamped with all sorts of peculiar jetsam seeking asylum in the West, offering to sell secrets at an exorbitant price. Most of them were worthless.

But Asgharian was a big fish to land. He'd been a devil to smuggle out of France. The Iranian intelligence officers were all over Paris. He'd come pummelling two-fisted on the embassy door on Friday 14th December. *Le Dinan* had whisked him out late in the afternoon of Sunday 16th December.

'So, Dr Asgharian. What was the last post you held in Paris?'

Asgharian removed his spectacles and rubbed his eyes.

'I was head of the ballistics programme in Iran's ministry of defence.'

'I see. Answerable to whom?'

'Direct to Najjar. Sometimes to the Revolutionary Guards.'

This guy was big. He could have whatever he wanted. A little cottage in Dorset. New wife. New kids. Andy was tempted to keep him under wraps for a while. Naturally he would share him with Max and Avi, but not quite yet. If they didn't fancy a wet Monday in Plymouth, that was their problem.

'I see. And your training is as a physicist?'

'No. I am an engineer. Sharif University.'

'And you were recruited into this ministry in what year?'

'Full time, that would have been in 1990. Two years after the war.'

'You were then, I take it, a full member of the Shahab-4 missile programme.'

'Sure.'

'At some stage we will need names. We want to know about all our old friends from Russia who are now working on the Iranian ballistics programme. We'll need you to trawl back through your memory for the results of launches. We need to know the results of experiments with solid fuel. Estimations of range. How quickly the weaponry can be deployed. Jesus, you know what we want better than we do.'

'Naturally. That's all stored in the files,' Asgharian said, tapping his skull. 'The second I become an English gentleman with an English flat and English car, then that's all yours.'

'We may need a few tokens of your sincerity before that. Some Russians, just to show you are who you claim to be.'

Andy pushed a sheet of foolscap across the table. He pulled a biro out of his inside pocket and laid it gently before the defector.

Asgharian grinned.

'It would be a pleasure.' He wrote for two or three minutes, covering the page with his cursive, flowing hand.

Lafarge brought over a couple of mugs of tea.

'There,' Asgharian said. 'A beginning.'

Andy took the page. A couple of the names were familiar. Many were not. He would have to pass it over to the Russia house.

'If you want to know whether we can hit a football pitch in Riyadh, for that I will need a little something from your side.'

'I'll talk to the accountants. It'll probably come out of my pension.'

'Hah, I do apologise.'

'Not your fault. So, why are we the lucky ones, Dr Asgharian? Why did you not just decide to sell all your rocketry secrets to the French in Paris?'

'Oh, who knows whose side they are on? They are too socialist. The French are inherently untrustworthy.'

Andy was warming to rocket-man. He sympathised with anybody who allowed themselves to get hopelessly out of their depth.

'As I am sure you'll understand, our big question in these circumstances has to be why? Whom did you piss off back in Tehran?'

Exhausted by a night retching into the English Channel, Asgharian clenched the damp cushions beneath him and stared at the table. He gestured towards Andy, crooking his index and middle fingers.

'Have you got a cigarette?'

'Sure.'

Andy passed the Gauloises.

'Keep the packet.'

'Thanks.'

He lit a match nervously, only striking the phosphorous on his third attempt.

'My life, sir, hangs by a thread. Naturally you will be aware of the bloodshed that has ripped my country apart in the last two months. To some extent, of course, you were complicit in the manner in which things unfolded.'

Christ, this guy was very high up. Asgharian didn't break his stare from the table.

'Tehran was always bad. But it's hell now. No one knows who anyone is any more. I hardly know if I can trust my own brother. After the military rising, it's been a witch-hunt. Every old enemy suddenly becomes a potential informant. The only way to stop him is to inform on him first. People are dying, sir. People are dying on the very flimsiest of evidence.'

'And who was informing on you?'

'I don't know. I didn't hang around to find out. There were just signs. Even my wife and children noticed them. The dark cars when I dropped the kids off at school, the strange echo on the telephone, the top level documentation at the ministry that suddenly became unavailable to me. In my country, sir, these are signs that you need to be considering a new career path and a new home.'

Andy nodded.

'And where are your family now?'

'That is something I have vowed to tell no one. No one, you understand. When I have reached some arrangement with you, then I will bring them over.'

'But are they in Iran?'

'No. That's as much as I'll say.'

'Sure. There's no pressure upon you. Certainly not at this stage, at least. Now, why would you, a loyal, diligent and talented servant of the Islamic Republic have anything to fear? Surely the importance of your work could protect you. They will always need you. What could an informant have that would make you so toxic?'

Asgharian looked up.

'I have no idea. I really don't.'

Andy puffed out.

'But I do. It's just an idea, but tell me what you think. As head of ballistics at the ministry you were in a constant dialogue with the Supreme National Security Council. In fact, for the most part, they were a pretty dumb bunch of politicians and village mullahs. You must have been pretty popular. You were a bit of a national hero. You were the man who was actually building the bomb. They courted you, they feted you. You were a source of intense national pride.'

Asgharian appeared almost nostalgic.

'Indeed, I was an important man.'

'Indeed you were, Dr Asgharian. So important, in fact, that you must have come to the attention of Baharvand. You must have dealt with him a lot while he was the secretary of the Security Council, no?'

Asgharian looked impressed and laughed generously.

'Oh, you certainly know your stuff, don't you?'

'And these aren't the best times to be a protégé of Ayatollah Ali Baharvand, are they?'

Asgharian this time laughed in earnest, shaking his head as he stubbed out the Gauloise.

'No, they aren't. That is something of an understatement.'

'Did you know he was plotting a coup?'

'Not at all. I had absolutely no idea. I was entirely peripheral. I thought that I was obeying commands that came straight from the top. How was I to know that the old bastard would go off and start waging his own personal war? He's caused a lot of trouble. He's almost got me killed. He's almost got my family killed. I am safe now, aren't I?'

Andy nodded reassuringly.

'When did you first meet him?'

'That was back during the war. I was just a humble engineer at that stage.'

'But working in ballistics?'

'Naturally. That's all I have ever done.'

'And what, exactly, was your relationship with Baharvand at that stage?'

'This is a sensitive issue. Maybe we should have this conversation later.'

'No, I'm not going anywhere. You're safe enough here, for now. If you want to ensure that you stay safe, maybe you should start at the beginning. Those must have been tough days back in the war. Backs up against the wall. There must have been all those questions, those moral dilemmas. Iraq is using mustard gas from Germany, we've got to hit back. Can we use chemical weapons? Can we use biological? Can we use nuclear?'

Asgharian pulled another cigarette out of the packet and tapped it against the table.

'Oh, sure. I was right in the middle of all that. It was a colossal mess. As you know, even under Khomeini our nation struggled to find one true defining voice. The morality of such weapons was always brought into question.'

'It was also a strategic question. It still is.'

Asgharian lit the Gauloise, far more confidently this time. He was getting into his flow.

'Of course, you never want to provoke an enemy. But don't forget that our country defines itself by being run by men of the cloth. One day, one Grand Ayatollah will tell you that chemical weapons are a morally acceptable means of defending the Shi'a. In the same way, subterfuge and dissimilation can be acceptable. The next minute, chemical warheads are expressly forbidden. Even mentioning them is taboo. Believe you me, if it's your job to fit out our missiles, you've got to be damn careful that you're on the same wavelength as the latest religious thinking.'

Asgharian took a couple of swigs of tea.

'And the whole confusion persisted into the nuclear age. Half the leadership reckons nuclear weapons are the only way we save the nation. We were on the brink in the Imposed War; it wouldn't have happened if we were a nuclear power. Look at the position Pyongyang is in now. They certainly got due respect once they had gone atomic.'

'But half the leadership disagrees?'

'Sure, much of the clergy falls into the dissenting group.'

December's National Intelligence Estimate from the US suggested that Iran had developed a distaste for weaponisation in 2003, possibly because of international pressure. Much of the intelligence community was far less generous, but it was certainly possible that the vicious divisions inside Tehran had re-opened four years before.

All in all, it mattered little. Iran was still pushing ahead with ambitious rocketry projects. In addition to this, undeterred by UN Security Council pressure, it was working on uranium enrichment at a scale entirely disproportionate to its ramshackle reactor down in Bushehr. Even if the prudent voices advocating no warheads had gained the upper hand in 2003, there was no guarantee that their wise heads would prevail for ever. All it takes is a nod of the turban and the ballistics programme will once again advance in tandem with the production of highly-enriched uranium.

'And Baharvand? Which side was he on?' Andy asked.

It was almost light and the rain had abated to a drizzle. Lafarge had holstered his pistol and was filling in Sudoku grids.

The Iranian slapped his knees.

'Baharvand was always on his own side. That's the first lesson you've got to learn about Baharvand. He's always looking after himself.'

Andy had learned that in 1980.

'But did he ever discuss with you what he thought about the nuclear programme? Did Baharvand think it was counter-productive? You must know that surely?'

'Hah! Is that what he told you? Is that what he said to you? Support me and I'll give up the nuclear programme and we can all be friends?'

'Answer my question.'

'The old man's dead now. It hardly matters.'

'It matters to me. Answer the question.'

Asgharian shrugged as if to suggest that history was useless.

'OK, no, to start with, no. Back in the war, Baharvand was a big supporter of the nuclear programme. Hell, anybody who had any sense was. He'd been one of the main catalysts behind the heavy-water programme, bringing back plans and technical advisers from eastern Europe, the Danube. Later, just after the ceasefire, Baharvand and I were two of the principle point men for the father of the Pakistani nuclear bomb, Abdul Qadeer Khan. Now Khan's got this shady reputation as a black marketeer and proliferator. But, God, to us then he was as much of a hero as he still is in Pakistan today. The very survival of the nation seemed to depend on him.'

'But he went off the idea?'

'It was more that he got frustrated. We were building up the know-how and we were using the junk that the Russians and Pakistanis didn't want. The IAEA has documented our technical difficulties in uranium enrichment pretty well. What Baharvand wanted was an immediate success story. On all questions, whether it be gasoline imports or atomic weapons, his primary concern was national security. So, if he came to the West before his coup saying that he was willing to suspend uranium enrichment, it was because he was frustrated. He had bigger plans. He thought that, for the time being, you could just buy the weapons.'

'From where?'

'Pakistan. That place is coming apart at the seams. There are all sorts of rogue elephants in their ISI.'

'Shi'ites?'

'No, that's not important. Religion has no part in this. He

261

was using the North Koreans as well. This is about the money.'

'And the deal was done?'

'Oh yeah, all sealed. Parts of the Ghauri-II would be shipped in from Pakistan, fully-armed versions of the No-Dong from North Korea. The arms bazaar is getting pretty turbid these days. Some of the warhead components would be Pakistani or Korean. Other parts would just come from under the counter. There's stuff in Central Asia, you would not believe.'

'And is this why he fell out of favour with the Supreme National Security Council?'

'Sure. They wanted to keep the whole enrichment programme on Iranian soil. He wasn't opposed to that, in theory. He simply reckoned that we needed to buy in the weapons on the sly, just to tide us over.'

'But was he going to declare these weapons?'

'I don't know. I wondered about that. The viper was an elusive man to read. Some days I reckoned that all he cared about was the defence of the republic. To Baharvand all that mattered was that we had the nuclear arms to deploy if necessary, to wheel out if we were threatened. The uranium enrichment could creep along at its pathetic pace or even be suspended. All that mattered was Iran got the bomb.'

'But Baharvand was also a showman, wasn't he?'

'Exactly!' Asgharian exclaimed, stubbing out his second cigarette. 'I reckoned he might follow up his grand bargain with an even greater fait-accompli. For a couple of years, Iran could go back to what it used to be: America's big friend, Israel's big friend. We'd sort out any trouble in Iraq. We'd be nice to our students, our Bahais and our gay-boys. That's when Baharvand would wheel out the nukes. He knew what national pride meant. What's all this rubbish that Ahmadinejad is spinning about how we should take pride in our civilian nuclear programme? Please!

It's an embarrassment that we have screwed up the programme so massively. Does any nation really take pride in its reactors? Do the British really feel a great national pride in Sizewell B? No, national pride derives from Trident missiles and two hundred nuclear weapons.'

'That would have been unlikely though, surely? It's too much of a risk just to present Washington with a fait-accompli. It might undo all the good work.'

'It might but the States has got used to all sorts of disreputable individuals with nuclear weapons. Pakistan for one. If the oil-men are raking it in, nobody's going to worry about five or six nuclear missiles.'

'Maybe not.'

'Definitely not! Particularly when Baharvand knows that you have bombed an orphanage. Definitely not when he can prove that British and American submarines launched an illegal raid inside the Islamic Republic. Those little children, sir. So very, very sad.'

Andy leant back against the back of his bunk. The viper had completely outwitted him again. Islamabad station had missed it. This had flown right under the radar of the Kim Jong-il watchers.

Andy took back his packet of cigarettes.

'Lafarge. Two more teas would be great.'

Asgharian rested his wrists on the edge of the table.

'You know there are all sorts of curious, circular patterns of fate in my country. I believe in such things, sir: a country's repeated tragic destiny. You know the story of Cyrus the Younger? That was the Cyrus who used foreign mercenaries, Greeks, to help install him on the throne?'

Andy nodded.

'Well, the foreign mercenaries won the battle and almost got everything their hearts desired,' Asgharian continued. 'There was just one problem, Cyrus managed to get himself killed. Bahravand was your Cyrus. The whole plan was perfect. Only without the man nothing would work.'

Andy was glad that his Cyrus had been slain.

It was a dull, colourless morning. The docksides were becoming more crowded. Seagulls picked at the shells of inedible crabs tossed aside by the fishermen. Two more teas arrived.

'You knew Alef Baa?' Asgharian asked.

'I knew of him. We never had the pleasure. One hears things.'

'You will not be aware that he died a few weeks ago.'

'No. How?'

'Prostate cancer. Apparently he must have kept it under wraps. The end was all very sudden. We had no idea.'

Andy registered the information. It should be fairly straight forward to confirm.

Asgharian sipped his tea.

'When do you get me out of here? I can't live on a bloody fishing boat for ever, you know. I am a senior official of the Islamic Republic.'

'At half past nine, you'll be moved on by car. To begin with, you will stay in a military facility. You'll be safe there. They may even do you Christmas lunch.'

Andy knew the bases around Plymouth all too well. They mainly belonged to the Royal Marines and were universally grim. As a green recruit into the service, he'd done combat training and marksmanship there. They were dreary, depressing worlds of freezing Nissen huts lashed by the winter rain. The roads had speed-limit signs of ten miles per hour. Such institutions didn't have a summer. Asgharian would wish that he'd stayed in Tehran and tried his chances with the intelligence.

Asgharian thought that sounded a little desperate. He enjoyed his luxuries. From what he'd seen of it, he wasn't inclined

264

to believe Britain was going to be his kind of place. It smelled of fish and diesel.

'I feel, sir, that we could be good for each other. What we've been talking about, it's just history. But you look after me, and I'll look after you. I know things, really good things.'

'What sort of things are those, Dr Asgharian?'

'Oh, I know far better things than rockets.'

Andy looked at his watch, then crossed his legs and linked his hands. He had all the time in the world.

'There is a great conspiracy afoot. A very great conspiracy. It concerns British interests in the Caucasus. It concerns energy supplies to the whole of Europe. And they have pulled the wool over everyone's eyes. If you help me, I can make you very famous.'

'Fame is not a sought-after attribute in my line of work, Dr Asgharian.'

'So you don't want to know?'

'Oh no, I want to know everything.'

In the endless pine forests outside Smolensk, a heavy snow was falling, squalling in the breeze, like a mainsheet flying loose. The black sky was weighed down, pregnant with hours and hours of pristine flurries. The green of the pine boughs had been entirely smothered by heaps of white powder.

Out by the wood-pile, a dark bear of a man was cleaving logs with an axe. The sharp cracks were the only noise to split the perfect, ancient stillness of the forest. His sleek gun dog waited erect and dutiful, resisting the temptation to gambol in the fresh blankets of snow.

They went back into the dacha. The dog shook the icing sugar out of her rusty red coat and lay by the stove as her master fed in the logs.

The man flicked on the radio. It was the first headline.

'Russia has delivered its first consignment of nuclear fuel to Iran, the foreign ministry announced today. About eighty tonnes of nuclear fuel were delivered yesterday after Russia gained further guarantees concerning the peaceful nature of Iran's atomic work.'

So, we won, he thought.

He stretched down and rubbed the dog between her ears.

'Come on Laika, let's have some sausages. You like sausages.'